ESCLAVE THE 2ND AGE

Cleveland Maximil
To Margalie Orleans
Great to Meet you

ESCLAVE THE 2ND AGE

CASTE OF NOBILITY

TRIBUNE BURDEN

iUniverse, Inc.
Bloomington

ESCLAVE THE 2ND AGE
CASTE OF NOBILITY

iUniverse books may be ordered through booksellers or by contacting:

iUniverse
1663 Liberty Drive
Bloomington, IN 47403
www.iuniverse.com
1-800-Authors (1-800-288-4677)

ISBN: 978-1-4620-5111-3 (sc)
ISBN: 978-1-4620-5112-0 (ebk)

Printed in the United States of America

iUniverse rev. date: 11/30/2011

To the Philadelphia

Church of God

CONTENTS

Born in Greatness, Forged in Destiny . . . made in the

Image of God.

Enrich my mind, feed my soul, my heart skipped a beat or

time literally froze.

The one thing you Fear the most.

Who I am you may not understand. What I want to be you may not accept, but when it is done the world will know . . . finally . . . it is done.

I wrote this novel based on a dream I had several years ago that could no longer be denied; it compelled me in a way that changed my life. I needed years to understand this dream, and even now it is still somewhat mysterious, allowing me still to learn something new. Thus far, it has taken years of study in the Bible, molecular biology, some physics, and lots of world history to complete the work you see before you, which has taken ten years of my life.

NOBILITY

I remember my life as the Living Busara, conduit to the spirit realm for those that follow in the faith of Chideria. One night a believer came to me with an armored box; in it was a creature known as the *sanscoeur*. It had been attached to his great-grandfather until the day he died, and the believer wanted to know of its history as others gathered around. Taking the box in my hand, I called for the phantom spirit, the former Living Busara from that time. At first I feared the spirit, for he is one of the twenty-five war phantoms that carry a dark secret. The war phantom took my soul, and it was then that I witnessed the End of the Age.

I saw it all—the deviant race of man be born into cruelty and fear by those of Noble descent. Victors of the War that Ended the Age.

Each time the phantom spirit took my hand, my essence was taken to a different period of time, where I would see the oppression. I saw the faces of enemies who brought our defeat, and walked through the suffering ancestors who could not feel my presence but yet I shared their pain. A burden that carried into the next life. I watched as the history of three nations unfolded.

"These humans will not answer to us," said Sceptor as the last sanscoeur was placed on the condemned, those who still had the courage to resist oppressive rule. I saw that the creature was placed on the human prisoners so that it would bestow torment to its victims.

It was here that all hope had been taken away and the human race was ruled by another. Those who fought back were shackled and made examples of.

"Where is the Tomb of Creation?" asked Sceptor, a general of the Noble Army. But none of the prisoners would answer.

"They will not speak; throw them into the sea. Let death be their reward for silence," said Sceptor.

His soldiers pushed the prisoners back using the Orum-Spear. They tried to fight for survival, but the sanscoeurs stopped any chance of that. They had become crippled with pain and their senses dulled. Violently they were pushed over the edge while chained to one another. As one fell, others would grab onto anything they could find, even if it tore the skin off their hands. But nothing could prevent their descent as the enemy watched the fall of the deviant race.

The phantom spirit took me again, and I saw as their bodies fell against jagged rocks; some were killed instantly. I closed my eyes to look away, but when I reopened them, I was underwater; the phantom had taken me to see their final resting place. I stand in a graveyard filled with the bodies of those who wouldn't submit, and now others join their camp. Those who survived the fall crashed into the water and were hurt beyond belief. The sea was cold and dark, and the condemned sank deeper into the water as light began to dim. Some struggled to live as they fought against the weight of the dead, but the chains were too strong. It seemed that in moments to come it wouldn't matter anymore. Heavy rocks fell from the surface right on top of them, pinning them down. But by chance and a merciful God, the chain was broken, and two of the prisoners escaped, leaving the rest behind. One was the great-grandfather of the believer.

The ones that lived went on to fight another day and gave thanks to those that took death in their place. The phantom spirit shows me more. All other humans are captured and their homes burned; from this moment on, they will only know permanent bondage—they are esclave. Any resistance is met with persecution, and the land of Kiskeya is brought into the next Age.

I ask the war phantom to show me the Tomb of Creation. But the phantom refuses to do so. The events marking the 600-year war (the

War that Ended the Age) would be kept secret, a mystery until the next age. All phantom spirits of that time were sworn to secrecy and their souls bound to that oath.

"Spirit, what were the secrets kept in the last Age?" I asked, but the phantom only shows me this:

For your people to be free, a sacrifice must be made . . . you must suffer.

3rd World Order

My hand is released, and I am sent back to my own time. When I awakened to tell the believer how his great-grandfather escaped, they were all dead, the Noble Soldiers had found us, and my life had ended that night.

That was 120 years after the war. That night I died as the Living Busara and became the phantom spirit of sorrow. I had witnessed the suffering of others and relived my own. Now another has called me to know my story. My spirit is now a guide for others to follow.

I can only show them what I know, but each time I am called by a Living Busara, our spirits are one, so that they feel my pain and know the agony given to me.

"Thank you for your help. But the mystery of the Age is still kept hidden," said the now Living Busara. After I have seen her death, the sorrow phantom releases me and my soul is sent back one thousand years to my own time. The next Age . . .

By the position of the sun, it was early on the morning of Homage, a day of rest and learning. There was a cool breeze and the sky was blue. But on this day, the serwans (a race of Noble Ones) were very anxious over the future of Kiskeya and her citizens. Usually the very critical teacher Kesi was late, but on this day she was the first person to appear. Everyone was curious about what would be said, and as always, she had to report to the officials the topics of today's class. Recently, there had been some uprisings in the land of Kiskeya (Mother of all Lands) by Uhuru, leader of the Maroons, a rebel army that had been around since the First Age and gained control over some of the territories outside of Kiskeya. Periodically, they would infiltrate the land to grant free will to other humans in exchange for joining the rebellion. But the latest controversy was about Nyack C'Kre; he was a human who claimed his own free will and was now being placed on trial at the Citadel in Peponi, the capital of Kiskeya.

The room was now filled with every level of esclave; even though it was mandatory to attend, it was still unusually filled. The first thing that is expected of all esclaves on the day of Homage is to pledge their allegiance to the Nobles and the land. From there, Kesi continued the lesson.

They gave us purpose. Before the Noble people, we were savage, brutal, vicious. They showed us a way outside the heathen ways, delivering us from chaos and showing us the mercy of order. Our ways were continually carnal, but by surrendering our wills to them, we have received salvation from them. Hopefully, through our own contribution, all of the deviant races can be saved from their own damnation.

Testaments of the Last Age

"So, whatever rumors you hear about rebellion, you must immediately report them to your master. Do not wait to let yourself be accused of conspiracy for keeping silent, or you will risk the lives of yourself and your family, or even worse, banishment to the Lougawou Mountains, the great void of the earth," said Kesi.

Kesi reminded them not to risk themselves for the Maroons, who are deceitful in nature. That the Maroons prey on the heathen urges of the lesser races, who are weak-minded and easily confused. "The Maroons have only the purpose of breeding anarchy and bringing destruction to all the good the Nobles have bestowed upon this world. For these reasons, we must be truthful to our masters: to save the land and continue to gain their favor," said Kesi.

Just then Amari, a small young boy who wore a black fabric around his head, asked about Nyack C'Kre. "What about the trial?"

Kesi moved toward him with a demonic stare, as though to boil the flesh right off of him. The insolence of an esclave (human) to ask that question! Even though Kesi was an esclave herself, she was an amanche, which is a person of mixed descent. But in a graceful tone she answered, "He has been deemed chagrin-guedado, an outcast."

"Nyack, the outcast, has no purpose; he has forgotten his place. We belong under the authority of the Nobles, for they are blessed," continued Kesi. From childhood, humans are taught to relinquish everything they have into the hands of the Nobles to gain the favor that none of them deserve. "It is easier for esclaves to do more evil than good; the thoughts of the Nobles are not our thoughts," she explained to them.

"We cannot be trusted with our own devices . . . . Now, don't forget about the play we have some preparing to do over the next few days," said Kesi. From there, no questions are asked and the lesson ends.

Just then the Noble known as Adversary was standing by the entrance. He had just bought an esclave called Nassor and brought him in for Homage just as it ended. Adversary was coming from a rally about citizenship for Noble women. Adversary was an elderly Noble from the Sceptor clan, who was stout, powerful, and like all Nobles, had wings that allow them to fly. His wings were very notable because they carried the marking of his family: black, purple, and some yellow. Unlike most serwans, the Adversary had birth markings of a particular design all over portions of his body. They indicated the origins of his family; this is seen as a true mark of nobility.

His clan was one of the three oldest families (Sceptor, Abyss, and Obsidian), descended from three Generals that were known for valor in the Sentient War, which lasted for 600 years and laid waste to the lands of the humans. Upon surrender, the humans were claimed as the spoils of war and their territory divided. Praise was given to the generals for bringing order into a world of chaos at the end of the Orum-Spear, a weapon that shows an ember glow upon use. The land of Kiskeya was over time split into three major areas based on class. The capital cities, such as Peponi, are areas of major commerce and history; they are where most of the Nobles are known to be. The next major areas are the rural territories, which consist mainly of miles of forestry and farmland worked by the esclaves. Last are the Lower Levels, whose inhabitants are made up of guedados (the homeless) and the Innocent Race.

After the war, monuments were built in honor of the generals for every capital city, and museums were filled with trophies that depicted the entire history of the war. It is expected for every citizen to make pilgrimage to those monuments; it is mandatory for any esclave. An annual celebration is held to commemorate the War that Ended the Age. The celebration would start soon.

On top of one of the monuments in Peponi is a weapon, the *Akin-Eno (Anointed Gift)*, used by the Final King of the Humans. It is said that during the battle, the Final King took the Akin-Eno and plunged it into a tree, turning it to diamond. The only evidence of this is that every morning when the sun rises, a display of light is illuminated from it that shows every form of color visible to the eye. Some say it is a sign of achieving victory over the Nobles; others say that it shows how Nobles belong in authority over man. The Akin-Eno itself is a legend, a weapon so great Nobles refuse to acknowledge that it has human origins. To esclaves the Akin-Eno is a gift from Heaven that was given to the human race sometime after creation. It is Mankind's greatest legacy.

As for the esclave known as Nassor, he will learn a new fate and purpose at the hand of Adversary, whose rules of labor and punishment are as sharp as his orum-spear carried down through the age. Most new esclaves are marked to distinguish the master they are in service to. The custom of the three clans is to chain a heavy log to the ankle for as long as they desire as a way of teaching submission. The only way to move around with it is by carrying it on one's head. Nassor's fate had now been sealed.

HEED TO THE LAW

People in Kiskeya must live by two things: the caste system and the law. The caste system is based on the three peoples that exist in the land. The *Caste of Nobility* is for the serwans, the *Caste of Innocence* is for the kenyetta, and the *Caste of Deviance* is for humans. People are born into their caste, and the only way it can change is if you are of mixed descent, usually human and serwan.

All those of mixed descent are given the Caste of Deviance from birth but can earn their way to a higher caste, except nobility. People of mixed descent are always born with a gem on their forehead that has an enticing glare, yet they are never born with traits of the higher caste.

As for the laws of Kiskeya, they mostly apply to humans and serwans. The Purpose of Law is for Nobles, and it only applies to those who could take flight. The gift of flight grants a Noble all rights and privileges to have a joyous life. This includes the right to vote and own property, which makes them citizens. This law only applies to Nobles since the name of their people was written on the Great Obelisk, proof that their people were the only ones who would ever know liberty.

The Law of Purpose, also known as Labor and Punishment, is for esclaves. Since they have no free will, it dictates that the best way to serve their purpose is to obey, submit, and sacrifice for their master. Near the river, where most trade and commerce takes place, Kesi showed how dedicated to the law she was. Weekly, she would hand out articles concerning the law.

To obey, you must heed to the voice and design of your master, never questioning his authority, for the decisions he makes are for your own benefit; those decisions are not meant to be understood by you, but put into action by you. By submission, an esclave must be ready at all times to humble themselves before their master and acknowledge that we are the weaker race, whose authority should not take precedence over those to whom we are in service. Above all, sacrifice is the most Noble thing an esclave can do to show loyalty; do not be afraid to give unto them whatever is needed to please your master by your own hand. Remember the sacrifices that have been made for you, to free our people of our vicious ways. It is the true test of the mind and body. From these, you will learn a degree of self-restraint and discipline that has been withheld from us. Look for the purpose that will extinguish our deviant ways.

Testaments of the Last Age

While at the river, Kesi noticed a serwan buying some food from a merchant who was a kenyetta. One of the young esclave boys asked, "What law do the kenyetta people have to yield to?"

"There is no law that exists for the kenyetta; they are neither citizen nor esclave. Because of that, they only know free will," replied Kesi. "Usually most people will ask about the guedado, but they are not really seen as people by law; they have no caste."

Of course, not everyone agreed with either law. Some of the citizens felt the laws were too strict and demanded too much. Even the kenyetta have felt that for a long time, they were at a disadvantage because they couldn't vote or own property. Some tried to rally and protest for more rights, but not enough of them would ever work together against a common problem until recently.

The next few days in Kiskeya went by peacefully as the celebration started; it was the one time out of the year that people of all castes were able to accept each other. Shouts were heard for the biggest day of the year, and people came from far and wide to relive the time that the Noble race won the Sentient War. Two thousand years of history is retold in one day, but people remain festive for the whole week. A parade is even held; people fill the streets wearing grand costumes, and kenyetta vendors open up street shops as calypso music is played. At the center of the celebration is the monument, where people gather. Those of Noble descent wear the battle armor used by their forefathers and display ancient weapons from the last Age.

Yet it is also a day that is kept as a reminder of people's place in the world. Each caste is brought to light. The rich Nobles stay high up in the monuments and trees. Even though they provide most of the funds for the celebration, they avoid participating because they feel above it all. Most of the people that fill the streets and parade are poorer Nobles, who are too ignorant to realize how looked down upon they are. Others, like the amanche who may hold the Caste of Innocence, prove their loyalty by volunteering; Kesi, for example, is having a play that retells the story of creation. Esclaves like Nassor, known for trouble, are made to work the celebration from dawn until dusk. This is one of the few times the log is unchained from his ankle. All other humans are herded to the monument under close watch from the Ona (Noble soldiers); once there, they are allowed a small amount of freedom.

The best thing about this day is it allows those of secrecy to remain hidden in plain sight, even those with devious designs.

From the east, the rays of the sun touch the monument, and people take witness to lights of glory. It is a perfect way to celebrate. But then the sun is hidden behind the clouds, "We shouldn't be here; this is their celebration, not ours," said a believer.

"We have to be here. Otherwise our absence could draw more attention," said the Living Busara, who works to keep up appearances. The last thing any human wants to do is make the Nobles more suspicious.

Then the Living Busara senses something and becomes faint; a danger approached from the west in the form of a storm. It grew to take greater shape and filled the sky as the people stood in wonder. Lightning and thunder poured from its belly; each time it roared, its true form is known and the world becomes silent. The sun made itself known again so that the two could come for war at the top of the monument. The lights of glory met thunder and lightning in a fight for the Akin-Eno. Intense powers struck the diamond tree, which fell to earth like a fireball. The people who had come for celebration ran for their lives as the top of the monument began to fall. The sound of thunder shook the trees as heavy debris fell everywhere. A giant crater opened in the ground, and in it the Akin-Eno, the anointed gift, it burned with an eternal fire. Finally, it had been set free.

Suddenly the Living Busara became aware of her vision; none of what she had seen had occurred.

"Are you all right?" asked one of the believers.

But the Living Busara had no answer—nothing like this had ever happened before. This was a revelation from the book of *3rd World Order—SkyBreak*.

"You come here, esclave," said Chisulo after snapping his finger at Nassor. "Get me some water." Nassor happily did it; the last thing he wanted to do was offend a member of the Hunters. He did as Chisulo asked, proving that he could be obedient. As Chisulo drank to satisfy himself, two esclaves working with Nassor laughed to themselves.

"Why are you two laughing so hard?" asked another esclave.

"Because that is the third one Nassor got," they replied. "They are drinking water from a bucket that Nassor bathed in," they said as they continued to laugh.

"Unbelievable; that fool will get himself thrown in prison," said another.

"Ah. Very good. Now get back to work," said Chisulo as he threw the cup back at Nassor.

When Nassor came back to join the others, the only thing he said was, "Okay. What's the next dare you have for me?"

Then they all laughed. Nassor was always the one who didn't take things seriously. Even when things looked bad, he handled it with a sarcastic attitude.

But even with all the fun and games, they had to keep their guard up. Groups like the Hunters were on patrol, making rounds throughout the parade. Some of its members had separated into teams to cover more ground, working to find any rebellious activity. Two of them were down among the street shops looking for free food to eat. One of them was Kumi, an amanche. The other was a kenyetta who hoped to get a handout from his brother.

"So, what's a hero like you doing here?" asked Falun, a street vendor.

"Just came to see my brother and his wife. Wow, that baby looks like it's coming soon," said the Hero to Falun's pregnant wife. But Falun seemed insulted, since his brother knew that this was his last day before his shop was closed down forever.

"Hey, Kumi, come here. This is my brother and his wife," said the Hero, but as Kumi came over, Falun's wife turned away. Something about Kumi made her uncomfortable.

"We should leave; there is still plenty more to see on a day like this," said Kumi.

"All right, let's go. Take care, little brother," said the Hero as he took a piece of bread and left with Kumi.

"Why does your brother call you a hero?" asked Kumi.

"Ah. It's something my family calls me ever since I got into the Hunters," he replied. As the two went about their business, Kumi noticed several amanche. He had seen them before and thought they looked suspicious. When he walked over to confront them, some children ran into him and Kumi fell into the mud. "You stupid children, come here!" shouted Kumi.

Fearful of what would happen, the children kept running and disappeared into the crowd, as did those amanche. Covered in mud, Kumi picked himself up and tried to clean off the coat given to him by his father. Kumi wore it everywhere, and he even put the colors of his serwan father on it—colors that burned in a blaze of blue and green around a family crest. He wore it with arrogance. Being so concerned about the jacket, he didn't notice that he was still being watched by others.

In another area of the parade, Nassor was cleaning up the garbage left by people. Most of it was taken by the guedado. That's when he saw Khumani walking by with her father, a member of a Noble family. "Oh, dammit!" said Nassor. He didn't want her to see him like this, so he hid himself behind a tent. As he tried to hide, Nassor fell through the tent into a bunch of women who were changing for the parade. "Well, this could be a good thing, at least for me," said Nassor.

The women didn't appreciate his sarcasm, and they beat him with the sharp ends of their costumes. They chased him out of the tent; the leader, Kesi, hit him several times with a broom. "I better not catch you here again," she said to him.

As Nassor was being taught an important lesson, Khumani was talking with her father about Hasani, another Noble. "I think you should start taking Hasani seriously. There are many women who would like to have him," said Khumani's father.

"Oh, I know. They tell me all the time how handsome and tall he is. The same women who would stab me in the back to get to him, but why don't we talk about something else," replied Khumani.

"Okay, then . . . . So, why did their family insist on having this parade? It leaves our city very vulnerable to an attack," said Khumani's father.

"I don't know. Hasani says we shouldn't live our lives in fear. This parade has never been canceled, and we shouldn't miss out because of the rebels," said Khumani.

"Well, let us not stay here long. I don't like being around all these 'people.' They are up to something," said Khumani's father. Like most Nobles, Khumani's father felt that something would wear off if he spent too much time with the other castes.

"We won't stay too long. I just want to see the play," said Khumani.

People were still trying to settle in when the stage was finally ready for the play to start. Behind the curtain, Amari stood excited about his part in all this. He was one of Kesi's students and had been asked to play the role of Affliction. The other children got into their costumes while Kesi began to narrate their parts from *Testaments of the Last Age*.

In earlier times, the serwans shared a single faith about the origins of life. In the beginning there existed two forces; one was called the Cyano, who were capable of harnessing light and using it for energy. The second force was the Karyon, who wielded the ability to store pure knowledge. Together they birthed the first being capable of thought, who were named the CyKar but are remembered as the Noble Gods. Using the sun as a source of life, the Noble Gods could now pass on their pure knowledge to those that descended from their line. It was through pure knowledge that the Noble Gods became aware of an even greater purpose, a legacy that must be passed on.

As time passed, the ones known to be the Noble Gods began to change, and the earth did as well; they lived long enough to see the sun step into its next phase. It was the light from the sun that they depended on, using this life energy to further their advancements. Civilizations sprouted that were based on their physiology, great monuments capable of harnessing light. With that light, the Noble Gods were able to put all their thoughts into action; no idea was held back from them, and they lived in peace for many, many Ages.

But one day the Immortal Strain appeared, those who carried corrupt knowledge. Being different from the Noble Gods, they were called the Immortals because once they emerged, they could not die. At first, the Immortals were seen as a marvel that should be embraced in the world. The first Immortal who emerged was given the name Immortal Sage because his knowledge was far beyond that of any other; he possessed wisdom and abilities like no other Noble God before him.

Many lifetimes had gone by before the Immortals were seen as the threats they were. Their knowledge had been so changed that sunlight didn't provide the life energy needed to sustain them; without death, their need for that energy grew. They hungered for it so much that they began killing for it. The Immortals became a scourge among the Noble Gods, crying out at night whenever the sun went away, like a child without its mother. Over time their knowledge continued to become more corrupt.

The Noble Gods' greatest thinkers worked night and day without rest to eliminate the Immortal strain, to fix the corruption. The Noble Gods believed that the strain was caused by the changing sun, and over time the sun would not be able to sustain them, putting their entire race at risk. Hope was eventually found in the archives, an old reference to a substance that was shot up through powerful vents from the earth. It was able to produce life energy in a way that marveled the Noble Gods. This new energy was called Lewe Energy, the substance that created the atmosphere and made life possible for future species.

The Noble Gods studied it, and with each step there was gradual success that led to the creation of all the hierarchies of the animal kingdoms. Soon the Noble Gods began implementing plans to create a source of energy like that found in the Kingdoms, the Lewe Orb.

But as they worked to save themselves, a ruling by the Sovereign God, Leader of the Noble Realm, placed all Immortals in exile. Their hunger for life energy had become dangerous to the Noble Gods, whose numbers had started to dwindle. Access to all birth-chambers was forbidden so that the strain could not be spread further.

The Immortals felt victimized and turned to the Sage for help. They felt that the real plan of the Noble Gods had always been to banish them so that they would eventually feed on each other.

Secretly, the Immortals led by the Sage began to think of plans to overtake the Noble Gods; they would no longer be the victims. They were desperate; most of them were starving for new energy. Everything seemed hopeless until the day when one of the Sons from the Last Kingdom came with the Lewe Orb.

Their time had come. This new life energy brought an end to their hunger, but it had not done the same to their banishment.

From that day until the end, there would never exist peace between the Noble Gods and the Immortals ; their only hope of freedom had been taken. Now rebellion had become the only course of action.

The Sage's disciples renamed him Eternal, the chosen savior of his people. As the first true Immortal, having abilities like no other being before or after him, Eternal soon became boastful, believing that it was his destiny to rule over the Noble Gods.

As the Immortals and Gods came to the brink of war, the sons of the last kingdom continued to learn and grow. From them were born four nations: one kenyetta, two serwans, and another whose name was not remembered.

The last kingdom was the greatest creation of the Noble Gods; in them was the gift to produce lewe energy.

Each nation was given a destined purpose, and the second serwan was placed into servitude; he would be the one to deliver the Lewe Orb to the Immortals.

He resented his brothers for the favor that had been bestowed upon them by his creators and hated even more to be the one to deliver the Lewe Orb to the scourge of the Noble Gods. When he would come back from helping the Immortals, his brothers would call him Affliction, as he was a plague among the kingdoms and should be exiled to live among the Immortals so that he would not spread his sickness. They told him that he was unfit to be given the knowledge of the Noble Gods, which was why he was sent to deal with the Immortals and one day wouldn't be allowed to return.

Eternal became aware of this and befriended him, showing Affliction the suffering that had been endured by the Immortals for so long.

"The Gods see us as a plague among them; they've denied us everything," said Eternal and tricked the boy into betraying the Gods.

A cataclysmic war broke out that fractured the earth into pieces and made the Heavens cry out in anguish. Casualties wore on both sides, and in the end neither side prevailed. Because of his betrayal, Affliction had his wings torn off; as punishment, he would never be given forgiveness in this age or the next.

This marked the day of the coming of man, a Deviant Kingdom forever ostracized by his brethren. Man would now be a scourge among the kingdoms, seeking favor that would never be given to him; it was in servitude that he began and in servitude that he must end under the cautious eye of his brothers, who would be his keepers. When the war had ended, both the Immortals and Noble Gods realized that neither could be saved. The remaining survivors had no choice but to seek refuge in the heavens; they ascended up into the sky and became stars to live out the rest of their lives as part of the constellations. They would be a constant reminder of man's betrayal each time he looked up into the night sky.

Testaments of the Last Age

Many of those that came were pleased by the lessons of the play. It had fulfilled its purpose, reminding them of the necessity of the caste system. When it was all over, Amari ran to his sister Menee and left to go home. Nassor waited for Khumani to leave with her father; it still hurt for him to see her. But just as everything was moving along, people in the parade began running for their lives. "The Maroons are attacking!" they yelled. People were panicking as they ran in all directions; street shops caught fire as the Hunters and Ona came to help. In the midst of people trying to save themselves, Kesi was knocked down. She would have been trampled to death, but luckily Nassor came and kept any harm from coming to her. He carried her to safety; Kesi had been hit hard, but nothing too serious. Before she had a chance to thank him, Nassor was gone.

THE TRIAL CONTINUES

The people lived in fear for the next few days with no real proof that what happened during the parade had anything to do with the Maroons. But it served a purpose: the people needed some sort of peace of mind, and it would come from C'Kre's trial. A guilty sentence would take their minds off everything else. But until then, Nyack C'Kre couldn't be kept in the same cell—the people were becoming more of a danger. He looked out his window and noticed the guedado making their way back to the Lower Levels. Around this time of the year, they made themselves scare; the parade was a joyous celebration to others but a danger to them.

Guedados were the biggest fear for humans, which is what Nyack C'Kre had been called. Guedados were former esclaves who had no master and roamed the territory begging for food. They wore filthy clothing and were covered from head to toe in dark cloaks. You could actually smell them as one approached, and it was even said that they would not come out in daylight unless it is for food. Unlike the Maroons or Lougawou Mountains(the Great Void of the Earth), their suffering was seen every day by everyone; citizens wouldn't even look at them out of fear that they would be followed home or catch some disease. The guedados are known for talking to themselves; the belief is that they are conjurers, who use dark magic to cast spells on people. Most guedados are executed or sent to the Lougawou Mountains; only a handful will linger around to serve as an example to any esclave who wanted to have free will.

One particular group of guedados is led by Gina Ifosia, an old woman who had been around so long no one even remembers who her previous master was. She wanders the city all day with two young boys. Almost like a mother, she takes care of them, making sure that they have as much to eat and drink as possible, even providing them safe haven at night somewhere in the Lower Levels. People of each caste would come by to persecute them, humiliating them by throwing garbage or rocks, and she had to step in to protect those she called family, taking the punishment in their place.

Every day she struggles with the two boys because their minds are lost. A look of confusion could be seen in their eyes, which hold a glassy stare. They never remembered anything from the last few days, which was probably why their master let them go. For some reason one is always distracted by the Nobles. He watches the Noble caste with deep thought and amazement, and he always denies knowing who Gina is in front of them even though he is seen with her every day. "Who are you? . . . I'm not your child; leave me alone," he would say to her. But she doesn't mind; she treats him the same regardless. The other boy always clings close to Gina, making sure that he and his brother keeps up when she is on the move; otherwise, they might get lost without her.

Until now, Nyack never really thought about the guedados, yet he had shared moments with them, particularly Gina. He remembers times when Gina would talk to herself about the Sentient War, the War that Ended the Age. Nyack remembers because it was one of the few times where the things she said made sense; he actually enjoyed hearing her talk about it. She would say that as the war came to an end, there had only been a few human kingdoms left that still posed a threat to permanent control of the land of Kiskeya. One Kingdom managed to unite neighboring territories through bloody civil wars, and another had possession of the Tomb of Creation. It contained mankind's history and origin of life, but only the most sacred priest could enter by performing a host of purifying rituals. If they weren't performed correctly, the punishment would be death.

Even as a child, Nyack had heard similar stories from family and friends. That in the Tomb were four crystals called **Kyah** and the Akin-Eno, which had been birthed from the sun, each gift bearing unique inscriptions. When the crystals were placed in the path of direct sunlight, their story of how creation happened would appear. So much is unknown about the crystals—there are rumors that they were born

from oblivion or that life exists in them—that no one can separate fact from myth. Whoever had possession of these crystals would wield power like no other. Supposedly, Abyss wanted the tomb because it was where the first spirit of man resided and whoever had possession of the tomb had control over all human life. Using human traitors as spies, the Nobles devised a way to infiltrate the territory. Eventually the kingdoms fell in a climactic battle between the Final King and General Sceptor, but the tomb hadn't been discovered. One of the spies had been captured and revealed the plot. In the end, the tomb had been hidden and to this day it has never been found.

As Nyack sat in his cell thinking about Gina and the crazy stories she told, he began to sympathize with her situation. Like him, she was despised and her children accursed, but even so in all his years, Nyack had never seen her give up. Because of that, he will not either.

The following day . . .

It had been another long day for the trial at the Citadel that had been built around the largest tree stump in the land. Nyack the Outcast began to tell his side of the story for the first time before the judge, while the rest of the courtroom wondered why they wasted time like this instead of just sentencing him. The only time a human was even seen in a courtroom was over issues of ownership when one serwan disputed with another over an esclave. Because of this, tension began to rise between humans and serwans, but surprisingly between kenyetta and humans as well. For decades, the kenyetta had tried to prove their right to full citizenship before the court systems of Kiskeya, but they had always been pushed aside; now some human, through an act of defiance, had gotten further in a few weeks then they had in years. To the kenyetta that was a spit in their face, a complete disregard by the Noble Regime to every effort made to help them become citizens. So the kenyetta took matters into their own hands, and riots began to explode everywhere between them and humans. In their minds, they had a greater right to become citizens than the humans, and for that someone had to be punished.

As for the trial, the Noble who represented Nyack started by allowing him to speak. "I grew up with a family of ten siblings. My father was an blacksmith, so I was too. My mother was the cook and seamstress for Shard . . ."

In the middle of his testimony, the prosecutor interrupted by saying, "Don't you mean *Master* Shard?" with a great level of disrespect.

But Nyack C'Kre looked the prosecutor right in the eye and responded, "I have no master . . . only a serwan who destroyed my family."

C'Kre made it clear that his master had become obsessed with C'Kre's older sister, that Shard suddenly began to make subtle attempts and advances but never got what he wanted from her. Nyack's sister wasn't naïve and she found ways to avoid him, but he was clever; Shard plotted to have her. One day she was gathering firewood when Shard approached her, but C'Kre's father stumbled upon them. Shard had not realized he was there helping her gather wood. If Shard wanted to just take her, he could have but he had his pride; he felt that as a "Noble," he didn't have to force her to do anything. He felt she should be grateful for such an opportunity; he would be doing her a favor.

It was a story that spoke to the hearts of many esclave families.

"What I don't understand is why make an issue of it now? These events took place almost three years ago—why didn't he do something then?" said the prosecutor, with the attention of the courtroom focused on him. "Clearly this deviant human, like all humans, wants to cause disorder and chaos, which is in their nature," continued the prosecutor as he looked for ways to discredit Nyack.

But the judge allowed Nyack to finish his story.

"I don't know what happened after that—whether my father exchanged words with Shard is still a mystery—but afterward the entire season went by uneventfully. But then my father was sentenced to a fate worse than death, the Lougawou Mountains, for a crime he didn't commit; and out of guilt, my sister took her own life; some believe she took it with Shard's unborn child. My mother wanted vengeance and tried to poison Shard, but her plot was discovered and all of my younger siblings were sold away, but he kept me because I was the only blacksmith left outside of my father," said Nyack C'Kre.

Now Nyack had little tolerance for the law, as did his father. He explained the hardships he had witnessed and even took part in. He had helped the enemy do harm to his own people, creating conflict among his people that he swore never to take part in again.

"Harvest season is the busiest season of the year. Kenyetta merchants keep their shops open longer to sell the crops and goods of Nobles, keeping the citizens rich. It is also the season where esclaves experience the most cruelty from their masters. The Ona keep their eyes open for anything suspicious because Maroons are more likely to act during that time of year. For this reason, humans are worked until the point of exhaustion . . . Shard once thought one of his esclaves was conspiring against him, and he had me *take care* of the situation. I never even thought twice about it," finished Nyack. Truly, humans have learned a lot from the serwans, but nothing of which they are proud. As Nyack finished, he felt contempt from the eyes of all those in the room for condemning the Noble people in such a way.

After hearing what C'Kre the Outcast said, the prosecutor scolded him for that portrayal of Shard as though it was an attack on their entire race. "What makes you think you can judge us, look down on your master as though he is as deviant as you? He has all the authority needed, and it has been granted by the law."

"The Articles of Purpose are clear. Humans are bound by law to submit to their masters, which your family wasn't willing to do, assuming that anything you have told us is true," continued the prosecutor. He made everything that Nyack said seem as lies, even accusing him of working with the Maroons, who to the Nobles are a bunch of savage kenyetta and runaway esclaves.

"The law is clear about the duties that are expected of an esclave to maintain the fulfillment of the master and keep his favor. It's no secret about the dire condition of Shard's wife; for years she has been stricken with an illness that has weakened the use of her body. But obviously in his moment of weakness, your sister took it as an opportunity to take advantage of his grief. Shard is the true victim, who had been looking for relief and in the end lost wealth in valuable esclaves," said the prosecutor. In the end, he made it seem as though Nyack's sister was obsessed with Shard but was rejected and for that she took her own life. The citizens weren't even concerned about the other details of the story.

CHIDERIA:
THE SPIRIT OF MAN

After the Sentient War, life for the humans took a drastic turn. Their culture, traditions, and religion had been destroyed. Nothing had been spared that was of their own creation; everything from cookware to cattle was burned to the ground. The Nobles wanted to guarantee that they would have no ties to their past, that they would only depend upon the culture that would be forced upon them. Nobles felt that destroying what made up the essence of man was as good as erasing the memory of him, and a man without a history can be easily manipulated.

But the essence of man isn't a mortal being that can be killed; it continues to live today in present-day people. What the Nobles thought was killed in the last age has survived in what is known as the Path of Chideria, the First Faith of man that has risen even in the midst of turmoil. Since the invasion, humans have learned to live with a dual identity, one created by their time in bondage. That restricts the part of them that is capable of greatness and shows humility for the peace of mind of the Nobles, and then the true identity that allows them to freely express the soul from oppression.

To the serwans, the concept of a soul is beyond comprehension; they feel it is a deception. The idea that there lives an eternal force inside a living being that can never know an end is something that couldn't be understood by their people; what plagues them the most is the notion that each soul will be judged to spend eternity either in heaven or hell. There was once a time that the serwans did have a God and faith, but they began to abandon their beliefs after they took full dominion in Kiskeya. It is possible that some still believe, but to reveal themselves would mean being persecuted by other Nobles.

The Path of Chideria is now a secret order, and rumors of it have always lingered in the air. Those who practice it have been very careful not to raise any suspicion; the meetings take place at secret locations called underworlds. If caught, they are known to face the worst form of torture, ones that are made public to quell any rebellious thinking. Most written history of it was destroyed in the last age; few documents survived, and even fewer have been found. But events are recorded by a chosen few that grow to become Living Busaras. Dozens are chosen from birth to be tested and trained, but only a handful actually pass. The ones who pass are expected to have the recorded knowledge of man from the beginning, which means the individual must know everything including wars, lineage, ceremonies, celebrations, and even the season of a person's birth. Usually Busaras are unaware of their ability to recall events; they must be placed in a dreamlike trance after inhaling specially made herbs and plants. Once they come out of the dream, they retain only some memory of what has occurred. They say that the Living Busara must be a conduit to the past by making contact with a previous Busara (phantom spirit), whose soul can come back to earth when needed to act as a guide. Whenever humans have questions about their past, the Busara from that time answers through the Living Busara.

Meetings for the Path of Chideria have now become scarce because of the Maroon rebellions that are happening more frequently; serwans have been keeping a closer eye on all esclaves and placing even greater restrictions on them. They feel that any human can be a potential spy for the Maroons, helping them infiltrate the territory. The last meeting was held by the High Priestess Faizah, another high rank of the path; almost anyone can become a high priestess, but the training is very arduous and one must be committed to the cause. For some time now, High Priestess Faizah has been hiding her identity with a dark purple cloak and gold pendant at the neck; only the oldest members may be aware of her true identity. It's the only way to be cautious, since some of the latest members could be spies for the serwans, infiltrating for a reward. Another reason for caution is to protect the members; the less they know about the higher ranks, the less they can hurt the cause if they are ever captured.

A ceremonial dance by the women is done at the beginning of each meeting. Each female who participates bears the markings of the four Kyah crystals, but only one female will bear the inscriptions of the Akin-Eno. The markings extend to a great portion of their body, and they wear a fabric that allows them to dance effortlessly to the sounds of drums. The dance itself can represent a harmony between Origin (the Creator God), creation, and man. These ceremonial dances are all meant to tell a short story, but today was special: the High Priestess Faizah realized that the time was critical to keep hope alive in the members.

"We have not held a meeting in some time. Many may have become reluctant in their loyalty to the cause," said Faizah to one of the older members.

"Good, then—we need to know who is for us and who is not. Let's see how they feel after the dance," said the member.

In this meeting, there was the addition of new dancers that told of the invasion by the Nobles and centuries of bloodshed at the end of the orum-spear. The next story told of the Lost Lineage, a human kingdom that managed to escape before being taken by the serwans but whose whereabouts are unknown; the idea of a lost Kingdom still gives hope to esclaves.

At the end of the dance, they all gathered around the Living Busara as Faizah began to speak. "I realize that we are living in hard times, in fear that we will be punished for our faith or chastised for ties to the Maroons, but we have been living in hard times since the last Age. The serwans have taken away a great deal from our people, even trying to demand our own free will, but free will is granted by the soul, not from soaring in the sky."

As Faizah spoke, she knew that there were those who believed that they could still find favor from their master if they followed the law—that one day they would be given the Caste of Innocence, the closest thing to freedom a human can know. But she felt they shouldn't have to earn what was rightfully their own. Mankind had done enough submitting to last until the Final Age.

"Every day I heard promises made by my master, but those promises were an illusion. They were a deception made to distract me from my true calling in the Path of Chideria; no matter what we do or how we do it, we will always seem deviant to them," said Faizah. She knew that she had captivated them all. "But since I confirmed my faith here, I realized that "deviant" is not what we are but what they made us to be; and now when I hear that word I cringe, because I know it doesn't define me or any of you." She paused for a moment while everyone looked around in agreement, thinking of all the times where they did more than expected but all that they got in return was a scornful look for wanting gratitude for a task they were meant to do. She continued, "Maybe some of you think that all this is futile, that we have been planning rebellions and having meetings since before the monuments were built, but if this was really all futile, would the serwans be as fearful as they are now, looking over their shoulders at every group of esclaves? Right now, Adversary has created a new coalition called Hunters, who work to hunt down any esclave expected of working with the Maroons, hoping to keep us in fear. But I tell you that they are the ones who are in fear and they should be."

"Believers remember that fear is inevitable, but it should not hold us back; have courage. A commitment has been made that must be honored. We who have known bondage should help the Maroon army; let freedom be the only purpose our souls know," Faizah reminded them. But it wouldn't be easy with new threats around like the Hunters; there are enemies at every corner who would betray merely out of hate and jealousy, and humans must be on their guard. In times like this, almost no one can be trusted.

Even so, some of their spirits had been rekindled. On their minds was the story of the Lost Kingdom. The notion that there are humans out there living a life free from the burden of servitude, who have never had to bow before the will of another, was like a dream that had yet to come true. It didn't just give them courage; it confirmed their faith.

ORDAINED:
THOSE WHO ARE PREDESTINED

"Mother, what is the Akin-Eno?" asked Nassor.

"The Akin-Eno is many things, my child, and you are too young to understand such things . . . But I will tell you anyway," replied Nassor's mother after seeing the curiosity in his eyes.

"The Akin-Eno was formed from the teardrop of the Creator God (Origin) and a star to show how it would last forever with man. It was a power that would flow like water with whoever wielded the gift . . ." continued his mother.

Years later . . .

Nassor finally had the log removed from his ankle; it had been so long that it felt strange to move without it. He will never forget the pressure it put on his back or the way it gave him a terrible limp because at night it would stop the flow of blood in his leg. Carrying that log was a burden that reminded him of what he had lost. He missed his old home, where all the people he cared about still lived. He remembers growing up close to his mother, but she had been taken away from him. For a long time he was depressed, and there was only one person who could make him forget how much he missed his mother. Her name was Khumani, a serwan.

She was amazingly beautiful, the kind of woman a man would risk anything for. Her hair was like a dark fire and it grew from her head, resembling the feathers on her wings. Patterns of gold covered parts of her body like a birthmark; within the serwan people, an inscription is passed on by the females to indicate the maternal lineage, while the colors of the wings are passed on by the father to show the paternal lineage. Most of the markings were on her face, arms, and back, but at night those markings seemed to make her glow. To Nassor it was like her beauty came to life.

They had known each other since childhood, and when her siblings would do whatever they could to make life hard for Nassor and other esclave children, Khumani would always step in to defend them. They grew to be very close; she would even leave him extra food after a hard day of work. There was nothing that they kept from each other, providing needed hope and understanding. Khumani and Nassor felt that they could relate to one another, since neither one of them could be a citizen. The law was clear that only if you had taken flight were you given rights and privileges. As of now, without wings no human could ever become a citizen; and even though Khumani had wings, it was taboo for women to vote. Kiskeya was very much a patriarchal territory, and males were the only ones entitled to the right of citizenship. It was even encouraged for Noble women to keep their wings covered in public so as to not draw any attention to themselves. For a male, his wings were like a badge of honor; but for a female, they were a mark of shame if displayed.

Khumani was a woman who could see things for what they were. She lived in a world where power was limited to a select few. It irritated her how most serwan women agreed with the law, that the right to vote was the "great burden" of Noble men and that Noble women wouldn't know what to do with such a privilege.

"Society has it so that everything is taken care of for us one way or another. Even if it's not what we want," Khumani would say. But she vowed to change all that. One day women would leave their mark on the world.

Nassor understood exactly what she was saying because there were humans who feel that they belonged in servitude. They felt that the human race was unfit to know anything else.

So many times they would come together and talk about the burdens they carried and emotions they felt. But one day it all came to an end, because as careful as he and Khumani had been to keep their relationship a secret, they had been discovered by Kumi. Kumi had the same mother as Nassor but the same father as Khumani, making him half brother to both. He had been suspicious of the two of them for a while. One day he found them together and demanded, "What are you doing here with this deviant esclave? What are you doing here with my sister?" It was because of that moment that Nassor was sent away.

Kumi recollects his close relationship with Nassor as a child. They even had the same wavy hair, a trait from their mother. Kumi remembers when his serwan family would throw rocks at him; sometimes Nassor was there, but most times he wasn't. "You dirty half-breed!" they would say. Those children were made to hate Kumi and any other human child fathered by Desever. It was his wife that ordered the children to punish Kumi; she was jealous of every infidelity committed by Desever with a human female. But what Kumi wanted most was to be accepted by those who despised him, and over time he began to hate his human family and do whatever he could to cling to his Noble heritage.

He began to follow the law until he earned the Caste of Innocence, which was bestowed on amanche esclaves; it is a method of giving humans free will without giving them citizenship. Under this status, Kumi didn't have to follow the articles of purpose, and his way of thinking continued to be admiral to his father. He then gained favor by betraying other humans, acting as a spy. As Kumi grew older, he made sure to despise the deviance of humans even more than the serwans, even spitting on those who looked at him. Kumi even took pleasure in taking out his inner hatred on the guedado. Luckily Gina and the young boys she looked after were never his victims, yet he would always put a cloth over his nose whenever they came around. It was that self-hate that allowed Kumi to join the Hunters. As one of its first members, he tried to prove his loyalty anyway he could, even changing his hair so he could look less deviant.

The Hunters are an elite force funded by the Noble Regime and led by Hasani from the Obsidian family. Since their creation, the Hunters have worked relentlessly to find anyone working with the Maroons; they even employ people from the lower castes for better infiltration.

In other parts of Kiskeya, growing up an esclave is different. Humans of mixed descent like Kumi are born hated by the world. But the saddest thing about being an esclave is being born one without knowing it. For the first few years, people don't know that they are struggling in a world that despises them, thinks less of them. It's like being born with that log attached to the ankles; many don't realize the burden it is. That is what life is like for Amari and other esclave children, who eventually gain a true understanding of life at a certain age. Amari was given a degree of wisdom through harsh experiences; seeing adult things at a young age forced him to make adult decisions. He even remembers several years ago seeing his first dead body after his sixth birthday with his sister, Menee; it was a little guedado girl who had died from hunger and infection. Since that day, they have felt an obligation to help the guedado any way they could.

Amari has yet to deal with the serwans other than running errands, but eventually he will. One of his jobs is to tend to the animals. He goes into the forest with a group of other children hunting for all sorts of woodland creatures, such as baby deer, squirrels, and rabbits. Once the animals have been captured, Amari has to put them in cages for breeding or eating. It's tough for him, being raised in a world where everyone that looks like him is treated as cattle while others, because they are of a different caste, are treated as people. What's worse is that Amari doesn't question the life he has because he was brought up in it. He believes this is the way it should be. The feeling of liberty is something he has yet to know.

Amari spends most of his time helping his mother maintain the home. He tries to keep up because a lot is demanded of her. "Let me do this for you," he often says. His mother is mostly stressed out from her duties of having to be a seamstress, cook, and the like, but still her family comes first. Amari is a big help in carrying her burden, but there are times when that burden causes her to take that frustration out on her own children, Amari and his sister, Menee, in violent ways.

Most days for this family are difficult, but the one who suffers most is Menee, and she suffers in silence. Menee is almost old enough to have a small child of her own, but that may never happen for her. Years ago there was a fire with her father and two other siblings, and Menee was the only one to survive, with permanent burns over her body. Everything was gone, and their home burned to the ground. Their mother had been away at the time, and it wasn't until after that, she realized she was pregnant with Amari. Everything that defined them as a family was taken that night, and Amari would be the first one born without those attachments. They had to start over, broken. The only thing left from the fire was the scars on Menee's back, a constant reminder of what was lost.

Since then, their mother has always felt guilty, thinking that the responsibilities for their master caused her to neglect the family. As for Menee, the scars made her very insecure, and she always covered them up to hide her shame, thinking that no one would accept her for who she really was. She doesn't hope anymore to have a family, but even if she did, it wouldn't matter; once a female esclave reaches a certain age, she has to be sterilized. Many excuses are used to justify this evil, but the main reason is that it allows Noble males to continue with their infidelity without fear of having a human child. Even female Nobles see the good in making the deviant caste barren.

Menee's only escape from her suffering is her knitting; she has become a skilled seamstress. At first, the designs outlined the scars on her body, but now she is able to design an array of beautiful clothing. She even once made a scarf that burned red and orange for her mother, who now wears it all the time. Eventually, their master took notice of her skill and saw it as a way to clear his debts. So for three days out of the week, she is escorted someplace by a petite serwan female with a bronze skin color; the profit of whatever work Menee does is given to her master.

Whenever she returns home, Amari always asks, "Where do you go?" She always replies, "None of your business; it is a secret."

Amari never seems to notice the distress in her eyes, dreading the next time she has to leave. Menee is able to conceal it well; the insecurities she has felt since the fire taught her to do that. All Menee is ever able to tell her family is, "I just teach other children how to make clothes like me—that's it."

As for their mother, she now lives with such anxiety that her children are careful not to agitate her. She has been known to talk to herself at times, and the abuse she receives from the world she takes out on her children.

No one has much in the area where they live; just because a Noble may own a few esclaves, it doesn't make him rich. Many of the Nobles in the area have debts, and they are willing to do anything to clear those debts. Menee is basically rented out to do service for other serwans to help out her master. One day Amari ran up to tell Menee that Malade was here.

"Who?" replied Menee.

"That serwan girl who takes you away," said Amari.

"You mean Mala . . . why would she be here? It is too early in the day for her to take me anywhere. Maybe you are just confused about who you saw, Amari," she said.

But the two of them went anyway to see why she would be here. Even before they saw any faces, Menee knew that it was Mala by the sound of her voice, so they quickly went back to their duties without being noticed. They realized that it had nothing to do with Menee, that their master had been invited to a gathering too important to miss and Mala wanted to make sure he would be there. It wouldn't be until later that Menee would have to leave. As they turned back, they were startled by a random kenyetta. "Watch where you are going!" he said while giving them a look of resentment. He continued on his way muttering under his breath, "Dirty humans."

They had no idea why he was there, but for some reason both Amari and Menee started to laugh, "Isn't he that *scab* whose street shop closed?"

The kenyetta who had just walked by them heard their laughter and knew it was about him, which infuriated him more, but he continued on his way to the main house.

That same kenyetta didn't leave their home until it was dark. He was still there even when Mala had returned with Menee. They came back early after another day of teaching some children how to knit. That kenyetta vendor was there to talk to their master about some business venture; his name was Falun. Frustrated from the failure of his own shop, Falun sought the help of Amari and Menee's master. In Kiskeya, for a kenyetta to have a stable life, he must work in accordance with the law, which says that the only way for a kenyetta to legally run a business is through a serwan; kenyetta can't own anything. So their people can have a business and sell whatever they want, but everything is under the name of the serwan they work with. One of the reasons why Falun's business failed was because he tried to run it by himself, but that didn't work out.

"Now it will be harder than ever for me to start a business. I have lost loyal customers since that half-breed opened his store. More of these amanche are taking over areas that were ruled by us," said Falun, who was frustrated that more amanche were being given free will.

"What would you have me do? All I can do is put my name down, and that doesn't mean much of anything," said Amari's master.

"I have no other choice. I must start all over to support my family; they depend on me as their provider," complained Falun. In the kenyetta culture, it was a disgrace for a male not to be able to care of his family.

In anger, Falun knocked a chair over. "It's not fair. My people have always been loyal to the laws of Kiskeya. We have never given trouble, only asked to be given what we deserve. We have earned that much." His people felt that nothing had been made fair for them. After all, they weren't the ones planning a rebellion or plotting to kill a mass of people. They were not walking around begging for food like the guedado. It was the humans that were doing all this.

"Over the last hundred years, the Noble Regime has done more for the humans than they have for the kenyetta people," continued Falun.

Then there was a knock at the door, and a note was delivered to Amari's master. He took the note and put it down as he spoke with Falun.

"I understand your frustration. My own grandfather, before his death, told me that when he was a child, there was no such thing as becoming an innocent. An esclave was human and a human was an esclave, a caste that could never be changed, no more than water being wet and fire burning bright. But things have changed. In his time, you could purchase ten esclaves for a cheap price, but in this day and age you can't even get one for the same . . . you could do whatever you wanted, and it was all kept secret; otherwise, they would be sent to the Lougawou Mountains. Back then, humans would cringe at the thought, but now it is a subject of laughter among their children. Yes, I understand your pain, friend. The humans have become too bold and been given too much, and for that we have suffered. I will help you start a new life . . . you can count on me," said Amari's master.

With that the merchant and the master shook hands in agreement. Who knows what plot ran through both their heads.

"Oh, and before you go, can you get rid of those furry little scabs? I don't want them coming near my garden," said Amari's master to Falun.

When Falun looked, he saw a few kenyetta children and his eyebrows raised a little, but he told Amari's master that he would take care of it right away.

Later that evening, Amari's master began packing his things. He had been in a rush to leave ever since he read that note. In it was a warning about victims being killed by an Assassin, victims that he had been involved with.

EXILED TO PERDITION

"Come here, my son. Let me tell you a story of Legend," said Uhuru's father. "Long ago when the Tomb of Creation fell from the sun, containing the Kyah crystals and Akin-Eno, it created a deep chasm in the earth. Inside the Tomb were many gifts, but the one that was of greatest importance was the *Book of 3rd World Order.* It opened the destiny to faith and religion. When it fell, its power was imbued within the earth itself. Three men of legend then ventured into the chasm and found the Tomb. Their names were Dessalines Maroon, Zumbi Quilombo, and Nyanga Palenque. They were the first Maroons, the forefathers that led the way to an even greater legacy. They witnessed what the Tomb had done; it had changed this portion of the earth in a profound way. They called it Earth Eno (Organic Eno); and when the forefathers brought the Tomb to the surface in sunlight, the Earth Eno had become solid. As they carried the Tomb up, the Earth Eno shimmered and vibrated, so they realized that the Tomb was special and mystic in origin."

Years later . . .

In the outer territories, the Maroon leader Uhuru was implementing the final stages of his plan, which would involve the main territories of Kiskeya. But there was still one thing he needed—a Living Busara.

"The best chance to defeat the serwans is on land," said one of his advisors.

"By air they would have a tremendous advantage," said another.

"With what the Living Busara knows, we may be able to even the odds. A rainstorm would do just that," said Uhuru. No clear-minded serwan would ever think to fly in bad weather; changes occur in the air that can restrict their ability to fly, and Uhuru knew that. "Maybe we can time the battle just as the storm hits and take down their forces," he continued.

His troops had been waiting for this moment for a long time, and the brotherhood that existed among them was eternal, each willing to sacrifice himself for the cause of free will. Watching his men join arms and ready for combat made Uhuru think of the events that led to this moment. He remembered stories of his mother, that she was a spy for the Path of Chideria, working with the Maroons to relay encrypted messages and help them gain access in and out of the city—that was how she met his father. His mother's pregnancy was kept secret because she was an esclave. No one could know because his father planned on taking his son to be raised in the Maroon camp, but she was obligated to her cause in Kiskeya. Uhuru's father was a dedicated soldier but impatient; and if it had been up to him, they would have gone to war against the serwans long before Uhuru was born. Yet after his time in perdition, he realized that life follows a particular path, things must follow a greater design, and he wasn't going to be the one to alter that plan for any reason.

As a young man, Uhuru's father hated the fact that his people had to live in hiding. Why did such an honorable group of warriors have to hide in the shadows from their enemy? He felt that it was better to die in battle head-on instead of planning all these acts of deception. He felt like a rat coming out at night scavenging for whatever resources he could find. Many of his friends tried to convince him otherwise, but he wouldn't listen even to his own father, Uhuru's grandfather. When he was finally exiled to perdition, he learned a heavy lesson at a terrible price.

During his own time among the serwans, Uhuru's father found a group of esclaves who sought to steal the Akin-Eno, which sat atop the highest monument in Kiskeya. It was a bold and dangerous plan that quickly intrigued him. "The Age of Defiance is now!" he remembers them

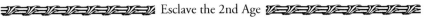

saying. All he could think of was the honor that would be bestowed upon him if he returned to the Maroon camp with the Legendary Akin-Eno, the gift from Origin. He would become a legend even among the serwans, the Maroon who defied the greatest of empires. With the Akin-Eno, his brethren would surely unite under a new breath of hope and start the Final Sentient War against the serwans.

Life isn't easy as a Maroon, especially for children, but Uhuru's father wanted to make sure that his first child wouldn't be brainwashed by the serwans into thinking he was nothing, only slightly above the dirt they walk on. At an early age, Uhuru was raised for a life of secrecy, being taught not to be suspected in any way so that he wouldn't draw attention. Children must get used to living this life, and the Maroons are always on the move, never staying in any one place for too long. Attacks by the Noble Regime were uncommon but had happened in the past. To be a Maroon is a birthright that is passed down from the father as a rite of passage. It's something that Uhuru has trained for his whole life, to take on his father's mantle.

On the day of Uhuru's birth, his father began fashioning a Safiya-Eno, which has been a tradition for over two thousand years. His Safiya-Eno was engraved with his entire lineage, all of whom were members of the Maroons. The substance used to make the weapon was found within the deep chasm of the earth, the Earth Eno. Once it had been brought to the surface, it was crafted using the forces of fire, water, and the blood of the Maroon who would wield the Eno one day. When all that had taken place, the Maroons believe life had now been imbued within the Eno, that a portion of a Maroon's spirit now lived within the gift and was now one with Origin, the God who allowed the Akin-Eno to descend to earth.

The Maroon camp always had an atmosphere of trust. Uhuru grew up around humans, amanches, and kenyetta who were all brothers to him. No amanche or kenyetta had ever been initiated into the ranks of the Maroons, but they still lived among them as family and were vital to the war as soldiers. Every Maroon was expected to go through a Rite of Passage in order to become a Safiya Maroon, the most supreme status. The rite chosen by Uhuru was named Exiled to Perdition, and it was a test that most declined. It was a period where a Maroon was exiled to live among the esclaves for three years in order to understand the nature of the Noble people. If the Maroon passed the test, he would receive his Eno.

The day Uhuru left, he remembers hearing, "This test is meant to instill contempt toward the enemy so that none of those who have allied themselves to the cause will ever betray us or show mercy when the time comes." It guaranteed that any Maroon who survived the test would become fortified in his conviction to defeat the serwans once and for all. The only other rite of passage was to live in solitude in the chasm; those years would be spent focusing on spiritual guidance. But Uhuru choose the unfamiliar path as a tribute to his grandfather and all those in his bloodline that followed the same path.

During Uhuru's time in perdition, he lived as a guedado, keeping a journal of the things he experienced, *Today I see suffering beyond understanding, beyond the teaching that was told to me in the Maroon camp. Life at the heart of Kiskeya is no life at all. Entering the city, I am no longer a Maroon, but now a guedado.* He remembers struggling to find food that wouldn't make him sick, and being taunted and pushed around by people of Noble descent. *There exists no brotherhood among the guedado, and they never stay in any place for too long. Like for the Maroons, danger is ever present for them. Even though they all share the same struggle, each one would betray the other for survival. Loyalty is a luxury that most guedado avoid; to live among them, one has to be ruthless, merciless.* The only time Uhuru saw any kind of loyalty was among guedado who were family, but their kind rarely survived. Yet he still felt sympathy for them, thinking of the guedado as a sibling who had lost his way. Their behavior toward one another was a direct result of serwan influence; they were the victims of a crime that had yet to be corrected.

It's been almost a year since I left, and still I am amazed at how the major cities of Kiskeya are constructed. The cities are composed of massive trees, redwoods that grow to heights beyond the scope of the human eye, with branches that interconnect like veins of the body and can extend from one tree to the next. The branches are so thick and rugged that one could easily walk from one tree to the other without fear of falling. Above the branches—truly a beautifully intertwined network of nature—is where the serwans live; they call it "nests." Below the branches is where most guedado and some kenyetta live, yet the kenyetta have homes; this is the Lower Levels. The cities make the best place for the guedado to survive because the trees provide some shelter and they collect any garbage disposed of by the serwans from up above. This is how they get some food and clothing. It is also how disease is spread among the guedado, which adds to the fear of them. The only other places where the serwans live are farming areas close to the ground that are maintained by esclaves. A good farming nest may have up to a hundred esclaves, while those in the city can have as few as fifteen. Humans are kept under tight watch. The only time they move around freely is through the Lower Levels on the Day of Homage or to the monument. On those days, the number of Ona on patrol triples.

Uhuru's Journal

One day while Uhuru was walking through the streets near the Citadel, he saw a young woman around his age fighting with a group of guedado. Uhuru wasn't going to intercede because this was a common thing to see in the Lower Levels, but then it got serious. The group of guedado was actually attacking the girl. They were trying to rob her, and when she refused, one of them slapped her right to the ground. "Give me what you have or you'll regret it," said the leader, who turned out to be a girl with a deep scar that went through her left eye.

The young woman got up from the ground and said, "I'm not going to give you anything." She was ready to fight back, but the attackers held her down. They were getting ready to teach her a lesson. But before they could give their next blow, Uhuru stepped in and hit one of them in the face with his elbow. He turned around, expecting a fight from the rest, but they just ran off, with the one who had gotten hit in the face slowly following behind.

Uhuru helped the young lady back up and asked, "Are you all right? Did they take anything?"

"No, I'm fine . . . . Thank you for your help. That was the third time they robbed me," she said. She then stared at Uhuru. "Why did you help me? Is there something you want?" It was a rare thing to get help in the Lower Levels.

"Nothing. I just saw you in trouble and thought I could help," Uhuru said.

At that moment, a group of Ona were flying above, probably looking for some innocent guedado to throw in prison. They were a special elite guard that was privately funded by the elite clans. They did the bidding of the Noble Regime for a variety of missions. They had at their disposal the most advanced weapons, designed to apprehend any individual through lethal means. Uhuru and his new friend didn't want to risk being captured, so they ran as though their life depended on it.

"This way—they won't check over here," said the young woman. They waited until the Ona were no longer near. But they had to be cautious, because sweeps of the Lower Levels were made periodically to keep the number of guedado to a minimum.

"What's your name?" asked Uhuru.

"Bijou," she said. She didn't seem like the other guedado. Most of them are broken down by a life of poverty.

"How did you get here?" he asked.

Bijou started by saying how she left in search of her little sister Bisa, who was about thirteen and had been missing since the last drought season. "She was sold away by my zwanga (master) for a profit," she said. For a moment she paused to keep an eye out for the Ona, but then continued, "At first I wasn't suspicious. Esclaves are sold all the time, but you can always expect to see the ones you love at the monument or during the Day of Homage to know they are well taken care of."

It gave Bijou peace of mind knowing that she would still see her sister. But weeks went by, and her family got worried. Bijou finally got the courage

to ask her master if there was any news about Bisa. He said it wasn't her business and he could only concern himself with the esclaves he owned. Bijou persisted every day, and it didn't matter that she got punished for it. She had to know. In her soul, she knew something was wrong. Bijou became relentless, even to the point that her master beat her with a stick and locked her in dark rooms. But no punishment was severe enough, and he still needed her to complete her duties. After a while, she realized that the more time passed, the chances of finding her sister would lessen. Bijou had to escape.

"My grandmother, the only family I have left, tried to convince me not to do it, but I was too stubborn and she wanted to know what had happened just as much as I did. Nothing was going to stand in my way, so my grandmother gave me as much food and money as I could carry, even some rags to blend in with the guedado," said Bijou.

Bijou was given the names of trusted esclaves and kenyetta in the area that her grandmother knew. It wouldn't take long for her master to notice that she was gone, so Bijou had to move fast. The last thing she did was tell her grandmother she loved her, and gave her a hug good-bye. She'd been searching for Bisa ever since.

At that moment, Uhuru thought of how he had gotten to this place and time. He weighed the chances that he would have met this girl in dire need of his help. He had been taught that with every task, a lesson must be learned. Some form of wisdom must be bestowed on you that will heighten your understanding of life. He now believed more than ever that he was meant to help her, and that by the end of his test, he would learn things to change his life forever. He held onto every word that Bijou said, completely fascinated by the small portion of her life that was told to him.

Afterward Uhuru wrote something new in his journal: *Life in the outer territories with the Maroons isn't for every person, but I always had a good sense of who I was and what was expected of me. Life was more nurturing instead of being dictated by others; never once did I feel less than anyone or some kind of possession. There were times that I struggled, but that is expected in any life, and especially if you want to become a true Safiya Maroon. But here in Kiskeya, I witness the degradation that takes place as the serwans find new ways to further cripple human beings . . . . People ask, "What is the meaning of life?" To me, it is to give life meaning.*

Several weeks passed, and during that time Bijou began to trust Uhuru, eventually showing him where she slept and introducing him to the people that had helped her in the efforts to find Bisa. They met every day and worked on the same thing, the last known whereabouts of her sister. Even though they trusted each other, Uhuru never revealed anything about who he really was; he didn't want to do anything that would jeopardize his final test before becoming a Safiya Maroon and receiving his Eno. Whenever Bijou asked a question, he would either lie or change the subject as he had been told to do, but she was aware of what he was doing. Growing up an esclave, she had learned how to be a little deceiving and secretive to protect herself. But she never held it against Uhuru because in her heart she knew he was a good man.

More time passed, and the leaves on the trees went from green to brown as they followed other leads to the whereabouts of her sister. They went about bribing every merchant that had information. Bijou's biggest fear was that her sister might have been kidnapped into underground labor dens. The merchants that they had met said such dens were filled with children who were either sold or kidnapped into them. These dens existed in all major cities and were against the law, but no one bothered to enforce it.

"These dens make up a substantial portion of the profit in Kiskeya, and no citizens want to lose their money," said one merchant. Currently, this was the third labor den they were about to encounter and still they hadn't found Bisa, but their hopes remained high. They journeyed through the Lower Levels looking for dying, abandoned redwoods, because underneath them is where the labor dens were usually located. They knew they could be captured at any moment and killed for trespassing, but that didn't matter; they hadn't come this far to turn back. They were prepared for the worst, carrying daggers under their cloaks and even small blades beneath their tongues.

They soon found an opening and journeyed into a deep corridor, in their hearts hoping to find Bisa. Torches were placed on the walls but only gave enough light to see a few feet ahead. They continued walking through until they came across another group of children in a dimly lit chamber. It was a depressing sight. All of them had been working until their fingers bled and were chained to their stations by the ankle. There was no way of knowing how long some of them had been there.

"Please don't hit me; I'll work harder!" Their first reaction had been to shield their faces as they heard the approaching footsteps. "Will we eat today?" asked another child, who seemed delirious.

"Look at the wounds caused by their chains; many of them will never walk without limping" whispered Bijou. Uhuru noticed but knew for some it didn't matter; infection would take them first.

It was a sad sight for them to see. For some of the children, it was too late; death was upon them. The children didn't even look up to see who had come into the room; they had been beaten into submission and taught never to look their tormentors in the eye. Food and water were scarce; but disease, fear, and pain were bountiful.

Bijou began by picking the locks on the children's ankles; she and Uhuru knew just what to do. "Don't worry. You all will be set free soon. My friend Uhuru and I will get you out of here." Bijou and Uhuru were lucky that the den master wasn't there; on their first mission they were told that the den masters return every few days to pick up the products made and hand out food. But that might soon change when the den masters hear of their laborers being set free.

After every child had been freed, they were taken back down the corridor that first led Uhuru and Bijou to the chamber. Bijou then lit a torch that set fire to the whole place. "This place will never be used again, never," she said.

As they were running back toward the entrance, Uhuru began thinking to himself, *Most of these children may not even have a home or family to go back to. All we really have done is freed them from one hell and placed them into the next. How will they survive now?*

As they reached the exit, the children struggled to look up at the sky. It had been so long since they'd seen the sun. Its powerful rays strained their eyes, but that was a pain they were grateful for.

Bijou saw the look on Uhuru's face. "What were we supposed to do? At least this way they have a chance," she said.

"A chance at what? Being kidnapped into another den, having no one to depend on because there is no one willing to take care of all of them? They are still going to struggle for food, but this time it will be harder because they will have to fight each other." Uhuru took a deep breath and looked up at the sky; he didn't want to say anything with contempt in his heart while Bijou was near him. This was an argument they'd had several times, and it always ended the same way.

. . . Three teardrops I have cried today after seeing the suffering of children deprived of life. My anger toward the serwans has reached new depths. They are to blame for all this, and I wait for the day when I return to the Maroon camp and get revenge.

Uhuru's Journal

The next few months went by as they comforted each other, making sure that neither got discouraged. Uhuru made every effort not to get attached to Bijou, realizing that one day he would have to shed this part of his life. But for now he was going to be supportive in the situation every way he could. They'd learned so much from one another. Bijou was a fine poet and dancer, traits that were passed down from women in her family, while Uhuru was a cook and skilled Hunter. She loved it when it rained. Whenever it started to pour, Bijou felt as though Origin understood her struggles and cried with her; but even in the Creator's sadness, there were blessings, because the raining waters seemed to wash all the sorrow away from the Lower Levels. All of the filth and frustration that existed in the land would be gone, and her heart seemed to be cleansed by his merciful tears, at least for the time being. Uhuru liked the rain because it was safer; the serwans were

reluctant to come out during a downpour, so the inhabitants of the Lower Levels could let their guard down.

Two years had gone by before Uhuru and Bijou found Bisa in the latest den. This time when they called out her name, she responded in a whisper that struggled to form words. Bisa had lost a lot of weight and hadn't eaten in weeks; they also discovered that she was blind in one eye. This was the most devastating and horrific den they had encountered; it was more like a tomb. A smell of death filled the air, and the scurrying of vermin could be heard in every direction as they chewed on the toes of the children chained to their stations, spreading disease and fear. It was too late for some, but those that were still alive were set free. By the looks, it was a place that had been abandoned by the den master, and they wanted to leave this dreadful place as soon as they could.

Weeks passed before Bisa was able to stand on her own, but Bijou was hopeful that she would make it. Uhuru knew that neither of them could go home, but luckily he knew of some trusted Chiderians who would be able to take care of the two sisters. This was a complete violation of Maroon law since it put the lives of people working toward free will in danger, but it didn't matter to Uhuru even if it meant being punished. Bijou and Bisa were taken to a safe location, and Uhuru stayed as long as he could to make sure that both of them would be okay.

When it came time to say good-bye, it was the hardest moment of his life and something that Bijou couldn't understand. "Why is it that to gain the life of my sister back, I have to let you go?" Bijou said with sadness in her voice. So much had happened since they met each other, and Bijou had never realized that she would be without Uhuru to lean on. "Why do you have to go? Where will you go?" For a moment everything was silent, and then she said, "I know neither of us have talked about how we feel, but I love you and you love me. I thought that one day I would bc your wife."

When she said that, a tear had fallen from Uhuru's face as he said, "I love you, too . . . . I think of you as more than a wife, as a reflection of

Origin's love for me. But I can't marry you; that is a promise that can't be kept . . . . I have made oaths and sworn my life to a greater cause."

Even though he never said it, Bijou understood what he meant, that he was a Maroon.

That was the last time he saw her, but he thought of Bijou every day. He was a young man when he had met her, but now he was fully grown and had risen to the rank of leader. The only thing he had left of her was a poem she wrote during their time together. He keeps it with him, remembering one of the lines that read, "Sometimes I feel like I'm drowning, struggling for air, but when I feel I can't last much longer, the Creator God Origin reaches out and gives me a last breath . . ." It made him think that she was his last breath that Origin had given to him, and it was the same for her.

On his first day back from his rite of passage, a ceremony was held as he was given his Eno. It was a beautifully crafted weapon; his father had put all his soul into forging a gift that would be suitable for his son. As Uhuru wielded the weapon, he loved it immediately; it had his entire lineage on it, and even his time in exile. The way Uhuru saw it, the Eno was crafted from the suffering he witnessed in Kiskeya; it was as if the Creator had worked to give shape to that suffering in the form of this Eno. Now he was a true Safiya Maroon. His weapon was shaped in the form of a flame. It had the capability of splitting into equal halves for a blade in each hand, and then becoming whole again when necessary as a spear. As he held his gift, Uhuru felt a connection to the weapon: it didn't just bend to his will but was an extension of his will.

When Uhuru brought his Safiya-Eno together at his ceremony, its vibrations resonated with only a few others. Only the true Akin-Eno can make them all vibrate; it holds the true purity needed that all other Enos are only variations of.

After his initiation, he heard that Bijou's sister had passed away; her time in the labor den had taken more of a toll than anyone actually knew. Bisa would wake up at night dripping with sweat, dreaming that she had been sent back to the den. She might have been physically set free from that underground prison, but her mind was forever trapped and whatever had blinded her one eye spread to the rest of her body. Uhuru made efforts to see Bijou, but by the time he arrived, he was told that she had left without saying good-bye to anyone or telling them where she was going.

KHUMANI

It was late in the evening as Khumani began picking some fresh fruits and vegetables from the garden behind her home. She had an array of organic food, with plants that grew to all sorts of heights. A barrier was constructed around the garden to protect it from hungry insects and animals; that was during the time after Nassor was sent away, and the barrier had been built to resemble a fortress. Tonight Khumani would be having a dinner for some very important guests. Even though Nassor had been sent away, it didn't deter her from trying to get Noble women the rights of citizenship. She felt that if she could gain citizenship, it would be possible to help Nassor and other esclaves gain free will. Tonight she would be having a meeting at home with other serwans who felt the same way. Only a handful would show up, but each had some sort of influence in Kiskeya. This would be a decisive meeting, one for which she had been preparing herself a long time. She almost didn't believe that this was actually happening; everything was set, the food was ready, and her speech prepared. She was ready for whatever concerns they might have, knowing that a few of them might still be reluctant in their association with her.

The time had finally come as all of those who had been invited came in one after the other and sat down to enjoy the feast before them. Most were officials of the Noble Regime or members of distinguished clans. One guest was Hasani, this generation's first descendant of the Obsidian family and brother to Chisulo, second-in-command of the Hunters. Their family was so respected that even the banner of Kiskeya was based on their family crest, born in the colors of white and gray. If Khumani was able to convince him, the others would follow his example.

For a moment, she began to doubt herself, wondering how she could change something that had existed in the system since the first age, both culturally and politically. Even if the law were to be changed for women, it wouldn't matter if the people didn't change with it. Having citizenship meant nothing if a woman refused to use it or worse, wasn't allowed to. *This may all just be futile*, she thought, but even so, an oath had been made to change things and Khumani would honor it. She reviewed her speech for the last time and decided that she would close by noting some of the most memorable Noble women who had been held back by the lack of citizenship.

Everything went the way she had planned, and she made sure to wish them a safe journey home as the night came to an end. The only person who stayed behind was Hasani, who said, "You did wonderfully tonight. Now they must take you seriously." Even though this meeting was about the rights of women, Khumani made note of the concerns of all those who were here tonight, and Hasani admired her for that.

What Khumani hadn't noticed while being with Hasani was that Nassor was watching them from outside. He took a great risk sneaking away from his home. At the time, he wasn't thinking about the consequences of his actions; it had been so long since he had seen her. The wounds on his head and ankle had completely healed from carrying the log during the entire drought season, suffering day and night with it chained to him. That was in the past now, and his back and leg felt good again. It only took a day to get to Khumani's home. With the amount of esclaves Adversary owned, no one would notice that he was missing for a while. He even had other esclaves do his work while he was away.

Nassor didn't know what to expect when he got to Khumani's home, whether her feelings had changed. Even if she were able to hide him, it could only be temporary. He would be risking a lot by getting her involved. He thought about turning around and going back. Even if it meant being punished severely, he would not let Khumani take the fall for his actions.

Suddenly, Nassor noticed that Hasani was leaving, and so he thought his chance had come. He waited until Hasani was out of sight and snuck in to see Khumani. She was cleaning when he came in and asked, "Would you like some help?"

Khumani was startled by the voice but immediately recognized who it was—the voice that reminded her of hope.

"Nassor, how did you get here? Are you in trouble?" she asked.

"No, everything is fine. I just had to see you," he said while stroking her cheek with the back of his hand. Then he pulled her closer. Everything was beginning to feel just right as both of them began taking deeper breaths from the tension and excitement they felt for each other, feeling their hearts beat harder and faster. Khumani had forgotten what it was like to be in his presence, feel his embrace. She closed her eyes and for a moment couldn't resist him and was ready to give in.

It was like instinct when she began caressing his ear and neck, bringing back moments of their secret love affair. The next thing that was said was a soft whisper and moan, " . . . missed you so much, hmmm." From there no words were needed; everything was said with touch alone. The candles around the room gave her skin an innocent glow, the perfect temptation. His touch was like warm water pouring down her back; every kiss given was made to be remembered. Who could deny such pleasure?

Nassor knew exactly what he wanted as he kissed her on the cheek and down to her neck tauntingly, playfully. They both possessed full lips as Nassor kissed her softly in a way that was soothing; it just felt so right to her. Khumani felt so seduced that for a moment she was letting go all of her inhibitions. Nassor continued giving her soft and enduring kisses on her forehead, cheek, even her eyes. But he wouldn't stop there as he attempted to go further.

Suddenly Khumani came to her senses and moved away from him. Softly she said, "We cannot do this; I cannot do this. There is just too much at risk."

At first puzzled, Nassor responded, "Is this about that Noble I saw you with? I knew one day you would find someone else; I just didn't think I would be around to see it.".

"This is not about him. This is about me and the things I want and need. This is about succeeding in a goal I swore to accomplish, citizenship for women, and *I will not let you stand in my way*," she said.

It was Nassor's greatest fear come true: Khumani regretted ever having been involved with him.

"This was a mistake. If anyone ever found out about our relationship, they would kill us and burn down the home of my family," Khumani continued. She knew that out of disgrace her family would have to leave and be socially ostracized; they would lose all respect and influence they held in the land. Her name would be stricken from the ancestry of her family as though she had never existed. She even mentioned that esclave males, his people, would face harsher laws because of them.

"Sometimes I thought you were worth the risk, but that was before. I have almost reached my purpose, and I will not throw that away for you. No one can find out about this; it ends tonight." She then turned her back to him so that he would leave.

It was the most hurtful thing that Nassor had ever heard: the one person he was willing to sacrifice all for wasn't willing to do the same for him. But he still loved her, and in his heart he already forgave her for what she said. The only thing left was to say that which was in his own heart. "Sometimes I close my eyes when I am with you, and I forget *what* we are and remember *who* we are. Khumani, you are a reflection of the things I want and need. We share the same thinking and understanding. I could never let you go; I love you." Nassor couldn't deny it. Khumani was a mirror image of the Origin's love for him, but neither one could ever experience it. Tears were brought to both their eyes.

"Nassor, you have to understand that I have a purpose, and the time is now. What we share as love is an abomination to others, serwan and human alike. I've just begun to gain serious influence, but all that could be lost . . ."

Khumani was interrupted by a sudden knock at the door. "Hello . . . Can I come in?" It was Hasani!

Nassor's face went from sadness to anger instantly. Khumani was really scared now!

Before Nassor took one step toward the door, she blocked his path. "Please, don't do this," Khumani pleaded, and then with seriousness in her voice she continued, "I won't let you; I need him!"

Hasani continued knocking. "Khumani, let me in."

"I will be right there, Hasani. Give me a moment," she said.

"Nassor, he is a good one. Even though he doesn't agree with everything I believe in, he is still open-minded about my needs. He even thinks that esclaves shouldn't be burdened by the law, that they should have free will," Khumani said while looking in Nassor's eyes.

She trusted Hasani. With him, her life wouldn't be one of struggle, regret, and mourning. Nassor realized she would have all the things with Hasani that she could never have with him.

Then Nassor, with a sadness in his voice, said, "You've said all the things that make your relationship with him seem perfect, except that you can't love him . . . not if you love me."

"I can grow to love him," she responded, "and maybe you don't care about your life, but I know you care about mine. You don't want to see me get punished, so if you care about me, leave now."

With that she turned her back to Nassor without guarantee that he would actually leave as she moved toward the door. But by the time Hasani was let in, Nassor had snuck out the back. He didn't even bother to look back as he headed home, discouraged. The last thing he heard as he left was that Hasani came back for some documents.

It would be a long walk back to Adversary's home. Nassor couldn't think about how punished he would be and didn't care. But the journey home did make him think and reflect about his life, about the decisions he had made thus far. These thoughts came to Nassor heavily as he tried not to be seen by any Ona patrolling above.

Nassor was now halfway home; he could tell because he was near the city limits. Suddenly, he heard some faint screams. Nassor looked around to see where they were coming from. As he got closer, he could hear people crying, "Leave us alone; stop hitting him!"

It was Hunters, three of them, including Chisulo and Kumi. They were assaulting a group of guedado for fun. Gina and her two boys were being questioned about the Maroons and the Path of Chideria.

"Tell us what you know. Are you conspiring against the government of Kiskeya?" asked Chisulo.

What frustrated Nassor the most was that the Hunters knew that their victims had no association with any plots against Kiskeya; these people had lost their minds long ago living in the Lower Levels. By now Nassor's hatred for his half brother Kumi had been taken to new depths as he watched an innocent group of people being humiliated. When they still considered each other family, Kumi and Nassor made efforts to help the guedado, even Gina on a number of occasions—but that was another life.

He watched as the Hunters continued their onslaught, punishing them with no regard. It was sad to hear the cries for mercy.

"What do you know of the Maroons?" asked one Hunter, who was kenyetta.

"Nothing, we know nothing," replied Gina.

"I think this one is a spy," said Chisulo, pointing at one of the boys. Then they grabbed him, the boy who had been always fascinated by the Nobles. He was the one who caught the Hunters' attention.

"Don't hurt him, he's a child, innocent . . ." pleaded Gina as she tried to step in. But she was restrained by Kumi, who in his heart struggled to do the right thing.

Chisulo pulled out a dagger, and the situation went from bad to worse. "I won't kill him, but he must be taught a lesson and be a symbol to all esclaves who wish to betray their masters, their saviors."

Kumi felt that Chisulo was going too far. He was thinking that this could easily be him one day, but he dared not intercede, especially not for any guedado. To the Hunters, Kumi was still of a deviant race, regardless of his caste.

The other boy attempted to stop Chisulo to protect his brother, but the kenyetta Hunter kicked him right in the face and he fell to the ground.

Chisulo had already begun making incisions on the boy.

That was it for Nassor. With all that had happened recently, his rage was now like a fire that couldn't be snuffed out. He sprang from the shadows, catching the Hunters by surprise. He attacked Chisulo first, taking the dagger. With his free hand, he slammed Chisulo's face into the side of a tree, knocking him unconscious.

"Get away from here, *now!*" said Nassor as Gina took her boys to safety.

Nassor then took the dagger and plunged it into the leg of the kenyetta Hunter, whose cry was loud enough to alert all others who were still in the area. As much as he wanted to get revenge on Kumi, he couldn't spare the time. Nassor ran back into the woods, thinking that if it weren't for his half brother, he wouldn't have been sold away in the first place.

Kumi stood there shocked by what just happened. When he realized that the person helping the guedado was his brother, he stood frozen. Seeing his brother risk his life for a group of people who were considered scum by society, he just couldn't understand why Nassor was more willing to sacrifice for them instead of the serwans, a Noble people. He hated Nassor with a passion for having the courage that he didn't, for trying to be the hero and doing the right thing. Every time Kumi was in a situation where he had to choose between his loyalty to the serwans and mercy for the humans, Nassor would always step in to make him look weak and cowardly, just like tonight. That was the way he saw things happen when it came to his half brother.

At that moment, more Hunters showed up to go after Nassor. As they left, Kumi shouted, "Be careful, this human is a dangerous *Maroon*."

THE TRIAL SET FORTH

Life is meaningless without a reason to live it; being alone and unloved is the worst punishment for any caste. It was a punishment known very well by Nyack, who sat in a dark prison chamber below the Lower Levels. He had been confined there for eight weeks, not even allowed to see sunlight or the courtroom. His enemies were determined to see him break and fall before their might. They made every attempt possible to confuse and humiliate him, all because they felt entitled to do so. Whatever hope he had of seeing the outside world had been taken away since the city was placed under quarantine; an alert was placed over Kiskeya since the Hunters were attacked by those they believed were Maroons.

Nyack overheard a prison guard talking about the incident earlier, that the Hunters had gotten some information on a Maroon gathering that would be taking place within the city. They had come across some suspicious activity and went in to investigate. A fight took place, but the rebels managed to get away when the Hunters stopped to save some innocent civilians. Times were becoming dangerous, and people were beginning to protest.

"They are worse than deviant; they are vermin," said one of the guards, trying to insinuate that the Maroons who escaped used deceitful methods to get away.

"One of the Hunters was stabbed in the leg; it got in deep. I believe it may have been amputated because of infection. For his patriotism, he will be given the medal of valor," said another.

Nyack had just finished recounting what he had heard when the prison door screeched open. The guards were bringing in food for him and the inmate that was recently brought in. Nyack didn't get a good look at the prisoner when he first came in, only heard the sound of shackles rattle

against the floor. It was a surprise to Nyack to have someone to share his burden with because this level of confinement was reserved for the most heinous criminals. He had never expected to have a cellmate; there was a greater chance that he would be left down here to die alone.

The guards left after giving the two prisoners their rations of food and closed the prison door behind them. It was dreadful each time Nyack heard the sound of that door, because it made him think of the day when he would hear it close for the last time. Shaking his head, Nyack tried not to think about the dismal situation he was in—what's done is done. Even if he didn't accomplish what he sought, he still got very far. The sacrifice he made dealt a major blow to serwan law and inspired humans against their masters. For the first time since the Sentient War, the war that ended the First Age, humans knew their place, and it wasn't under the foot of the Nobles. Nyack took comfort in that, and his last act of redemption would be to reach out to the inmate next to him because whatever he did, it must have been as serious as Nyack's crime.

The first few days Nyack tried everything to talk to the other prisoner, "Why are you here?" said Nyack, but the prisoner wouldn't answer. "My name is Nyack—have you heard of me?" he continued, but the other prisoner was silent. "Friend, we share a similar fate, so we must have a similar understanding for one another. This place can be very lonely when you have as much time as I have to think alone. Sometimes I don't know whether I am asleep or awake because, whether my eyes are opened or closed, I am surrounded by darkness. I don't even know what time of day it is until the guards bring food, I haven't seen the colors of light that reflect from the monument in a long time. But it is a blessing to know that I have you to share this burden with, a blessing beyond measure. You may not want to talk, friend, but I have plenty to say for the both of us." After pausing for a brief moment to see if his new cellmate had anything to say, Nyack continued.

He explained how over time this place had started to drive him crazy. Between the trial and this dark prison, he was exhausted and his mind began to wander. Nyack started to hear little whispers that were incoherent, but over time the voices got louder; they would groan at night as though they were in pain and wanted him to share in their suffering. Maybe it was the guards taunting him, just one more way the law wanted to see him suffer. But then the voices would say things, things that were personal that no one else could have known. He had lost so much already, and the voices took every opportunity to remind Nyack of that.

"The voices haunted me, trying to convince me to commit suicide, even taking the appearance of my enemies. Even in the courtroom, I struggled. But the voices were a whole new form of punishment; they called themselves Legion. They convinced me to do things in the darkness of this cell, things that were against my nature, even telling me that my food had been poisoned. For a while, I truly lost what I held sacred . . . my spirit," said Nyack, who realized these were his inner demons brought to reality at his most vulnerable moment.

But one day another voice started to speak to him, one that was different from the others. A voice that protected him from the others. It told him that he was being tested, that he had to be prepared for the final days of the trial. The guards thought that they were witnessing him going crazy, but Nyack was really more ready than ever. Now each time Nyack went to court, his arguments became much more effective. The questions and statements made by the judge were the same as the voices; his enemies felt weak now that they were at his mercy. Now no punishment brought down upon him would be enough to deter Nyack from revealing the truth, that humans are the true heirs of Kiskeya.

We were made from the dust of the earth with the breath of the Creator. We are a reflection of his greatness . . . and one day we will cleanse the earth of the abominations that exist against his will.

3rd World Order

A week later . . .

"In the beginning, when the serwan race first discovered Kiskeya, it was a treacherous land, where we found a creature so evil and vicious that we called it man. The creation of man is not a wondrous act, but a fateful mistake of nature. Life was not breathed into the humans from an omnipotent force that makes itself known only to the humans. No, they are the crust that was dusted off from creation, as a blade is crafted by removing all impurities . . ." stated a new Noble prosecutor who seemed more manipulative than the last.

"As it was written, there exists a weakness in man, a corruption that he refuses to accept, but we ourselves cannot be blinded to it. Our forefathers witnessed it during their conquest of the land; this flaw that lives in his very being is their truest enemy. They were not created for greatness, but only for deviance. But through us, they have found a purpose in servitude." The prosecutor then directed his attention from the citizens to Nyack and continued, "It is their deviance that makes them incapable. Nyack, like all humans, lacks the mental understanding and physical capability to have dominion over the land. If there is some divine creator that the humans have faith in, why would it make false prophecies of them ruling over the earth? Surely a prophecy of this caliber would have been reserved for a more superior people."

Nyack suddenly felt a weakness in his legs when the prosecutor approached him further to say, "Whatever this force is, this God, it lied to you. It was merely a myth created to give humans hope of usurping serwan order, Noble order, but in reality it was a deception that has inhibited your people."

Most serwans stopped relying on the assistance of Gods centuries ago; allegiance to Gods in the past created enemies among their people. They now see that the prophecies given to mankind only show their weakness, that they need to be dependent on something other than themselves, whether it be a God or a serwan authority figure.

"Even now, as Nyack stands before us, his answers come from voices instead of himself, unlike my people who forge and walk their own paths, not the paths dictated by others," said the new prosecutor. He was very persuasive in his arguments and had an arrogance that pleased the Nobles.

"There are a lot of citizens who seem to sympathize with humans. They say that it's time to free them and whatever discord that exists between our two peoples must be buried. But the citizens who say that don't own any humans; they don't have to deal with them the way most of us have to," said the prosecutor.

Nyack watched as the prosecutor continued to condemn the right of humans to live their own lives.

"Like any creature, if you give them a hand, they will take an arm . . ." the prosecutor continued. "Free will should only be given to those who have earned it from their master." The more the prosecutor spoke, the more he convinced the other serwans.

"The truth is, I fear for the leadership and future of Kiskeya if we were to let humans have their way. We must continue with our current course and never deter from laws that were forged by our ancestors. Whether we agree with them or not, those laws have led to a safe and prosperous society. More than anything, my loyalty lies with Kiskeya and its citizens; my lineage has inhabited this land for nearly an entire age. I am bound to this land, and I have a patriotic duty to uphold its greatness and extinguish those who would hinder that greatness. To change the law would be to change history, to change ourselves, and I am not one for change," said the prosecutor.

Nyack listened to every word that the prosecutor was saying, but he didn't notice the three most elite in Kiskeya that were sitting above him; it was rare to see all three of them make an appearance in one place. Clearly, this trial was more than just about a disgruntled human trying to upset his master; it had now disrupted the fabric of serwan law, since half of it only applied to humans.

All three of the elite—Obsidian, (Adversary) Sceptor, and (Desever) Abyss—sat together wearing cloaks that marked their social caste; they were treated as royalty in the courtroom. They were whispering to one another about the trial.

"It must not incite a rebellion within the esclaves of Kiskeya. If the Maroons were to attack at the same time as a rebellion, we would lose," said Obsidian, who preferred to be recognized by his family name.

"Don't worry," replied (Adversary) Sceptor. "I have set some precautions. As I have told you, there have been a few advances in our artillery that only the highest officials have knowledge of."

The three elite felt confident in their plotting. Each day the Hunters patrolled the cities seeking out the enemy like bloodhounds.

"Humans are scared; the slightest suspicions from them are dealt with harshly. The Hunters work to infiltrate, intimidate, and annihilate those who are against the Noble Regime. These methods of disciplining humans have never failed. They have been made subservient since the last age, with servitude instilled into their being. They only know to serve, and that will not change," continued (Adversary) Sceptor.

The trial went on as the prosecutor spoke to the hearts of the people, but if he wanted to remove any doubts they had about mankind, he would have to make things personal. When it seemed that the trial was reaching its peak, he brought up the story of creation, **the Great Conflict of the Immortals and Noble Gods**.

"Once, my mother told me of the Immortals, abominations remembered only as the strain or old affliction. In a time of prosperity, the old affliction made itself known to the world, becoming the one thing the Noble Gods feared the most, until they were imprisoned so that life would be preserved. For generations after, the Noble Gods lived in peace, knowing that this threat had been locked away. But their world, which was once united, fell into division when *Affliction*, the father of the human race, killed Sapient, the Sovereign God, and unleashed the old affliction once more. Then the Immortals went to war against the Gods, a war that broke the earth so that nothing would ever be the same again," said the prosecutor, who knew he had finally won the people over.

"This man, Nyack, wishes to have free will; but the last time man had free will, *corrupt* knowledge entered our world. The Noble Gods were once part of the greatest civilization; no greater society has existed before or after them. But whether you believe this as fact or not, the understanding that comes from it is simple: to be cautious of man's intentions and the destruction that will come from his free will." That was the last thing the prosecutor said.

This brought the trial to an end, and the prosecutor was very pleased with the reactions from the entire courtroom.

As a result of what the prosecutor said, the judge rendered a guilty verdict. The judge felt that for peace to be restored and for the safety of all citizens, Nyack must be immediately sentenced. "This trial has been a reminder of the deviance that man is capable of, and my purpose is to maintain order in the land of Kiskeya. Therefore, Nyack C'Kre, I sentence you to live out the remainder of your days in the Lougawou Mountains."

Immediately the people in the courtroom raised hands in celebration, and the protestors that were gathered outside the Citadel cheered in disbelief—order had been restored for them.

Kesi was near the Citadel at the time, and she watched as Nyack was brought back to his prison cell. For a short moment, they saw each other, and Nyack felt comfort knowing that he had fulfilled his role in all this. But in his heart, he also felt defeated. Humans were no longer part of the caste system. In the words of those who sentenced him, "A human cannot claim his own free will, and therefore can never be a citizen regardless of being born free or esclave."

It had now become law . . . humans were no longer deviant; they were property.

IGNORANCE AND ANARCHY

Watching as people gave praise to the prosecutor, Abyss shook hands with the ambitious, young Noble, as if to say, "You will go down in history, my friend." A swarm of people cheered his name while he walked among the clan elite.

Before, the serwan people were angry and frightened by the outright defiance of humans in Kiskeya. A mob of them had rallied in front of the Citadel demanding the immediate sentencing of C'Kre and the head of the assailants who attacked the Hunters. Distrust had spread among the citizens—how was it possible that the Maroons were still infiltrating the city to hold secret meetings and then escape after defeating the Hunters? The serwans had lost confidence in the government and began harassing esclaves randomly as intimidation tactics.

The judge thought that by giving Nyack a guilty verdict, he would bring back the harmony and order that had left the land, but news of the guilty verdict only empowered the mob. The power to maintain control over humans was great within the citizens. They felt the need to strike humans at their heart, so for days after the trial, they burned places known to be where humans congregate. The leader of the mob was a serwan female, Mala-Dek, who had encouraged the people for a guilty verdict and stricter rules against humans. She incited the protestors to raid the homes of humans and kenyetta, dragging them into the streets to interrogate them. They forced their prisoners to kneel down on jagged pieces of rocks and extend their arms outward like wings while bricks were placed in each hand. They had to hold that position for however long Mala-Dek deemed fit.

As she walked through the group of people on their knees for committing no crime, one of them looked her right in the eye. For that, she beat the young man with the inside of her fist repeatedly, saying, "A human has no right to look at me; no one who should be feared should be looked at in the eye."

She enjoyed taking away hope from her victims. Even the cries of a small child did not shake her. She approached a little girl clinging to her mother, who was on her knees being punished. Mala-Dek asked why she was crying, and the little girl held her mother tight and said, "Because of you."

There was nothing the mother could do but pray in her heart that no harm came to her child.

Mala-Dek then asked, "Where did your mother get that scar on her left eye?"

"She doesn't know," replied her mother.

Mala-Dek took a deep breath and looked at the little girl, realizing that she only wanted to go back to the safety of her mother's home. So Mala-Dek said, "Take your daughter and go; I will spare you and yours."

Quickly, the mother dropped the bricks from her hands and grabbed her daughter to run as fast as they could, but as soon as she got up she fell hard right to the ground.

Mala-Dek and the rest of the mob laughed at them. She said, "You must never show mercy to them—but let them think you will."

Kneeling on the jagged rocks had taken away all the feeling in the mother's legs; she couldn't walk and had to crawl away. It was no longer enough for the serwans to intimidate, but they had to demean the humans as well. With her daughter by her side, the mother continued to crawl until they were out of sight.

As a young girl, Mala-Dek was born with a rare disorder; she had a recessive disease that was the result of inbreeding. Her parents shared a common ancestor from centuries earlier, and it was the reason she had suffered her whole life. The disease gave her wings like a bat that had no distinguishing birthmarks, and in serwan society that was a disgrace. Even humans were bold enough to make fun of her, so for a long time Mala-Dek felt the sting of being ostracized by everyone. Even though humans had no wings, they still had each other, but she had no one who could relate to her.

As a child she was called Mala and did everything she could to be treated normally, but the more she tried, the more her family pushed her away. She remembers how all her other sisters and brothers got what they wanted because their features were considered acceptable by society—but not her. She would get into as much trouble as the rest of her siblings, but they got off easy while she was punished mercilessly even for the smallest offense. Her parents would tell her that she only got into trouble looking for their attention and that she should stop. But it didn't matter because they never gave her the attention she needed. Love couldn't be forced, her mother told her; it had to be given, but her mother still did more for the rest of the family than for her.

Only one person treated her well—Mala's older brother. Once in a while he would make fun of her, but that was something every child in the family went through. Sadly, though, he had been killed by a human some time ago. The news of her brother made her bitter and sadistic. She decided because of the pain caused from his death that she would repay that debt to all humans until she caught the one who murdered him, but her scars ran deeper than that. No one but her knew of his involvement with the labor dens. Since then Mala rose quickly in their ranks. Her ways of maintaining a productive den helped her become in charge of the whole organization in Peponi, and she hopes to eventually run the organizations in all the major cities of Kiskeya. Eventually she took on the name Mala-Dek, meaning "affliction," because her influence spread like a disease.

Later that day after Mala and the mob let all of their victims go, she planned on meeting all of the major den masters in Siek, the second largest city in Kiskeya. They were having a dinner to discuss what the threat of a war or rebellion meant for them and whether their profits in the labor dens were at stake. She arrived there late with her comrades; they didn't realize how much enjoyment they would get from protesting and lost track of time. By the time they arrived, everyone in the room was dead—their drinks had been poisoned. No investigation could be made because this was an illegal meeting. Mala-Dek knew that if any officials found out, she could be implicated and bring further shame to her family.

Without touching anything, she looked through the room and found a burned rose. Without a second thought, she left the room and set it on fire. Mala-Dek knew who had killed them—it was the same person that had tried to kill her, and this was the second attempt that failed. "You will never get me; I will get you first, do you hear me? . . . I will kill you first."

FIRST LOVE

Kesi had managed to get away from the mob of protestors before it had gotten violent. When she got home, she fought back tears felt for all the people she cared about that had been locked away. She then took a deep breath to compose herself and went to sleep.

The next day the rioting had gotten worse. The Noble Regime started to deploy the Ona as a warning to all those disturbing the peace, but the Ona seemed to fuel their rage, making the situation become deadlier.

Most of the serwans involved with the rioting were poor; they needed someone to blame for their struggles, someone to take their anger and frustration out on. They had no real control over their lives and decided to do something about it. Unfortunately, they didn't get what they wanted from torturing innocent humans and kenyetta, so they started to harass the government of Kiskeya. They accused the Noble Regime and all the elite clans of working with the Maroons. They claimed that there was no real rebellion but only real corruption of government, using the wealth of the people to fund a war that didn't exist so that the rich stayed rich and the poor stayed hungry.

"The Ona are nothing more than the government's puppets, who disguise themselves as protectors but are just another means of profit for the elite, profit that is taken from all of us," cried one protestor.

The Ona managed to arrest the biggest instigators of the riots and placed them in jail, hoping to eventually quell this idea that government was corrupt. The last thing that Kiskeya needed was dissension among its citizens.

Kesi hadn't been this scared since she was a child. She was born of a beautiful Noble woman that she never knew and a human father. While her mother was still young, she fell in love with a young amanche male who had been given the Caste of Innocence. It was still a very dangerous game they played, but the secret meetings they planned were easier since he could travel around freely. Kesi's father went across the land performing odd jobs for anyone that would pay him; he learned several valuable skills in his time. Word of his ability to do work in a timely fashion spread, which was how he met the mother of his child: he had been referred by a previous employer to her nest. His job was to help build an extension to their home that would make it twice as big. His employer at the time was Sorabi, the father of his love. Sorabi wanted something that was truly spectacular. It had to be a marvel to all who ventured by his home, and prior experience told him that his current esclaves weren't capable of such design.

But when Kesi's mother had gotten pregnant right after the extension to the nest was finished, the two of them feared for their lives and the life of their unborn child, especially since she had been betrothed to marry a rich Noble man. For an entire season, Kesi's mother wore loose-fitting clothing and went on as many trips as possible without anyone getting suspicious. Kesi's father tried to stay calm, but the thought that he could be separated from the people he loved most in the world was too much to bear. He refused to let that happen again. His plan was to run away with her, but Kesi's mother knew they would be hunted down—Sorabi would pursue them relentlessly. Their only hope was to give birth to their daughter in secrecy and give her to her father. The child would travel the territories with her father, while her mother would be forced to marry someone she could never love.

They thought that if Sorabi ever found out, it would be too late because his daughter would be married and he wouldn't risk telling anyone what he knew because it would ruin him. He would be forced to keep silent about the truth of his illegitimate granddaughter. It was a sad plan, but the only plan that guaranteed life for everyone involved. When Kesi was finally born under the tree where her parents had met so many times, it was the happiest moment of their lives but the last time they were ever together. They spent the whole day under that tree with their daughter, a moment that could never be taken away from them. The next day Kesi and her father left and never came back, while her mother stayed in bed every day crying herself to sleep for weeks. Sorabi was told that she was very sick and needed to recover in bed. Eventually she did get married, and for several years no one knew about what she did or the sacrifice she made for love.

Kesi's mother stayed in contact with her secret family. They left messages for each other in hidden places, just as they had before they were separated. She knew that her daughter was being well taken care of, and Kesi knew all about her beautiful serwan mother. It wasn't much, but this was all they had; the messages told her where they had been and where they were going next. If the message was really touching, Kesi's mother would keep it locked away to always come back to it at Sorabi's nest—any other letter was immediately burned. Each letter made her cry a little, realizing the happiness that was denied her, and life seemed miserable because of it. To be denied first love pained her heart, and *first love* was what they were. It meant everything.

As careful as they were, one of the human esclaves stumbled upon one of the letters and gave it to Sorabi, assuming that it must be for him. It was a recent letter, and it gave enough information to tell him of his illegitimate granddaughter's whereabouts, a deception that had been kept from him for some time. Sorabi wondered to himself that if he knew, who else did? "I can't let this turn into a disaster that will ruin my daughter; her shame can never be discovered." With a sympathetic voice, Sorabi soon confronted his daughter and told her that she would never have to worry about these vicious amanche humans ever again. "He has taken advantage of you, and he will be punished." Sorabi had convinced himself that Kesi's father was extorting his married daughter, keeping this horrible secret over her head for money. Sorabi felt this dark secret was the reason she was sad so often after leaving his home.

Kesi's mother panicked. She didn't know how to react to her father's discovery. Her mind kept saying, *Tell the truth, tell him that he is not extorting you but that you love him.* But as her lips began to move, she said, "Yes, Father, you're right about everything, and I don't know what to do. It was a mistake I made years ago. Can you help me get rid of him?"

Out of fear she lied. With each word that came out of her mouth, she struggled not to let the lie go any further, but it was as though something else was making the decisions. She broke down in tears before him. After hearing what she had to say, Sorabi assured her that he would take care of it. "You won't have to deal with this burden."

The last letter Kesi and her father got was a warning telling them that Sorabi knew and was coming after them. Kesi's mother was able to warn them in time as the chase began. She didn't go into details about how Sorabi found out; all she said in the letter was, "You can never contact me again for your own safety. Please take care of my daughter and know that my biggest regret is the love that I failed to prove I have for you both . . . Enrich my mind, feed my soul, my heart skipped a beat or time literally froze."

But now Kesi's father was faced with another hard decision. He had sworn never to give up his loved ones again, but life kept forcing him to do just what he hated most. By now most people recognized him and his daughter from all their travels, and he couldn't trust anyone not to betray them for the right profit. There were only two choices: live life on the run anticipating the day he and his daughter would be captured, or give his daughter away.

Kesi remembers that day, how hard it was for her and her father to go their separate ways. Even though she was young, she understood what was happening. Her life changed dramatically. Her father held her tightly, with his last words being something she would never forget: "Sometimes I feel like I'm drowning, and I can't breathe until God gives me a last breath . . . you were my last breath given to me by God when I was drowning, and I wouldn't have been in this world as long as I have if it weren't for you." That was the last time she ever saw him; Kesi was given to relatives on her father's side.

She was never treated any differently by her new family; they always had kind words for her, but for some reason she kept her distance from them. Kesi thought it would be better if she didn't get too attached in case they were ever taken away from her. Because of that, some of them assumed that Kesi thought she was better than them, but that

wasn't the case at all. Sometimes she got in fights with her cousins, and hurtful things were said. "You were left in the gutter by your father because he didn't love you; you were a mistake that he didn't want to deal with, and my father took pity on you." But eventually Kesi and her cousins grew up and put their differences aside, realizing that they all shared a similar fate as esclaves. She came to the understanding that the reason why her life turned out the way it did was because her father was human and her mother was serwan. Since that time, she dedicated her life to something greater, to a world where there was no caste system, just people. She soon found that greater calling in the Path of Chideria, rising to the rank of Faizah, the high priestess.

The order filled the emptiness in her heart and gave her life meaning. She no longer felt like the victim who needed aid, but was giving aid through scripture and love for the creator, Origin. One of her first acts was feeding those less fortunate, such as the guedado. Even people in the order didn't understand her deep concern for them, but it wasn't meant for them to understand. Her desire to help others was beyond herself and from the Creator, who now led her life. Through the Chideria, Kesi felt as though she gained back an identity that was taken away from her. For so long, the devices and history of humans were disregarded as a vicious upbringing before the serwan ways. Humans were expected to hate themselves and everything that made them who they were. They had to relinquish thousands of years of human tradition to be accepted, yet still be despised by their serwan rulers.

But as always, fear reminded Kesi of what she needed to do. She gathered some food and clothes, telling herself, "Everything will be all right. Calm down and think of the mission." She then opened a doorway beneath the floor to her home that led to a secret compartment. Inside was a shrine dedicated to the Path of Chideria that could house several people. Kesi would turn to this place anytime she was scared, happy, or just needed time to think.

"I have some food for you. You will need it when you leave tonight, and these clothes to disguise yourself," said Kesi.

"Thank you, High Priestess, you have done and sacrificed more for the cause than anyone. It will not be forgotten by the Creator," replied the stranger.

"It is my duty to protect the Living Busara with my life if I must. You are needed to bring an end to all of our suffering," said Kesi. "Soon you will leave to help the Maroons in the outer territories and bring free will to our people. Nothing else matters." Kesi was another woman willing to make the hard decisions and take the lead that no one else was willing to take as she prepared the Living Busara to be placed with Uhuru, the Maroon leader. Looking around the room to make sure everything was packed, she found a small sculpture carved to look like the diamond tree.

"You should keep it as a reminder of him; he has yet to fulfill his role in all this," said the Living Busara.

"What role can Nassor fulfill in prison waiting to be sentenced? He came to me needing help, but all I did was put him in greater danger. Now he is paying the price," said Kesi. So now, like Nyack, Nassor would be punished. A man who had suffered and lost so much already.

"Tell me, before it is time to leave, how did you get involved with him?" asked the Living Busara as she laid down to rest.

"I was in the forest very early in the morning, almost daylight, when Nassor came running toward me. He had been trying to hide all night. At first, he didn't recognize me because I was dressed so differently. When he realized that it was me, he jumped back as though there was no hope. But even so, he was desperate and asked for help from me, a stranger to him in some ways. Even now, I'm surprised he put his trust in me," said Kesi.

"Nassor looked so tired, like he didn't have any strength left to keep running. His clothes were covered in sweat, and he had blood on his hands. I wasn't sure what to do at first. I didn't want to jeopardize the mission, but then I heard the voices of the Hunters nearby. They were after Nassor because of his attack on them. Nassor immediately jumped to his feet; fear gave him the strength he needed to last a little longer." Kesi knew she couldn't risk being seen with him, especially with what she wore. Any Hunter would know that she was part of the order.

"I told Nassor to come with me, and we ran as fast as we could, following the path of a river. Not long after, we reached the waterfalls and climbed the rocks that led to one of the secret tunnels. It led us to a cave entrance, and we continued the long journey from there," said Kesi, who was thankful they got to safety.

Nassor was dismayed by the history of these caverns. They had been built long ago, hidden in plain sight by the most fearless of human esclaves still resistant to serwan law even after they lost the war centuries earlier. They kept the caves as escape routes, and only the most diligent believers of Chideria know of their existence.

"This place was built so that future generations would not forget why we fight. On the walls are a written history of all those who traveled these corridors. Our life stories can be told throughout the tunnels," said Kesi.

On the wall, Nassor had read aloud some of the writings. "Before I die, a piece of who we are and what we have done must be left behind if we are unable to free the human race." Kesi wrote one in memory of her father. "Sometimes we feel like we are drowning, struggling for air, but God gives us one last breath to live." Nassor told Kesi that he heard that one a long time ago, which surprised her as they continued down the path.

"There are other places built just like this throughout Kiskeya. This is one of the oldest and had been abandoned generations ago. More of the meeting places for the order are being discovered because of spies, and now we must resort to former installations. We call them underworlds, places of refuge for the coming war, the last home and final resting place of the Chideria Order," said Kesi.

"Welcome, brother, to the other side of humankind that has been denied to you," said Kesi as she and Nassor came to the end of the tunnel.

It was an amazing place built inside the edge of a cliff, and vacant as they entered. The room itself was coated with a reflective serum found in plants; with one torch everything could be seen. This was a place built to last through any disaster and big enough to house several dozen people. Nassor continued to notice all of the writings that had been engraved throughout; it made him curious about all its hidden history.

"There will be others here soon, so have some food and I will be right back," said Kesi.

Nassor then traveled even deeper through the underworld until he came across another level hidden behind a curtain. He pulled the curtain and jumped back, startled by a statue. He pulled the curtain even further, and found there were other statues made of wood and metal, with names carved on them. The entire level was dedicated to these statues and preserved by the plant serum.

Different areas of the room depicted different stories. On the ceiling was the statue of a Noble fused with the building; it soared overhead, chasing after a woman and her child who ran in fear.

Another one showed a group of humans who seemed to be crying out in agony, even sharing a similar marking across their bodies; they looked like giant spiders. Some of the statues were made as part of the caverns, carved into the walls and floors with portions of their bodies emerging.

The last sculptures that Nassor saw was a group of humans finding the tomb of creation, with three men leading the way. The tomb was sunk into the floor with two heads poking up behind it, as though they were ascending from a pit. Nassor didn't realize what was before him, but by the art and detail, it was something of great importance; he knew that these were heroes of old, *forefathers of a defiant race.*

"Nassor became mesmerized by all that he saw, and now I see him in a whole new way," said Kesi.

"Yes, he is a brave man. He must have been shocked to discover that you were part of the order . . . I'm just glad to have known him," said the

Living Busara, as they both became saddened by what had happened. After Kesi helped Nassor, she took him to one of the Chideria meetings, and they were betrayed by one of its members.

"If it weren't for Nassor, they would have taken me, too," said the Living Busara.

"I know. Many people were taken that night, but luckily Nassor remembered the escape route I showed him. We may never know who the traitor was, but what they did came at a high price," said Kesi.

"True. I may be the only one left now," said the Living Busara.

"If you are, then you have become a dangerous person to the Noble people," said Kesi.

THE WISHING STONE

Falun and his family lived the life of wealthy aristocrats. As a child, he knew the pleasure that came from wealth. His family held a firm hand in society and commanded respect even by Noble standards. His grandfather was especially known for being an advocate for the kenyetta people. At his prime, Falun's grandfather's resolve never waned before his foes. He was part of the first council that established a voice on behalf of their people. Even as a young man. Falun's grandfather searched to be the exception. Most kenyetta at the time were hired for construction because of their natural abilities to climb. But he used his talents as a musician to speak out against the limitations their people faced. In his time, his people were often thought of as *scabrous* because of the dark colors that ran at the ends of their arms and legs. The most common insult was *furry scab,* because of the amount of hair that covered their bodies. Yet historically their name *kenyetta* refers to the *innocent ones.* Back in those times, people still used the words *zwanga* and *nest,* but because of his grandfather, words like *scabrous* used to define his people are now seldom heard. Yet they are still made fun of because of their long tails.

As firstborn, Falun's father was meant to be taken under his own father's counsel; the eldest of his siblings, he would receive favor that none of the rest would share, or so he thought. It became clearer every day that his father had more of a connection with the second-born son of the family, and it aggravated Falun's father to see his younger brother do more for their father than he could. Over time, the second son was given the best of everything, and he could do no wrong before their father. One day the second son was given a gift called the wishing stone.

"Thank you, Papa," said the second son as he embraced his father.

The firstborn remembered that night well; he heard his father say, "You can keep this because it has granted me the best wish of all . . ." as he held his second-born son to him. Those words would stay with the firstborn for the rest of his life. That night guaranteed the second son would have dominion over the first.

Am I not your firstborn, destined to be the true heir of all that you have? he thought in rage.

When the two brothers came of age with their own families and success, their dying father gave all his authority and worldly possessions to the younger of his sons. The firstborn cursed his father that night and spat on him at his deathbed. He renounced all ties to his family.

When Falun became old enough to know the truth, he realized that his grandfather had betrayed his own son; it was just for Falun's father to renounce all ties to his lineage. Using that moment of betrayal, Falun found strength to become something better and go beyond the success of his grandfather. What was denied his father would not be denied to him.

Years later . . .

It was the night of a full moon, which has special meaning to his people, and it would be a night that seemed to stand still for Falun as he celebrated the birth of his first child. In kenyetta tradition, one candle is lit in the home of all neighboring people as a sign of life. Those who make up the immediate family dress in robes of white, while the mother-to-be is kept in a bed chamber with several midwives to help assist with the birth. Outside the bedroom, all invited guests enjoy themselves in this moment of celebration.

People walked around the room admiring Falun's beautiful home. He greeted the people as they handed him gifts. As the night went on, he thought of the promises he had made to his family, that he would protect them, provide for them. His children would get all that they deserved and more, but most importantly, he would love each one of them equally. Suddenly, a hand fell on his shoulder. He turned to see Khumani, who had been sent on her father's behalf.

"Congratulations. I'm so happy for you and your family," said Khumani.

"Oh yes, of course, I've never been happier, but this is just so much to take in," said Falun nervously.

"But at least you can be grateful that you're not in this alone; you'll have your wife and family for support," replied Khumani. But in his eyes Khumani could see a sort of desperation; he seemed worried about something, and it wasn't his wife. "Falun, you and your family have done so much for the land of Kiskeya, and our fathers have been close business partners for years. The citizens owe your brother a debt that can never be repaid. I understand he received a medal of valor after losing his leg while trying to apprehend a fugitive. Maybe one day, when there is one caste between all peoples . . ."

"All peoples!" interrupted Falun. A seriousness had taken hold of him. "The greatest achievement my brother ever got in his life was becoming a Hunter, and it was the humans that took that away from him, *forever*."

His brother had been firstborn, and his success was like a crown to their father—but it was ripped away. To Falun, humans were to blame for taking away businesses, privileges, and rights his people had worked hard for over the years. The only thing he shared equally was his disdain for each and every one of them. Noticing his change in behavior, Falun quickly apologized; but Khumani didn't take it personally. She just told him that right now times were stressful but he shouldn't hold onto the rage—it would become a burden.

"Remember, Falun, that right now you live for your family, and you can count on me to always be a friend in whatever way you need me," said Khumani.

A cool breeze from the midnight air swept through the room as one of the midwives emerged from the bedroom, saying she needed one more person to come help. When no one stood up, Khumani rose to the occasion—it wasn't the first time she had helped deliver a baby. Sounds of agony could be heard, showing that it wouldn't be much longer until the baby was here. Suddenly there was a knock at the door. Two figures walked in, one holding a cane; and Falun knew it was his father and brother. This was his brother's first appearance after receiving his medal, and everyone in the room stood in silence as the Hero began to stand among them. The guests cleared a path as they applauded him, while also offering their condolences for his loss.

It seemed that for the time being, all the attention would be focused on his hero brother. *He's done it to me again. I can never have a moment to claim as my own,* thought Falun while clenching his fist.

But as he watched his brother sit down, Falun noticed the expression on his face; he had never seen such misery before. Falun actually felt sorry for his brother, but couldn't help but feel grateful that with him out of the way, it would be Falun's time to shine. Let the Hero have this moment; it would never come again.

Most of the evening went by very smoothly. The midwives moved in and out of the bedroom like ghosts, and everyone seemed to be socializing among themselves—everyone but Falun and his brother, who seemed to be in his own world. But Falun hardly paid any attention; he had his own problems to worry about as he tried to conceal his agitation. For some time now, threats had been made against his life for unpaid debts, and he had nowhere near the amount needed to even pay the interest. All he had ever dreamed of was becoming the son his father wanted, the kind of son that would finally make his father proud. It wasn't until he met his wife that he wanted something more. One kiss from her gave him the strength needed, one touch was more satisfying than water in the desert, and her smile provided more warmth than any fire on the coldest night. Yes, it was true that he'd do anything for her, because she was the first thing that he had that his brother didn't. But even she couldn't help in this dire situation. Falun kept his secret dealings to himself. All he wanted to do was start his own business on his own terms without burdening his loved ones. Things were going well at first, until the Maroons raided shipments that he needed for his shop. Many people suffered as a result, and Falun just felt like hurting someone, anyone—but then came the sound of glass breaking from the bedroom, and he was brought back to reality. Not long after was the sound of a baby crying, and all his worries wasted away as he went toward the bedroom. The guests waited in anticipation to behold this new life as one of the midwives came out, standing between him and the door.

"Give us a few more moments," said the midwife.

"Why? Is the baby all right?" asked Falun.

But the midwife disregarded his questions and went back inside, locking the door. For some reason, they were stalling; and Falun couldn't understand why. It didn't matter to him what flaws his child had; he and his wife would face them together. Falun became impatient and asked calmly to come inside.

"Let him in. I can't keep this from him," said a soft voice from inside.

Falun opened the door and took a deep breath while looking around the candlelit room.

"A healthy baby boy, just gorgeous . . ." said Khumani.

Falun saw his beautiful wife weak and with a sadness throughout her. She was trying to hold back her tears.

"Are you okay?" asked Falun. But with each step he made toward her, the midwives backed away toward the door. When he reached out to his wife, she pulled away. "I'm sorry," she said.

He didn't understand so he turned to Khumani, again reaching out to the baby. He pulled the blanket from the boy's face to see the shock of his life. The baby was human. A weakness came over his entire body; he could feel his legs about to give out, and his stomach began to ache.

"Let me see my child," said his wife.

Betrayed, Falun left his house with all its guests and went toward his father's home, a walk that seemed to last forever. He thought this was all a dream, but it wasn't. In the quiet darkness of the night, the nightmare of his reality had just begun. Smoke was in the air, and he noticed a fire had been set at his father's home. Before he could run back and get help, a group of cloaked assailants grabbed him from behind.

They gagged his mouth and gripped his arms as he tried to struggle. One of them gave him a hard knee to the chest, while another gave him a heavy blow to the side of his face. Falun collapsed to the ground hard, and then another cloaked figure emerged before him. "This is the price paid by those who don't pay their debts. You and all those closest to you will be made examples," said the cloaked figure as the flames consumed his father's home.

"Please, I just need more time, I beg you" pleaded Falun.

"And you'll get that. You will pay with everything you have left, but as I said, an example must be made," repeated the cloaked figure.

Then the other assailants circled around Falun. He wanted to run but didn't have the strength to do so. He even tried to defend himself, but that made no difference as they began kicking him violently. No one was around to help him, or they were too scared to interfere; he was alone and at the mercy of those who might end his life. The pain was unbearable. Falun thought he would die tonight, but then the group was told to stop by the one in charge. With blood dripping from his mouth, Falun heard him say, "If we kill you tonight, we will never get back our money; and we want our money, so you get to live a little longer. Be grateful." Falun was already dazed and in too much pain to move, but he knew that his life had been spared. For a moment he thought the worst part of the night was over, but when he looked up, the leader of the group grabbed the back of his neck and pulled out a sharp knife.

"I was told that tonight would be a special occasion for you; it was the reason we stopped by unexpected," he said to Falun. Falun's eyes began to open wide. Had he been deceived? He didn't have a chance. If he fought back, they would only punish him more. As the cloaked leader came closer, Falun felt a tear fall from his eye, mixed with blood as his face was brutally marked.

Days later Falun found himself in a strange home recuperating. He wasn't sure how he got there or who had saved him. His whole body was throbbing with pain, but he soon realized he was in the house of his brother when his mother came in with water and food to eat. "I'm glad to see that you are awake; I'll go get your father and brother," she said as she placed the food down next to him. Falun tried to sit up as his father and brother walked in moments later. They told him that there was nothing left of his father's home but ashes. They had found him passed out on the ground with blood everywhere.

"We thought that you had been robbed and left for dead until we saw this," said Falun's father as he pulled out a rose carved from wood, which was the symbol of a big crime organization in Kiskeya.

"What kind of danger have you placed our family in? Why do you owe them money?" demanded his brother, but Falun refused to answer their questions. He had nothing to say that wouldn't upset them more.

"You realize we have nothing now; everything was burned in the fire. You've always been a disappointment," said Falun's father, who turned to see his wife standing by the door with hot water and a towel to change Falun's bandages. She looked as though she were going to say something as her eyes drifted from Falun to her husband, but he gave her a look that suggested that she should stay out of this. She then looked to the floor and stepped away. "Is there anything you can do to help?" Falun's father asked the Hero.

"I will do everything I can, Father, but for now let me talk to Falun alone. I will try to reach him as a loving brother should," he said.

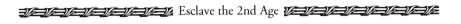

When they were alone, the Hero began to circle his injured brother. "I knew from the start that your wife would be no good for you; she has brought shame to this entire family," he said casually. "But if you wish for my help, Brother, all you have to do is ask, and it shall be done. I could easily relieve your burdens with the people I know," he continued as he offered his hand so that Falun would accept his bargain. But Falun boldly refused.

"Falun, if you refuse my hand now, it will never be offered again in this matter. Deny me now and forfeit any chance you have at settling your debt," said the Hero. "If not today, then at another time you will beg for my help."

"You truly believe you are some sort of hero even with only one leg. But on that day where I consider asking for your help, that will be the day that I let the bandits carve out my other eye," said Falun. "Until then, I will take my burden and suffer with it alone."

Several weeks passed as Falun's strength and vitality began to return to him. He basically had to depend on himself because he was too ashamed to look his family in the eye after all that had happened. One afternoon as the sun shone through the window and a cool breeze swept through the room, a visitor knocked at the door. Falun was lying in bed as she came in—his wife. There was so much confusion in his heart because every day he thought about her, how much he hated her. But when she came through that doorway like a majestic, divine being, all of his sadness and hatred melted away. They saw each other and locked eyes, and then she smiled at him. He wanted to look away, but something wouldn't let him. Could he ever truly walk away from her? In his whole life, she was the only woman he had given his all. A *first love* was all she could ever be to him.

She moved toward him slowly yet elegantly, and the room suddenly seemed brighter as the air carried her sweet scent. She removed the hood from around her head, and Falun remembered the shades of bronze that made up her hair. A woman's beauty was marked by that, and the length to which her hair ran down the small of her back. She took him by the hand and knelt down by his bed. He wanted to pull his hand away, but she kept it tight; in truth, he hardly put up a fight. She caressed his hand and kissed it gently as she looked in his eyes to find forgiveness, but Falun had none to give. Tears began to fall from her eyes and onto his hand; though he loved her, he could never forgive her. It was a truth revealed without saying a word. Both were unaware of the time that passed by in silence, but their time felt too short. He could sit in silence next to her like this for the rest of his life and be content, but it could never be the way it was.

"I know you can't ever forgive me, but one day you will understand that it was something I had to do, that I was forced to do it to protect my family . . . just as I had learned to do," said Falun's wife. "You've always been an inspiration to me, and if it takes me an entire lifetime to earn your forgiveness, then that is what I will do. I know I've hurt you, but I can't give up on you or us," she continued.

Feeling compelled and drawn to her like never before, Falun took his wife in his arms to kiss her. But in that moment of passion, the door swung open with a bang, and his hero brother limped through. The moment he saw Falun's wife, he yelled, "What are you doing here? Get out . . . my father told you to never come here."

She was so startled that she got up and ran out before Falun could even say good-bye.

"*Ha-ha*, how dare that girl show her face? What was she thinking, that we would let her make a fool of you again?" said the Hero.

An anger came over Falun so intense that he wanted to choke the life out of his brother. "You damn cripple!" he shouted. "You could never see me happy with her because she was the first thing I had that you didn't. You used to be something but now you are nothing, and you want everyone else to be the same," said Falun. "Now you are just as big a disappointment as me. The savior of our family, who became its burden!" said Falun. Now no one could save them.

Falun got up, feeling an amazing strength. But the Hero wouldn't just let his brother leave, not without teaching him some respect, not after such humiliation. Boldly and defiantly Falun looked his brother in the eye, but the Hero stood just as firm. "How does it feel to know that your greatest work cost you your leg?" said Falun.

Twhamp . . . Red blood trickled from his face, and like a child, Falun was grabbed by the back of his neck.

"How dare you speak to me that way! It is a privilege for you to even look at me, let alone be your brother. Or did you forget . . . I AM A HERO!" he shouted at Falun.

He raised his hand to give Falun a second blow, but Falun kicked the base of his brother's cane. The Hero tried to fight his fall, grasping at anything he could, but it was inevitable and he hit the floor hard.

"All my life I was envious of you, even respected you, but now I have only pity, the last thing that I will ever give you!" said Falun. And with that he left.

INITIATION AND CLASS

"Deploy more reinforcements and release the gas," Hasani ordered as powerful toxins were released that dulled the senses of the rebels.

"They must be reminded why nobility is the rule of the land," Chisulo said in agreement.

Metal clashed like thunder, blade pierced flesh, and the sound of agony became silent as they crushed the enemy without mercy. Those of the Maroons who were able to survive the battle were hunted down and taken to the Lougawou Mountains.

These were the moments Kumi relived that led to his newfound status. Their voices echoed through his mind as he sat in a most exclusive tavern. Since the confrontation between his brother Nassor and the Hunters, Kumi was able to advance his position. Not only that, but information was leaked to him about the next few raids on imports made by the rebel Maroons, information that was given to Kumi alone. He could now confirm his power, his destiny, his greatness . . . it could no longer be denied.

With what he knew, Kumi was able to further prove his loyalty to the Noble people. On the day of the raids, elaborate traps were set to capture the rebels. It was a heavy loss to the Maroon cause, but not every raid was a complete win for the Hunters. Hasani felt it necessary for some of his own to die so that the citizens would always sympathize with the government; the gas would be released only when he needed a decisive win. As for Kumi, with each battle that took place, he would stand in the distance with Chisulo and Hasani as Gods watching mere mortals do their bidding. They believed that they were above the slaughter.

It was after this that the Hunters and Kumi's own father, Desever, started to recognize Kumi's worth as a valued member of the team. Desever for a moment even acknowledged Kumi as his son, and that felt good. As he sat in the Hummingbird Tavern, Kumi felt a deep sense of satisfaction. There was a boldness in him, as though he could now accomplish anything.

The tavern itself was filled with high-class citizens, who were rarely seen among the common people. There was not a single candle lit in the room, but it was as bright as could be. At each table was a glasslike ornament that held an illuminating glow, just another reason why this place was set apart from ordinary life.

"Here's your drink—enjoy," said a pretty tavern girl. Kumi saw how magnificent she was; she was average height and had soft skin that went with the atmosphere of the place. The air carried her scent, and it intoxicated him more than the drink itself. When he got a better look, he noticed she was a mix of all three peoples, and she wore a necklace that he had never seen before.

The sound of whispers began to awaken him. "Where am I? How did you get me here? Do you know I work for the government?" said Kumi with heavy breathing. He had been passed out for some time and trying to remember what had happened but couldn't. Someone then pulled the hood off his head, and he was surrounded by dozens of people dressed in what looked like ceremonial clothing. Right in front of him was a candle burning incense, and it looked like he was sitting in some sort of grand temple that was very old. There were inscriptions written on the walls, and pillars unlike anything he had ever seen before—and then a flash of light. When his eyes readjusted, three individuals stood right before him behind a veil. The one in the middle had the higher authority just by the way he stood above the other two, together these three were the Eternals. With a God-like visage, he commanded the attention of the entire room as he said, "Welcome, Kumi. We are the Immortals, and we have been watching you for a very long time."

"Just as the Noble Gods were a fusion of two great forces during creation. We, the Immortals, are a secret society made of the two strongest races in the land, human and serwan," said one Immortal.

"And just as the Cy and Kar were brought together to create the first sentient being, stronger than the two before, which led to the first great civilization, we believe that it is our destiny to one day inherit the land and begin a new great society," said the middle one.

"No other has ever reached your level of status among the Noble people. We can use your position to infiltrate them, to guide the coming war in our favor. To aggravate the humans for rebellion and incite fear within the serwans. All you need do is join us, become the Immortal you are destined to be, and when the time comes do what is necessary to see that we succeed," said the third Immortal.

Kumi had never dared think of a world without the rule of nobility. Before he could give them an answer, he felt a dizziness, and the voices in the room turned to whispers again as he began to black out. He realized that the incense burning in front of him had the same drug as his drink. The last thing he heard was someone saying, "Remember, we are watchful of all things you do."

Kumi awoke in his own home and realized it was late into the next morning as he heard a banging at the door. "Go away," he shouted, but the knocking continued. He went to the door and found to his surprise that it was his half sister, Khumani, and in her hands was a newborn baby.

"Is that the seed of Nassor?" asked Kumi. "I won't help you keep this from our father; your shame is your burden to carry," Kumi callously said as he poured himself a drink.

Khumani then walked into his home. "You must be even more of a fool than I thought if you believe this child to be mine—but look at you, you are making quite the name for yourself. A beautiful home, accessories, even a nice gem to adorn yourself with. Life must be very good for you. Maybe this change in wealth could be used to support this child, your son," said Khumani.

But Kumi hardly paid any notice to the boy. All he thought about was the necklace that he quickly put away as he realized it was the same necklace the waitress was wearing. She must have drugged him; and if he had his own necklace, the Immortals must consider him to be a member, an Immortal.

"I'm talking to you, Kumi. This is your child, and only a few weeks old. He needs his father," said Khumani.

"You come to my home with a random child, saying it's mine, and expect me to just raise it on your word alone," said Kumi.

"You know he's yours, and the mother told me so. You remember her, the wife of Falun, an *innocent* who got caught in your deception. I know it's all true," she said. "I see her as often as I can concerning the child and you. Do you care that your actions have destroyed a family?" said Khumani as she caressed the child. "If I didn't take him, who knows what they would have done with him? It's their culture to get rid of the shame. Why did you do this? Did our father . . ." she started, but Kumi cut her off.

"Let me make this clear to you. Many children I have fathered, but none have taken refuge in this home. I may have children scattered throughout the province, and like this one, I don't care about any of them. Now take this orphan baby, get out, and never come here with him again," said Kumi, as he pushed them out the door.

"You have a responsibility, Kumi; you cannot abandon him. Who will take care of him?" cried Khumani. But the only response she heard was the sound of a door slamming in her face.

A few moments later, Kumi left his home with the necklace in his pocket. For a moment he looked around checking if he was really being watched. *I have better things to think about than some mongrel child, thought Kumi.*

When Falun returned home, a feeling of peril was in the air. He found his mother laid out on the floor sobbing, "My son, my firstborn son," she cried.

"Mother, what's wrong?" asked Falun. Then he saw his father sitting quietly on a chair with a drink in his hand.

"Look at what you have done to us. You took him from me and your mother . . . you are the cause of this misery," said his father.

Falun didn't understand until he walked further in and saw with his own eyes what had brought his mother to her knees. The Hero, his brother, the hope of the innocent, had taken his own life. Devastated by the sight, Falun couldn't find the strength to move. He wanted to look away from the lifeless body of his brother but couldn't.

"This isn't what I wanted . . ." whispered Falun, wondering if his cruelty had led to this.

"You took away our joy, years of love and hard work. You killed him, and in so doing you have killed me. I am too old to start over. I wait for death, where your brother waits for me. Until then, I will mourn and grieve," said his father. A curse Falun was to them.

"Father, I don't understand why he . . ." said Falun.

"Don't call me father! You have no father and no mother, and we have no son. Everything that has befallen our family . . . we have nothing left! Nothing in this world to give," said his father.

Falun looked toward his mother for compassion, but he might as well have been invisible; she had taken no note of him for years. She was like a ghost, with her presence felt but never confirmed, and he had become that to her.

"Now leave and do not come back!" said his father as he threw the medal of valor at Falun's feet. It would be a constant reminder of his regret.

At the funeral no one asked questions about Falun; maybe they already knew why he wasn't there. In the days to come, Falun would come by to watch his family from a distance, yet his burden of guilt was too great for him to ever confront them again. His father's last words became a dark omen in his mind; he knew that he had become a scourge to those around him. Tears ran down his mother's face every night and his father refused to eat, a final legacy for them.

One night when the sky had darkened, Falun came to his brother's grave. A vow was made as he cried in his native tongue to the moon. *There would be blood.*

REVELATIONS

It was a day like no other in the land of Kiskeya as dark clouds filled the sky from morning to evening. The warmth of the sun was blotted out, keeping its rays from shining though the Diamond Tree that sits atop the greatest monument in history, where the Akin-Eno rests. A storm was approaching that foreboded an even greater disaster that would strike Kiskeya and her people. The scent of a great downpour filled the air as serwans and kenyetta began to find safety in their homes; the Maroons took refuge in the chasms of the earth, while those of the Chideria Order retreated to deep spiritual prayer. From this day forward, nothing would be the same, as it marked the beginning of change not known in any other age. Amari, Mala-Dek, Khumani, and Chisulo would remember this day for the rest of their lives, as each one would take part in a mystery revealed; it would be a day of revelations.

Chisulo, the latest descendant of an elite clan, is known as a hero among his people. He is believed to be the next destined leader of Kiskeya. On the day of the storm, Chisulo never left the house after feeling fatigued. The last few months had been spent trying to crush any rebel incursions; he has a brilliant mind for warfare and is strategic in battle. One of his ideas was to use the sanscoeurs in efforts to create a soldier that could withstand pain. But with the news of the storm, Chisulo decided that a day of rest wouldn't be a bad idea. As he lay in bed contemplating the days ahead, his eyes began to feel heavy, and he fell into a deep sleep. During his revelation, Chisulo stood before the sun as it gave birth to a deity, whose power was so great and old it preceded creation—and in a blink of an eye, Chisulo stood before another amazing sight, the entire universe. The deity stood by his side and offered Chisulo the universe as a gift. Chisulo reached out to claim his prize, only to have a star explode before him. In the next moment, the universe was gone; it had been swallowed up into the body of the deity, who sought to have control of the universe for himself. For that, he had been imprisoned in a crystal for all eternity.

Khumani also saw the impending storm as a reason to stay indoors; she used the time to go over a speech she had written concerning the rights of Noble women. Every speech she wrote, every rally that she attended were done as though it would be her last, believing this could be the one, her catalyst. Khumani had dreams of going further than any other woman in history; at the very least, she wanted to open doors for those that would. She had always been aware of having to live a lucrative lifestyle; coming from the line of Desever was more than helpful to her cause. Even Hasani had been showing support by making some appearances at the rallies.

The weather gave her time to think about so much as she watched over the baby; she wasn't sure if she was ready to make a commitment like this, to be a mother when she already had so much to deal with. Even though she had servants, Khumani tended to her nephew at all times. She loved him and knew he shouldn't be abandoned as Kumi had done. In her arms she kept the child, having him lay on her chest as she caressed his back, making sure he was still breathing. She allowed herself to think of Nassor and what he must be going through right now. Oh, how she missed him. When she looked down at the baby, she wondered what if this was really her child and Nassor was the father—the thought made her smile.

Outside the weather was getting worse as the rain fell harder. Then there was a knock at the door. One of the servants got up to see who it was during a time like this. Khumani was surprised to see Falun, dripping wet.

"I'm sorry for coming to your home at such a terrible time, but I need your help . . ." said Falun. Looking at his face, Khumani could see that he was recovering from serious wounds, but she didn't want to ask how he got them. Then the baby started to cry, which drew Falun's attention. Immediately noticing the change in his face, Khumani had her servant take the child out of the room, fearful of what Falun might do to the child that ended his marriage.

"How can I help you?" she asked.

"This is embarrassing for me to ask, but I am in great debt and I need some money to pay it off. You told me that if I ever needed anything, you would help, and I need your help now," said Falun.

There was a look of desperation on his face as though Khumani might be his last hope, and she felt sorry for him because he had clearly been through so much. She had no choice, so she went into one of the rooms of the house and came back with a small box. It contained priceless gems, which she offered to him. "This should be more than enough to clear any debt you have, and I hope everything works out," said Khumani.

Falun was very grateful as he walked away, saying that one day he would repay her kindness.

Khumani felt exhausted; the baby had gone back to sleep in his crib, and Falun was long gone. So she went to her room to lie down, and it didn't take long for her to doze off. In her revelation, there was no ground to walk on. She found herself soaring high above the clouds, the radiance of the sun giving her power. She flew among majestic creatures not yet seen before, who also drew power from the sun. These ancient beings, who had been forgotten, then merged together, and a woman was brought forth with Khumani's image. The being wore a white robe covered in a golden armor that was made of the creatures that formed her, even glorious wings made from veils of light. The being turned to Khumani to show her that it also had the same birthmarks.

Khumani reached out to touch the one that had taken her image, but in her efforts she began falling to the earth. It seemed like forever before she ended up falling into a pit that swallowed her. She tried to struggle free, but it was pointless. Everything started to fade into darkness as the pit placed her in another realm. It was a completely dark land as thunder and lightning roared through the air. Khumani felt an innate fear of this place, but she was also drawn to it. In this realm, the forces of nature were wild, with no chance of maintaining life; the elements of fire and cold would descend and attack as though she were an enemy. The ground beneath her consisted of jagged rocks crystallized from lava that surrounded her in all directions. She ventured forward, hoping to get away, until she came across an ancient well, mystical in origin and surrounded by several pillars bearing the same markings that were on her back. She touched one of the pillars and activated them all, causing a reaction.

The ground started to rumble, and nations of men began to emerge from the molten land. They seemed as rulers and kings whose times had passed away, whose bodies were covered in the rocks that bore them; they had been waiting for her arrival. Once the pillars had been activated, they formed a barrier, and the well opened a gateway that allowed creatures to enter our realm. The light from the well became blinding as Khumani wondered what was happening before her. A great maelstrom touched the sky. Nothing could escape it as fire, wind, and even lightning were taken up into it; more creatures were brought forth, and then it exploded.

As the rain came down in Kiskeya, Mala-Dek stood silent in one of the many homes she owned. Beneath this home existed her own personal den chamber. She took a candle and went down to the chamber. Whenever she made her approach, bells would sound to signal the children, and they would hide like mice in the presence of light. To Mala-Dek, hiding was a sign of their fear and respect. If they didn't hide, she believed that their suffering wasn't enough, so she would lock those bold enough to defy her into a hole. "Come out! This work must be done on time," she said. Menee emerged from the shadows first, the only one without chains strapped to her ankle.

As Mala-Dek turned around to leave, she said to Menee, "You will have to stay until the end of the storm, but at least you will get plenty of work done before you do go home."

But Menee stopped her to say, "Mistress, nothing pleases me more than my service to you, but what of the child in the hole? If flooding starts, he could drown."

Mala-Dek continued to walk away and casually said, "Then let the deviant out . . . when I'm satisfied with the work." Mala-Dek grinned, knowing that nothing could be done to help the child.

By the time she went back up the stairs, there was a knock at the door. Without a second thought, she placed a dagger by her side beneath her cloak. Mala-Dek believed that her life was always at risk. When she opened the door, an innocent stood there with a box in his hand. "What do you want?" she asked.

He removed his hood while still under the rain, and it was Falun. "I was told to come here to make the last of my payment," he said.

Mala-Dek cautiously held her hand out, and he gave her the box. She took a quick look inside it, looked back at him, and then closed the door without even asking for his name. Mala-Dek then took the box to a hidden room that was always locked, a place where she collected all her debts that would be taken care of later.

She walked back to her room and lit some scented candles. There was a mat on the floor for meditation, which she would use for future plans. She had no intention of sleeping, just sitting quietly in her room. But as she was getting comfortable, someone emerged from the shadows and grabbed her from behind, wrapping an arm around her neck and holding a two-pronged dagger into her throat. The Assassin had come for her.

"Where is your den, demon?" said the Assassin, but Mala-Dek only smiled. The promise of a violent death only excited her, but she let the Assassin know that the children were several floors down. "Are there any others who work with you?" asked the Assassin.

"None but me; I teach these children myself," replied Mala-Dek.

Mala-Dek had no weapon she could reach in time without being killed; all she carried was a melting candle, so she took the hot wax and poured it on the hand of the Assassin. There was no scream, but the pain was felt enough to make the Assassin lose her hold. Mala-Dek then grabbed her enemy and threw her over her back. She reached for the dagger beneath her cloak, but the Assassin was already back on her feet.

Now that they stood face-to-face, Mala-Dek noticed the unique gauntlet and mask; the Assassin even wore armor on parts of her leg. "I hope that armor is tough enough to protect you from me," said Mala-Dek as the two circled around each other. Strategically Mala-Dek snuffed out every candle she came across. Fighting in the dark added to the thrill, made it more of a hunt. "What do you want with my den?" she asked.

"To free the children you keep in bondage, but first I will have to break you," replied the Assassin.

"What does a little woman like you plan to do with those mongrels? Were you once one of them? I think you were. I've had time to think about you and the vengeance you deal to those who do the things I do. I like that; the taste of vengeance is good—it frees the soul," said Mala-Dek.

"Yes, it does," said the Assassin as she made the first move.

The Assassin was fast. Her moves were devastatingly fierce, but there was a born savageness in Mala-Dek. She knew how to make her hits count and wasn't afraid to fight dirty. Blows were exchanged and blood was drawn. For every powerful hit by Mala-Dek, the Assassin returned with three of her own; but it didn't slow either one of them down, especially Mala-Dek, who became more excited as the fight continued. Mala-Dek broke a table leg and used it as a club, trying to smash in the leg of the Assassin, who blocked it with her shin. Even with the armor, the Assassin felt the pain go right through; if she hadn't been wearing it, the bone might have cracked. Mala-Dek came at her again, hitting her twice with the club. She now had the Assassin by the throat against the wall.

"This was fun," said Mala-Dek.

But the Assassin wasn't willing to accept defeat, and she hit Mala-Dek in the face with her elbow. Mala-Dek fell back quickly as a powder was blown in her face. In moments, Mala-Dek began to stagger; she fell to the ground, and her eyes dimmed into blackness. Exhausted, the Assassin was just about to give the final blow—and then she heard footsteps in the hallway. By the time the door opened, she was gone.

Mala-dek laid on the floor passed out. In her revelation, Mala-Dek found herself surrounded by children—both living and dead—that she had placed in den chambers. One by one they came to her asking, "Please, Mistress, let me go home . . . I just want to go home." But she struck them down, each one that came near her, with a stick covered in spikes. Harder and harder she swung to keep them away, but as they fell, they got right back up; the number of children became overwhelming. "Don't worry. I will teach you all a very important lesson about my power and authority," said Mala-Dek as she continued to break them down, but eventually the children mastered their punishment. They were no longer hurt by her violence. Suddenly one jumped on her and grabbed the stick in her hand, and then another child grabbed her again. They all began turning into ferocious monsters; demons they were. The heavens disappeared and the world turned to darkness as they continued to attack her from all sides, biting and clawing at her. Their touch was like fire, and in frightful voices they continued to say, "Release us, Mistress, let us go." To anyone else, this would have seemed like hell as the demons began devouring whatever soul she had left. But Mala-Dek never cried out in pain or begged for mercy; instead, she smiled, enjoying what was being done to her. She enjoyed pain and suffering, even upon herself.

The three of them—Chisulo, Khumani, and Mala-Dek—wouldn't awaken until lightning no longer struck the Lougawou Mountains, when thunder didn't roar through the clouds, and when rain no longer fell from the sky. But the very last revelation would be the one that was most profound of them all. Amari, a young boy curious about life, would experience the one revelation that would occur while being wide-awake. Moments before the storm ended, Amari felt a compelling need to feel the force of nature for himself, to experience its unbridled power. As he stood in the midst of

the storm, he looked up at the sky. Something began to open up like a whirlwind, and then there was a great explosion of light, with every color visible to the eye. It was the most divine thing he would ever witness.

As he looked deeper into this phenomenon, he could swear he saw a person, a God. After that, the storm was gone as though it had never come, and Amari ran back inside to tell all those he could that he had seen a God fall from the heavens. But everyone just laughed at him, and his mother beat him when she heard that he had gone out in such dangerous weather. Amari was sure of what he had seen; the only problem was that he was the only one who had seen it.

Falun still had one more thing to do after paying off his debt to Mala-Dek. He traveled to a facility where the Hunters operated. When he reached his destination, he was escorted by soldiers to Desever. Falun still had the medal of valor and placed it before Desever. "My brother took his life, and I want retribution. Help me get revenge by bringing in those who destroyed him," said Falun.

Desever grinned happily at Falun, knowing full well that Nassor had already been captured. That information was being kept from the public; it kept a sense of fear and obedience among the peoples. Desever took the medal, and in so doing, knew that this was the opportunity he had been waiting for. "I think I have exactly what you are looking for; come with me," he said.

Falun had no idea what he was getting into. He had hoped to take the position of his brother, but that was not what Desever had in mind. Taken to a secret part of the facility underground, Falun would be a test subject in an experiment for the Noble Regime. They drugged him with a toxin that paralyzed his muscles; the only thing he could do was blink, and even that was a struggle. Falun could hear voices say, "Don't worry; you won't feel a thing," as they placed his body in a tank filled with chemicals. They were readying him to be bonded to the ancient creature, the sanscoeur, which was used during the period of the Sentient War as a way of subduing the human race. "When a sanscoeur bonds with its host, it causes extreme pain throughout the body," explained Desever, but Falun paid no attention.

This form of torture had been abandoned sometime after the war. It was discovered that after prolonged contact, victims would develop abilities fueled by the constant pain felt from the creature.

"It was a power that couldn't be tamed; humans again tried to rebel. But ever since, the Noble Regime has been devising ways to use it as a weapon," said Desever.

"This is an untapped reservoir of power harnessed through the sun, the lifeblood that feeds the sanscoeurs," said one of the Nobles readying the process.

At the bottom of the tank were two rare gemstones forged in the crust of the earth; each crystal could store massive amounts of energy needed for the experiment. Three sanscoeurs were then put into the tank, and immediately something happened.

Falun felt a great pain. He was in agony from the chemical bath, but even more so from the sanscoeurs that attached themselves to his body. He wanted to cry out, but the toxin prevented it. From the outside it seemed as though the experiment was causing no discomfort. The solution then began changing his body. A power was being drawn into him as the sanscoeurs tapped into his aura. What was left wasn't the Falun that entered. When the procedure reached its end, the scientist drained the tank of its chemicals. As the effects of the toxin wore off from the energy that pulsated from his body, Falun slowly began to move.

"He will always experience a degree of pain from the sanscoeurs attached to him, but the chemicals raised his tolerance to it. Without that, the sanscoeurs would have killed him," explained one of the Nobles.

"How do you feel?" asked Desever as Falun was taken out of the tank still weakened. The scar through his eye was glowing as he responded in his native tongue, a language they didn't understand, and then he passed out.

BELIEF

Back in the prison of the Citadel where the trial of Nyack C'Kre was reaching its end, the defendant sat in his cell, once again conversing with his mysterious cellmate, whom he could now call friend. There was not much he knew about this stranger, only that he was a very spiritual person who prayed every night since his arrival, asking that he be ready for whatever test came his way. The only strange thing so far was the fact that he didn't have a trial date set after being here for so long. At times they would pray together. This unknown man began to slowly influence Nyack as he began to look for his own spiritual path and turn to a greatness beyond himself. "I think there is a reason we are both here; fate may have a design for us," said Nyack. The stranger would say, "I agree, Nyack. All of our days have already been written for us."

The prison guards opened the outside gates and walked in, escorting Hasani and Kumi. They walked up to the cell and faced the stranger. "You surprise me, Nassor," said Hasani. As Nassor looked up, he saw a gathering of his enemies who were ready to see him be punished. "It's not every day that a rebel Maroon like yourself is able to attack an elite group of warriors bound to the nation of Kiskeya and escape—well, at least that's what the people think. To the world, you are a fugitive at large; and since you are a fugitive, there's no need for a trial, but we can still give you a proper sentencing." Then Hasani had one of the guards open Nassor's cell door as he was held down, and another group of guards entered with an armored box forged of the strongest elements.

Kumi then gave the order for Nyack to be taken out of there. "Be happy; these are your final moments before being thrown into the dark void." But as Kumi mocked Nyack, secretly he hoped that he would never know such a terrible fate.

As they took Nyack away, Kumi helped open the box and then looked at Nassor. "Don't worry. Your friend will get one as soon as they tie up some loose ends about the trial."

Hasani used a metal prong and pulled out a sanscoeur. "This will hurt, a lot," he said with a look of satisfaction. Then they attached the creature onto Nassor's chest, causing him unbearable pain. The sanscoeur burrowed its tentacles deep into his flesh. His screams could even be heard up above, and the agony was so great that there was no moment of relief.

Tears of blood fell from his eyes, and then Hasani extended his hand. Instantly the pain stopped. He carried a spear developed by the Noble Regime to manipulate the abilities of the sanscoeur. With that spear, Hasani could control the level of pain that would be inflicted upon the prisoners. Nassor was his first victim. Even the sanscoeur's psionic powers could be controlled, and he used it to force Nassor to bow before him. "Don't worry. This is not your punishment; this is my way of having fun with you before you are sent to the Lougawou Mountains like that other criminal. By morning, after the sun strikes the diamond tree, you will know a different kind of prison," said Hasani.

"But that is the truth we know. In the next several weeks, the Maroon fugitive Nassor will be blamed for the deaths of several citizens and kenyetta, those who find sympathy for the deviant races. And in the midst of the chaos, I will single-handedly bring an end to your murdering spree and lead you into justice. But sadly enough, you will be killed in an escape attempt. The fear that others like you may be out there will keep the people in line, putting their trust in my Hunters, who work at all times to prevent any threats to Kiskeya," said Hasani.

"You know, I have thought of every scenario and placed all the necessary precautions. But you have even shocked me. Most of your kind are predictable, but you are different. Instead of being captured, you surrendered yourself, just turned yourself in. It was a surprise that fit well into my plans, and I'm curious to know why but not curious enough to ask. But I will let you know one thing: you will never have her the way that I will. In the coming days, I will poison her against you. Khumani is a rare flower that will not be corrupted by the likes of you," Hasani finished.

Up until her name was said, Nassor had nothing to say to Hasani because he had always known one day his time would come. But something about her name being uttered by Hasani's mouth forced Nassor to speak. "How do you know about that?"

"Kumi told me everything. Your half brother has quite the disdain for you," replied Hasani. "Open the doors this place detest me," ordered Hasani as he turned his back and left the prison.

While Nassor lay on the floor still feeling the effects of the sanscoeur, Kumi stood over him with a sense of superiority, a satisfying feeling. For the first time, he felt like he had won. No longer would he be tormented by the thought of Nassor standing over him, mocking him. It was a thought that had persisted for years. When Kumi was told that his brother had surrendered, that thought returned to him for the last time.

In his mind, Nassor was like a phantom who fought against Kumi because they had different fathers. He was a reminder that Nassor was a gift of love to their mother from Nassor's father. They shared a blessed union and were a family, but what Kumi was to their mother was something else. The phantom of Nassor would always persecute him. "Your birth was a burden to our mother, her greatest shame forced upon her." Nassor's voice tormented Kumi from every direction.

"My eyes, hands, and heart. When I look at myself, I see the traits of my parents, a blessing. Are your features the result of love, Kumi? No, it can never be. You are the result of something impure, and impure things must be cast out. When I look at you, I see his face, his eyes, and his hands. I see the person responsible for what happened to my family. Like a dark shadow that has loomed over us, a disease that takes hold unexpectedly, that is what you are," the phantom would say.

By the end of that thought, Kumi was about to leave the prison, but Nassor still had one final thing to say. "This isn't over, Kumi. One day you will have to answer to me, in this life or the next."

"Then I will see you in the next life, my brother," said Kumi.

Nassor returned to prayer to help ignore the pain he felt. He began to ask himself whether this was what Origin wanted. Was this his path to spiritual balance and awakening? It had to be, Nassor thought, or it would all be in vain. He began to think back to when he was a fugitive, hiding out with Faizah and the Living Busara. They were the reason he had started to believe. They taught him of the Chideria Order, and over time he developed a relationship with them, even sharing his innermost thoughts. They created a lasting bond as the Living Busara would share with Nassor spiritual advice, informing him that the creator Origin called for him and that there was something that needed to be done by him alone. Faizah helped Nassor with scripture. She showed him how every word linked us with the Creator and that it should be seen as truth and salvation to every obstacle set before us. She read to him one scripture that now meant so much:

When my enemies persecute me, my strength never wanes.

When my loved ones have abandoned me, my strength never wanes.

When all my possessions have been taken, my strength never wanes.

When all I have is my faith, my strength never wanes.

And when all I have is of the Creator, my strength never wanes.

3rd World Order

Faizah told Nassor that he would know no greater love or trust like that of the Creator God known as Origin, and it was from that moment he decided to give his life over to the creator, converting to the Chideria Order. So he prayed on the word, asking for a sign from the divine to help let go of the anger and vengeance in his heart. But the more he prayed, the more tormented he was; he would wake up at night dripping with sweat.

"What's wrong?" asked Faizah. The first few times he wouldn't reply; he would just go back to sleep. But one day Nassor revealed the terrible truth to her.

"A long time ago, my father was a carpenter who was lent out to help some serwan build a small bridge. But when the job was done, there was an accident and my father was killed. Later on, I found out the real truth from hearing a private conversation. I don't know who it was I was listening to, but they said that my father's death was no accident. It was over money that the serwan refused to give, so instead of paying, he killed my father," confided Nassor. When Nassor learned the truth, he told no one, not even his mother, but he waited for years until the time had come to deal with his father's killer.

"I confronted him, and he didn't even deny it. He gloated in fact, showing no remorse, and I went into a blind rage. We fought hard, but I fought much harder and more brutally. I put my hands around his neck. He struggled, but I could feel his throat crush beneath my fingers—and then he stopped struggling. Since that night, I was changed; my eyes opened for the day someone would come for their revenge as I had done. Living with that burden, I kept preparing myself until the day vengeance would be met," said Nassor with regret.

Faizah was the only person who ever knew what he had told her.

"You thought that by killing your father's murderer in secret, it was justice, but instead you lived a life of secret fear ever since and it has brought you no good," said Faizah. "No one can change what you did, but only you can let it go." After that, Nassor thanked Faizah for her help and went back to prayer.

As though reborn, Nassor felt like a whole new person. Who he was before had no ties to him now, but one day while praying with the Living Busara, Nassor had a vision. In it he was engulfed by a fire that didn't burn. He immediately told the Living Busara what he had seen, but the Busara

had no clear answer for Nassor other than to keep praying and that the meaning of this vision would soon come. The same vision occurred several times, and each one was more intense than the last. Nassor could see smoke rise from his body at the end. Both Faizah and the Living Busara agreed that Nassor should go on a fast so that it might open the gates of his mind. So Nassor, only drinking water for two days, asked for guidance. On the third day, the vision came to him for the last time. In it his body was again engulfed with fire that did not burn; its power came from within him, and it was controlled by his will alone. He commanded it as easily as he commanded his hand, and the fire looked like the sky. It was celestial, a fire that burned from heaven and was everlasting.

When the vision ended, that was when Nassor realized he must surrender himself over to the Kiskeyan government, that his purpose could not be fulfilled from the shadows hiding and running. Faizah wouldn't agree to it and argued, "You're insane. The most foolish thing you can do is give yourself up to them, your enemies." But Nassor felt compelled to do it, as though a darker fate was in store if he didn't. The Living Busara confirmed it as well. "The spirit phantom has spoken to me. Now is the time, Faizah. We must do whatever is required of us to help Nassor from this moment on."

The last thing Nassor asked Faizah before he left was, "What does it mean to know a *First Love* . . . ?"

Faizah answered and said, "When you realize that what you have wanted in someone your whole life has always been there since the beginning, even if you didn't know it. Even if you have gone to distant worlds and seen strange things, you still find your way back to it, because it has never left you. It is something written for you . . . that is *First Love.*"

As Nassor finished reliving the moment that led to his surrender, he looked to see that the guards were returning Nyack to his cell. Kumi came in as well to make sure Nyack received his own sanscoeur.

Sometime later, after the pain began to subside, the two prisoners spoke in the darkness of their cell.

"I don't know if I'm ready for what is going to happen to us next, but whatever it is, I accept it," said Nyack, as his sentence to the dark void really began to set in.

"We're ready. I've never felt more ready in my entire life. I don't know for certain what will happen in the next few days or hours, but I do know that it will be a great defining moment. For now, we'll pray, so that our strength may never wane when we need it most," said Nassor.

PASSION, SUFFERING, AND MERCY

The days that came after Khumani's revelation were spent taking care of her nephew, whom she named Nassor for reasons of her own. She spent so much time fighting for equal rights, she never took time for the little things. It was time for a vacation, and with little Nassor so helpless, she could truly devote her time to him. She decided to do something she hadn't done for quite some time—visit her father.

As she traveled, there were looks and stares because of her tiny companion. She realized what true ignorance was and that some people would never change. When she reached her father's home, he welcomed her with open arms and kissed her as though they had been separated for years.

"Come in, come in. Go, get us some food and something to drink," he said to one of his servants.

But that was before he noticed the child. "What is this? I hope no one saw you with this baby," he said while checking outside the window.

"What are you afraid of, Papa? That someone will think the child is mine?" said Khumani.

"Ha . . . don't be ridiculous. Like any of those fools would ever dare think that a daughter of mine would have a human child. But seriously, this is becoming a growing trend among Noble women, and I for one will not have my bloodline tainted," said her father.

"I've never noticed this trend," said Khumani. "The one that I have noticed is Noble men who father human and kenyetta children, but I dare not speak of such things in the presence of citizens," said Khumani sarcastically.

Her father smiled. Even though Khumani kept a straight face, he had always tried to hide his transgressions.

Khumani added, "It's always been an accepted yet unspoken rule that Noble men can violate their matrimonial vows, but not the women."

"Precisely, my child. You have always had an understanding of what things are and should always be. But anyway, why are you here?" asked Desever.

"I wanted to talk to you about Kumi. This is his child, and he won't raise him," said Khumani.

"Very sad but understandable. Few people know of my own relation to Kumi; no one wants that kind of embarrassment. But Kumi's affairs are his business; it has nothing to do with me," said her father.

"Your grandchild, who may not be your only, should always be your concern. You have been working with the kenyetta people trying to reach a level of trust; you even had me act in your place, which is how I found out about this baby. All I want to know is, did you have Kumi seduce that girl and ruin a marriage, a family? You had to know that it wouldn't help; and if anyone found out about your involvement, it could destroy any chance for open talks with them," said Khumani as she put the baby down.

Her father pulled out a drink, poured it in a cup, and sipped. He then looked at her and said, "And who would ever find out? I won't tell and you won't either. Yes, I spoke to Kumi and told him to enjoy his youth the same way I did, but I had no idea it would turn into this." Then he looked away from her.

"But none of this is making any sense," she replied.

"That's why I will find a way to rectify the situation, I promise. My first act will be to take you and my new grandchild out to buy him some clothes and whatever else he may need," said her father.

It made Khumani happy to see her father acknowledge the child, knowing exactly what to do to change the subject.

"What's his name?" her father asked.

"Oh, I haven't had the time to think of a permanent one, but it will be one that suits him," she replied. "Why don't we just go out shopping now so that we can think of one," continued Khumani.

"I'm quite busy today; maybe we can do it the next time you decide to visit," replied her father.

And with that, Khumani began gathering her things to leave. She could feel that her father wasn't telling the whole truth, but she definitely didn't want to remind him of the name Nassor—that name had brought enough trouble to the family.

After saying their good-byes, her father went into the next room and began writing a letter. When he was done, he sealed it with the family crest and gave it to a servant. "Go, deliver this to Adversary as fast as you can," he said.

Khumani spent most of the day out, and when she got home, she was surprised to see an unexpected guest had come by. Hasani was there waiting with a candlelit dinner. He had hoped to surprise Khumani, but he was the one caught off guard when he saw the small child in her arms.

"You should have told me you were coming. I would have prepared something special too," said Khumani as she laughed out of embarrassment.

"I wanted to surprise you; it feels like I haven't seen you in ages. We both have been so busy, but it looks like you have new obligations now," said Hasani.

She laughed at his small joke. "I never told you, but I hate surprises."

"I'm sorry; I just wanted this night to be perfect. I even asked your servants to give us some time to each other, no interruptions," said Hasani.

Looking nervous, Khumani asked, "But why? What is the occasion?" as she put little Nassor down right near her.

"Honestly, Khumani, we have been involved with each other for some time now, and we understand each other so much . . ."

But as Hasani spoke, Khumani began to stare into space, and the sound of his voice was drowned out by thoughts of Nassor.

The last time she had seen him was the night he became a fugitive. She remembered how his touch was like warm water pouring down her back, so soothing it was. She imagined him whispering in her ear, "It humbles me to be near you, like being the most strongest man, who is at your complete mercy. *I love you!*" She rubbed her own neck, thinking of him, knowing he wasn't around, as the sound of Hasani's voice brought her back to reality, " . . . be my wife."

"What did you say?" responded Khumani as she almost dropped her drink.

"I want you to be my wife, mine forever," said Hasani.

"You can't be serious!" replied Khumani.

"I have never been more serious, never wanted something so much," said Hasani, and he pulled out his family crest. A golden statue of a phoenix that could fit in the palm of his hand, the most sincere form of commitment. Giving this to Khumani meant that he was willing to share his family name with her forever.

So stunned she didn't know how to react, Khumani was brought to tears.

"So, does this mean yes, or should I start crying myself?" asked Hasani.

Hearing the question again made her hesitate, but she realized her answer would be, "Yes, Hasani, I will marry you, be your wife," and she fell into his arms.

The rest of the evening seemed like a dream as they held each other. He kissed her softly and caressed the back of her neck. Delectable fruits laid before them were dipped in honey and fed to each other. It was a very romantic evening.

"How would you imagine our life together?" asked Khumani.

"It will be one of nobility . . . a love story that puts all others to shame," he replied.

Hasani had always been the kind of person who got what he wanted, never leaving anything to chance, but as he talked about the kind of life they would have, Khumani knew that little Nassor would not fit into Hasani's grand design of an aristocratic family.

Almost sensing Khumani's feeling of confusion, the baby started crying, looking for the one person who would always take care of him. Hasani held onto her hand firmly, but it was ripped away when she heard the baby crying. As she moved away, Hasani's family crest fell from her lap. She had not noticed but Hasani did. No one could know what Hasani thought at that moment, but he picked up the crest and placed it gently back on the table before him. He quickly got over the incident; he didn't want to overthink anything, especially on this night.

The moment Khumani took little Nassor in her arms, he stopped crying and smiled; he was happy. Looking at him, she started to feel a sense of guilt, as though she had betrayed Nassor in an act of infidelity. Feeling left out, Hasani thought he should join in to show he could tolerate this child just long enough to convince Khumani. "Let me hold him; I'm good with children," he said.

Everything seemed okay until little Nassor threw up all over Hasani's clothes. Khumani couldn't help but laugh.

"I think it's time I left," said Hasani as he gave back the baby and wiped himself off.

"So soon? I hope it wasn't because of him; it was an accident," said Khumani.

"No, no, that isn't it at all. I still have some business to take care of that needs my attention," said Hasani.

"Okay, then, but the next time I see you, it better be to make wedding arrangements," said Khumani.

"Nothing would make me happier . . . . What's his name?" asked Hasani.

"He's my nephew. I named him myself, Nassor," said Khumani.

"A good name for a boy," said Hasani, who then kissed her on the cheek good-bye, which was weird because Khumani expected a little bit more than that.

Hearing that name had made Hasani's stomach twist. He clenched his fist behind his back to keep control; otherwise, he might have smacked her in jealousy. She was still attached to that deviant—Hasani knew this for sure. There were times when he was with her that he got upset just thinking of him being with her, but Hasani was careful to make sure that she didn't notice his mood change. Khumani had no idea at all that Hasani knew about her secret love affair. He kept those bitter feelings to himself and channeled his anger into a smile. He then walked toward the door, saying, "See you soon, my love."

"Have a good night," she replied back. As she retreated into the safety of her home with little Nassor held tightly to her, Hasani left, clenching his fist and cursing the name of Nassor. He looked at his ring and promised that for this shame, Nassor would be the one to pay for it, dearly.

When Khumani's father, Desever, reached his destination, a military base, he was taken to the same laboratory that had run the experiments on Falun, who was still in recovery. Placed in a separate room, Desever spoke privately with Obsidian. "Everything is going according to plan; so far there have been few setbacks," he said.

"Wonderful. Our latest weapon was a complete success. After his recovery, he will be deployed with very sensitive instructions," said Obsidian.

As they continued to talk, the scientists who worked on Falun were mapping his progress; he was getting stronger every day. Falun was learning how to control his power, but it was slightly unstable. At times he had to be sedated so that no one would be harmed accidentally. Suddenly Falun tried to thank the people working on him. He reached out and touched one of the scientists. When he did, he began to have visions; memories flooded into his mind that were not his own. He saw images of other experiments that had failed horribly, all but one besides himself. He realized that he was not the first experiment to succeed and that the first one had already been sent out weeks ago to kill the leader of the Maroons.

"Are you okay? Did you see through my mind?" asked the scientist.

"Yes, I did," replied Falun. "Is that normal? A side effect?" he asked, but the scientist only alerted the others.

"He can see memories just like the others," shouted the scientist.

Falun continued to ask more questions that went unanswered as Obsidian and Desever were informed of the news. "What does this mean?" asked Falun.

"It means that you are a complete success," replied Obsidian while he maintained a safe distance away. As for those experiments that had failed, some did survive long enough so that the scientists could perfect the procedure. They knew for certain that for the three peoples, there are a set of abilities unique to each race. But none before had survived past the point of fourteen days to gain further information.

"They tell me you know of the first one. So far you exhibit all the abilities that he had been gifted with. You can see into the minds of others, which we can use against the Maroons," said Obsidian.

"If that's the case, why haven't you crushed their forces by now? The first one was already sent," said Falun.

"The ability you share with him can't be predicted; it comes and goes. As of now, we are not sure if his mission was a success," answered Obsidian.

"Then how soon until I am ready? I want to test this power, bring peace . . ."said Falun.

"No one here is a fool, Falun. I know why you are here, and I don't care. For now, you must be patient," said Obsidian. He walked out of the room thinking that the time for peace would be determined only by him.

As Obsidian left, Falun stared at his hands. His abilities were amazing. He then noticed smudges on his palm that he tried to wipe off, but the marks couldn't be removed. He realized that they were not stains, but teardrops from when he last saw his wife and she cried for him. The experiment had left her tears as a permanent mark on him. Even the scientists couldn't explain it, but that didn't matter to Falun. Even though he was disowned by his parents and forced to face a new journey, it gave him peace to know that her love was now always with him, even when he hadn't realized it. To him, this was a *mark of first love.*

CONSPIRACIES

While eating at some elite tavern, Kumi came across an anonymous note addressed to him. It had markings similar to the pendant given to him by the Immortals. In the note was information about the next Maroon raids, and also an invitation to a party. The party was going to be in the Lower Levels, where no one would notice; things were known to get wild at these parties, rumor had it. Kumi knew he had to be there; he needed to know more about this secret society that believed they would inherit Kiskeya. He left for it as soon as possible, and by the time he got there, the party was even more than he expected. There was a big bonfire, and hundreds of people danced around it. There was drinking, laughter, and music, but danger still was about because if the Ona came by on patrol, everyone would get arrested. Public gatherings of the lower castes in this way was forbidden, but there was a thrill in defying authority.

Few esclaves came, and anyone else probably held the Caste of Innocence. This was an area that was usually flooded with the guedado, but most had made themselves scarce after seeing all these people who could pose a threat.

It seemed anything could happen here; all sorts of laws were broken, yet no one would have dared to deny themselves such pleasures—the atmosphere was filled with it. Kumi wouldn't have objected to enjoying himself like this more often. He had done some crazy things before, but nothing like this. It was an exhilarating feeling to be breaking the law right under the Noble Regime, showing a complete disregard for the law. It finally made sense why the Immortals brought him here so they could hide in plain sight, still having their way.

Time passed, and still there was no sign from the Immortals. Kumi noticed a little boy who was lost in the crowd; he had seen the boy earlier, enjoying himself among the people. He was even far more mesmerized by what was going on than Kumi. The little boy approached him, and Kumi could see that he was guedado by the smell and the clothes he wore. There was a compelling feeling that the boy needed help. It was unusual for Kumi to show concern for a stranger, let alone a guedado, but there is a first for everything. The boy stood right in front of him, looked in his face, and didn't say a word. Kumi asked, "Are you lost? Where are your parents?"

The boy's eyes were glassy, as though he was in a daze, but he answered, "I don't need parents; I can take care of myself."

Kumi laughed because a part of him felt the same way at times. "Someone must care for you; you can't be on your own, not at this age." The boy seemed frail. "Would you like some food? I have some in my bag," offered Kumi. The little boy's face lit up with joy, and he took the food without a second thought. Kumi would never admit to it, but helping that boy felt right, to just show compassion to someone in need. He even gave the boy some money just in case.

More time passed and Kumi offered to help the boy get home, but the boy said he couldn't remember the way and would be happier staying here. Suddenly it seemed that the boy didn't need Kumi's help after all, since the boy's mother grabbed him by the hand and asked, "Where have you been? Me and your brother have been looking for you."

Kumi knew they had to be his family. Who else would claim a boy that had no home? They even had the same glassy stare. The mother didn't seem to notice anyone else around but her sons, with one standing silently behind her.

"I don't know you. I'm not like you. I'm like them . . ." said the little boy to his mother as she dragged him away.

"It's nice to see that you made it, Kumi," said a voice.

Kumi turned to see who had called his name. It was the girl who had drugged him that fateful night. He looked back to see where the little boy and his mother had gone, but they had already disappeared. With all the music and people, a person could move around like a ghost and be unnoticed. It was strange, but for some reason, this family seemed familiar to Kumi. He didn't know it, but Kumi had helped that family before, a mother and her two sons, some time ago.

Oh well, he thought, *the boy is weak.* Now he could get back to what he came for. "I almost didn't come. Usually people who say, 'We are always watching,' are the ones I tend to stay away from," said Kumi. "Are you the only one, or are there others watching from a distance?"

But the girl only smiled with a small laugh and said, "I'm not at liberty to say, but it's best to assume so. It seems that you have been making a name for yourself."

"True. I would like to think it was because of my own ambition, but I see now that your people have had a helping hand," replied Kumi.

"Well, we are all friends now. No one chooses to join us; we choose them, and you have potential that hasn't been seen in a long time," said the girl.

"Potential or not, I still don't see the grand design. How do they plan on taking over the land?" asked Kumi.

"Simple; we divide and conquer. We have spies everywhere, in the government, the Chideria Order, and even among the Maroons. Our spies keep us informed with all that we need to know; and when the time is right, we will use that information against them—they will fight among themselves. In the end, there will be no victor, and that is when the Immortals will take all that they know and reign forever. But for now we remain patient . . ." said the girl.

"I admit, this is all very well thought out. This secret society may have a chance, and if so, they will know my loyalty is with them," said Kumi.

"Good, very good . . . We are also careful not to let too much information out to opposing sides, like that of the raids we gave you. Otherwise, one side may get the upper-hand with the right information," said the girl.

"How did this society start?" asked Kumi.

"Like any other. We were different, outcasts to both what is Noble and deviant. For that we were resented. No one was sure which side we would claim loyalty toward. We started hundreds of years ago and slowly began acquiring some power and wealth, but what really inspired us to call ourselves Immortals was a revelation. I'm not sure where it started, but do you remember standing before the Eternals in the Great Hall filled with ancient markings? On the floor was a drawing of two beings, Gods who would one day descend from a higher plane and rule us in the place of the serwans. But they will only come when we have made this world ready for them, and we think that day is soon to come," said the girl.

Kumi did remember that drawing: two Gods, a male and a female, that stood holding up a giant orb that was surrounded by a gold ring. The girl explained that the Orb was a symbol denoting the Firmament, or first level of heaven. Kumi would have to be baptized in the waters of the orb as a final form of initiation. The waters also had a second purpose of telling a person's age; it had been tradition that the eldest member be leader of the Immortals, but Kumi wanted to be more than an Immortal; he thought to be an Eternal one day.

He never did find out the name of the girl, but throughout the night, they ventured to see other exciting things that were happening. Hard to believe that such a culture went unnoticed here, but it did. At every turn there was something new going on, with magicians who played with fire, psychics, and the most acrobatic dancers to entertain.

"Do you want to go see a magic trick?" asked the girl.

"It doesn't matter to me," said Kumi.

They walked up to a magician who was trying to make a rabbit disappear but kept failing.

"This is the worst magician I've ever seen," said Kumi, but as he turned around, he saw the girl was gone.

"I guess I made your friend disappear instead," laughed the magician.

"She is good," said Kumi.

Suddenly someone shouted, "The Ona are coming!"

Then everyone with enough sense began disappearing into the darkness like ghosts.

Kumi was able to get away before the Ona got there. By the time he got home, he dropped right into bed but didn't fall asleep. He started to think more about his future, how much more promising and certain it was; he now had more to gain and almost nothing to lose, *almost* nothing.

Since the attack, Mala-Dek was as angry as ever, not from the attack itself but from the fact that the Assassin was able to free all the children from the basement den chamber. When she had awakened from her fight, it was Menee who was there watching over her, a human, which added further shame for her. Since that day, she left every window open and every door unlocked, hoping that the Assassin would try again and they could finish their fight. None of her wounds were too severe, and Menee was able to clean them up with some ointment. She got rid of Menee soon after, saying that her services were no longer needed, that she had taught the children all that she could. Mala-Dek's only goal now was to find this Assassin with whatever resources were at her disposal.

As for Menee, nothing made her happier than to be free of that kind of evil, but what made her even happier was the fact that the children were free because of her. Thinking scum like Mala-Dek need to know pain and torment for all the harm they have caused, they fear the Assassin. But to Menee and the den children, the Assassin is their lethal protector, and by now all ears have heard of her and what she does. It was Menee that helped her in, and together they found a way to free the children.

When Mala-Dek woke up, Menee told her that she had found her passed out on the floor with blood everywhere. Mala-Dek was unaware of Menee's involvement; she believed that Menee was much too fearful of her to come up with such a plot.

Going back to her family gave Menee new hope, and Amari seemed overjoyed. He was so excited to know that she wouldn't have to leave anymore, and he kept telling her the same story about how he had seen a God fall from the sky. "It's true, Menee, I swear it," he said.

"I believe you," she replied. It was good to be home, very good.

While Menee was home enjoying the company of her family, Mala-Dek continued making preparations for the next time she would confront the Assassin. She used her unlawful influence to put a hit out, and then had her servants contact other den masters to let them in on her plan. Unfortunately, most of those den masters were already dead, and their deaths were recent. Mala-Dek truly realized how skilled the Assassin was, even admiring her talent for punishment.

As for the children that were set free, no one can truly know what became of them afterward. Some might find their way home or end up in the Lower Levels, but there was comfort knowing that they had a better chance wherever they were now.

REDEMPTION

There was another celebration going on at the Maroon camp; even though they were a warlike people, they believed in times of enjoyment. Not everything had to be about survival; those were things done out of necessity, but it was not their reason for life. It was more important to create memories of happiness; otherwise, all they would know was misery. Without moments like this, what they were fighting for, any victory, in the end would be meaningless.

This celebration was known as Kissed by the Sun, a celebration that began at sunrise and wouldn't end until sunset. Small children would play at the river all day, and Maroon fighters would place their Enos in a direction facing the sun, a sign of respect for the source of their power. It was like an infant's kiss to its mother, a sign of affection to what gives the world life and eternal warmth. On this day, everyone forgets their worries, sadness, and regrets, because one must live for today, yesterday has passed, and tomorrow is yet to come. Some might also say it is a day for humility, just being thankful for what you already have, with no desire or goal to be met, nothing to cloud the mind but everything to free the spirit.

For some, this day is about evoking the creative parts of the mind through music, art, and folklore. One might walk by to see things that they have never used to describe a Maroon warrior, a sense of humanity. From both corners of the eye, a person can witness a valiant soldier rehearsing a romantic poem as a proposal for marriage to his first love, walk by to see a Maroon-to-be find courage to receive his first kiss, or see a bitter old man who may have been a legend years ago find happiness in the music he plays. One might see an ordinary man become a mentor to children and tell them that the world is their canvas and they can make it whatever work of art they want it to be.

These are the values that the Maroons held sacred and would keep until the next celebration. They would fight hard because they fought for a way of life. These are all the things Deathblow witnessed, the one sent for Uhuru, who walked hidden among the people.

But for Uhuru, leader of the Maroons, Kissed by the Sun is a day of remembrance. Unlike most, he will spend the entire time down in the chasm where the Earth Eno was found. On this day, he remembers those who have fought and died in this war, those that have been buried but whose hearts and minds remain with them forever. After death, a Maroon's Eno is placed back into the chasm, and without sunlight, it returns to its first form. Maroons believe there is a spiritual connection between a warrior and his Eno, and not even death can fully separate them. So even from the afterlife, they remain as a collective entity; warriors from thousands of years past remain as watchful Guardians to the next generation as their Enos are reforged.

Even now as leader, just to stand before their memory made Uhuru feel like a novice, and for that he was truly humbled. He took his own Eno and kissed it to think of his father, who had the greatest influence on him. He placed his Eno down next to him and concentrated on the spirits of the warriors who taught him the most, even those whom he had never met but were only told to him through history. There was so much he still had to learn, but he felt their spirits even if they couldn't speak to him, and that was satisfaction enough.

At the entryway of the chasm stood four Elite Guardsmen sworn to protect Uhuru; they were brothers, two sets of twins. They each carried an Eno of similar design, the only difference being in color, but they recognized their Eno by heart. The second set of twins were born a year after the first set, and that gave their father the idea of what their Enos would be. It would be a sword that could separate into two blades, and each blade could separate into daggers. Each son received one whole sword, and they were known to fight with a flow that rivaled some of the greatest warriors. Their strikes were known to be like blocks of ice, untouchable as vapor and surrounding their enemies like a flood. Each one was born with a natural fighting talent that was years beyond their age.

Yes, the people of the Maroon camp were in a festive mood, unaware of the malevolence coming for them, for their leader. Those that stood in Deathblow's way were crushed without mercy, but even with his powers, he knew that alone the Maroons would overcome him. He absorbed the memories to prove that. He had to devise a plan.

Deathblow came across a few empty tents and began lighting them on fire. The memories he had absorbed gave him knowledge of their territory, which he used to his advantage. It was divided into four quadrants, with a lookout post at each quadrant; they had ways of alerting others of danger days before it came using their Enos. What kept them hidden for so long was the fact that they blended in with the jungle terrain and the only paths to their home were hidden in streams and waterfalls.

As Deathblow prepared his assault, he became distracted by glimpses, flashes of memories of men he had killed. The drawback to his powers was that they were random and he couldn't control what memories he would get. For some of these men, their last memories were of their families, and he understood that. Some were expecting the birth of their first child, and others dreamed of not having to live in the shadows as scavengers; but all wished to see a day when humans didn't live under bondage. A touch of remorse started to fill him. Each man he killed had a loved one waiting for him, and now because of Deathblow they would have to wait until the next life. He did think to show mercy, but if he had let any of them live, it would jeopardize his whole mission and he couldn't do that. Deathblow had come to a point of no return; he had to see it through to the end.

But in that moment of distraction, he had left himself vulnerable. Two guardsmen approached him and ordered, "Stop what you're doing." Deathblow closed his eyes to concentrate as though he were charging up. The guardsmen readied themselves in defense, but they hadn't been expecting this. As Deathblow raised his hand, a force emanated from it, a sort of impulse wave. The two guardsmen were thrown into the air. Deathblow now had to move fast as the fire he started began to spread. He moved to the southwest quadrant of the camp, the place where they were most vulnerable. He got there to see children playing

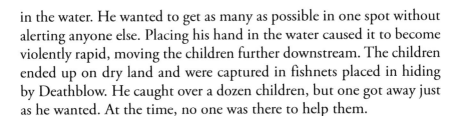

in the water. He wanted to get as many as possible in one spot without alerting anyone else. Placing his hand in the water caused it to become violently rapid, moving the children further downstream. The children ended up on dry land and were captured in fishnets placed in hiding by Deathblow. He caught over a dozen children, but one got away just as he wanted. At the time, no one was there to help them.

When he arrived, the children had cried for their mothers. Accidentally one child was touched by Deathblow, a small girl. He could sense her fear as it raced through his body. He had forgotten what fear was through the eyes of a child, and the little girl thought she would die today. "No, little one, you will not die. I promise," said Deathblow.

By the time Deathblow returned to the epicenter of the celebration, word had already begun to spread about the fires and missing children. Frantically people began to disband, hoping that it wasn't their own children and homes caught in this tragedy. It was obvious to most of them that this was some sort of an attack, especially during a time like this. Someone was responsible, but there wasn't time to figure out who. Most of the Maroon warriors headed to where all the danger was, but the rest would be headed straight toward Uhuru to inform him of what was happening. Those were the few headed toward the chasm in the northeast quadrant, and Deathblow followed them. He knew enough about the chasm to know of its great significance to the Maroon people; it was a sacred place.

As they neared the entryway of the chasm, Deathblow jumped out of the shadows and attacked the warriors with his impulse wave.

"Look out!" shouted one of the Elite Guardsmen. The group of warriors were able to jump out of the way just in time.

"Ready yourselves, men. The war has come to us," said another of the Elite Guardsmen.

But Deathblow didn't come to fight all these men. "By now your people are searching for some missing children, but they will only find six; the

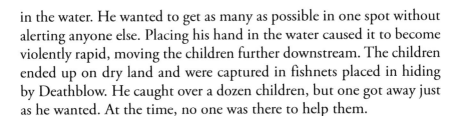

rest have been hidden away by me. If you leave now, you can save them from drowning in the rising waters," said Deathblow.

"Where are they?" asked one warrior.

"Outside the perimeter of the camp toward the edge of the river," said Deathblow.

One of the warriors said to the Elite Guardsmen, "None of us will leave your side to fight alone or leave Uhuru vulnerable. Someone else can see to the safety of these children."

"By then it will be too late. Now, all of you men go find those children, while my brothers and I deal with this one," said one of the Elite Guardsmen. The Maroon warriors who left did as they were told, but not without feeling a sense of abandonment. They were leaving their comrades to face an unknown enemy.

Deathblow was surprised that they believed his lie; he had sworn no harm would come to those children, and he meant it. But it would keep them occupied long enough for him to finish his mission.

"Capture him alive! We need to know who else he has with him and how far they have gotten into our grounds," ordered the eldest of the brothers elite.

"No doubt this is related to the raids that have left our warrior kinsmen dead," said the youngest.

This was it, thought Deathblow. It was really happening, and he would be the one to end a war that had been building up for thousands of years.

Down in the chasm, Uhuru remained unaware of the events above. His thoughts too were about the coming war and how long it had taken to come. It should have happened long ago, he believed. But there were times when the Maroons were under a leadership that didn't want to have anything to do with a world outside their own. That was a mistake, because it allowed an injustice to go on without challenge. He planned to change that.

Back on the surface, Deathblow removed his cloak and revealed who he was.

"What are you?" asked one of the Elite Guardsmen.

"Who cares? He is the enemy of our people and must be put down hard," said the brashest of the elite brothers. Eager for a fight, the two youngest brothers went in first, not realizing the full nature of the one they were fighting. "As long as we avoid that attack from his arms, we can get close enough to hit him," said one.

As they charged, Deathblow remained still. His body had been changed drastically from the experiments. He was like stone and not easily broken. Like Falun, he had three sanscoeurs attached to him; one was on his forearm, where most of his attacks were from. Another was on his chest, and the other was attached to the back of his head with extensions that wrapped partially around his face.

The warriors pulled out their daggers with the intent to wear him down through small injuries throughout his body, but Deathblow broke his stance and struck the ground with his fist, sending a surge powerful enough to shake the trees. To his surprise, it only broke their stride. He was in for an intense battle.

Deathblow defended himself as much as he could, but for the most part, he accepted the full force of their blows as they landed in vulnerable places. Deathblow couldn't tell the difference between the pain he was receiving now and that which he was already feeling as a result of the experiment. The serums had toughened his skin; with every hit, the shock was mostly absorbed and dissipated into the ground. He noticed that the Elite Guardsmen had a unique fighting style compared to their fellow warriors. They even dressed slightly different, but that didn't matter as Deathblow managed to grab one of them. The warrior broke his hold but was not fast enough to avoid the impulse wave. At such a close range, it should have killed him, but not enough energy had been gathered to do so. The young warrior fell to the ground several feet away, mostly with his pride hurt for being the first caught in an attack.

Another brother quickly reacted by striking Deathblow on the side of his head with the blunt end of his dagger. It dazed him momentarily, but Deathblow recovered like it was nothing at all. The two elder brothers followed into the assault, but Deathblow was living up to his name and was hard to defeat.

They now stood between Deathblow and the entryway to the chasm. "You will not step any further, no matter what power you have," said the eldest, and then through his will alone, he fused his daggers together to form his blades and raced into combat. His other brothers followed his lead and fused their daggers as well. The first brother jumped into the air and kicked Deathblow in the face, but it only staggered him. The next brother came and slashed Deathblow right through the stomach, the first injury to draw blood. He followed with a kick to the chest right where the sanscoeur was placed, but the force of the attack was deflected back into him. Deathblow then grabbed the Elite Guardsman and countered with a knee to his face. The Maroon elite fell back while his brothers engaged Deathblow.

"Does anyone else find it strange that his movements are starting to look like our own?" asked one of the brothers. As their fight raged on, Deathblow was gaining knowledge of their techniques with each blow that made contact; this added to the limited knowledge he had gained from other Maroons he had encountered. But to fight like a Maroon would take years of training, and no matter how much of their memories he had, it would not match their skill as fighters.

It didn't take long for the fighters to realize how Deathblow had learned some of their moves, so they covered themselves from head to toe. Under different circumstances, a challenge such as Deathblow would have been exhilarating; to face an opponent who knew all their moves would be a true test of their skill. Yet the safety of Uhuru and their people was in jeopardy, and they wouldn't risk that. But now Deathblow couldn't absorb their knowledge, which was favorable to him as well; each time he absorbed a memory, it left him vulnerable.

Two of the brothers fought hard and were driving him back. They kept striking the same places, hoping that the damage would eventually take its toll even with his tough skin.

"Look, he is getting weaker, he has exhausted his power," said the elite eldest.

At long last, the brothers were able to surround Deathblow from all sides.

"Let's finish this," said the youngest.

"Remember, avoid his hand and chest," said another.

They came at him all at once, thinking he would lose, but a shimmering glow emanated from his chest and Deathblow unleashed an impulse wave from his entire body. Moments later, all four were on the ground passed out, while Deathblow struggled to his feet, a dangerous move. That attack took more of a toll on him than the entire fight; he wouldn't be able to do that again, but he was left with few options. Yet he still had all he needed to face Uhuru.

As Deathblow journeyed into the chasm, the light seemed only to get brighter not dimmer; he needed no torch to guide his path. Finally, at its center, he saw the man whose life he must bring to an end. Uhuru had his back turned, his head bowed in prayer. "Prepare yourself, Uhuru, leader of the Maroons, for this temple will be your final resting place," said Deathblow.

Uhuru barely reacted to the threat. He just raised his head, took a deep breath, and said, "Whoever you are, you have made a grave mistake by disturbing me and desecrating the place of my forefathers, and for that I will show you no mercy."

Uhuru rolled and grabbed his Eno like a bird catching the air beneath its wings, so natural were his movements. But Uhuru had not realized that he faced an enemy who was a living weapon dedicated to his destruction. The vicious battle had begun. Using the blunt end of his

Eno, Uhuru hit Deathblow on the surface of his kneecap, causing him to collapse backward. As Uhuru and Deathblow continued their fight, they were unaware that the battle was being sensed by the Earth Eno, which reacted heavily. Sparks of light jumped into the air as Uhuru struck Deathblow two more times with the Eno; he was ready to finish this once and for all. Deathblow refused to be beaten; however, there was only so much trauma his body could take as Uhuru punished him.

Exhaustion was beginning to take effect, but with the little energy he had left, Deathblow released an impulse wave straight into Uhuru's face.

"Aghhh!" screamed Uhuru as he fell back, disoriented at a defining moment.

Suddenly the lights that had flickered before began to surround Deathblow. They were drawn to him. The Earth Eno was making itself known to him, something that had never happened before. Somehow through the sanscoeur, Deathblow was able to make a connection with the Earth Eno. The most amazing event happened next, giving shape to something unexpected. The memories, history, and collective consciousness of the Earth Eno flooded into the mind of Deathblow like a waterfall into a bucket. Uhuru stood in awe of this incredible sight, and then there was a great flash: both Uhuru and Deathblow had emerged from the chasm forever changed. Deathblow, the great enemy of the Maroons, had now pledged his life to their cause, calling himself an Emissary of the Eno. The scattered memories from thousands of years past resided within this one being.

The warriors who had been sent to save the missing children had just returned; they had gotten halfway there before being told that all the children had been accounted for. They found the Elite Guardsmen on the ground just before they had awakened, and feared the worst had occurred. But then their fears were placed to rest as Uhuru ascended from the chasm—and to their surprise, with Deathblow beside him. All the warriors kept their Enos at the ready to finish Deathblow.

"Stand down!" ordered Uhuru, whose hair had turned white.

"But he is our enemy; he threatened your life," said an Elite Guardsman.

"He tried, he failed . . . but he has become anointed, blessed with what we hold dear, Kissed by the Sun. What happened in the chasm, I cannot explain; but I need you, my soldiers and friends, to trust that our destiny is to let him live," said Uhuru. Deathblow now served a greater purpose that would be vital to their cause in the coming days.

Without question, they all heeded Uhuru's command. They believed something greater was in motion; they could feel it through their Enos, and all that was required of them was faith. But a burden still lay with Deathblow. He had done such terrible things, but with his will now aligned with the heart of the Earth Eno, his guilt could be carried no longer. "I have committed crimes against your people that must be dealt with. All I ask is that you wait until I have fulfilled my purpose, and then you can deal with me as you see fit," said Deathblow.

Knowing what had happened in the caves gave the people more of a reason to finish the celebration, but there were those who would never be the same again and would claim retribution for the crimes committed by Deathblow. For now, though, he would remain unharmed as later on he spoke privately with Uhuru concerning traitors in the Maroon camp.

THE ONE THING YOU FEAR THE MOST

Dawn came. Its morning rays entered every household, allowing all the glory of the sun to enter in. It was a day of anticipation, as Nyack and Nassor awaited their banishment to the Lougawou Mountains, a place thought to be hell. Neither was able to get a full night of rest, knowing that the end would be soon for them. Nassor had time to think about so much at that time. He of course wanted to see Khumani one last time, still feeling the undying love that could never be accepted in her world. The last time he had seen her, she had dedicated herself to another, Hasani, the one who would see Nassor punished. He thought of her deeply, so hard he heard the beating of his heart and the passing of air through his body. The room became silent. He felt a peace within him and wondered if she thought of him right now. In that moment, he no longer felt the pain of the sanscoeur, only his will that was determined to take control of his own destiny. He could make no promises, but he wouldn't submit to his enemies without a fight. Whatever chance he had, he would try to see her one last time. Nassor also thought of his brother, Kumi. He wished that they had not become such bitter rivals. So many years of animosity existed between them, and yet there was a time when they were close, inseparable as brothers should be. Even now there was a part of Nassor that would always want to protect his brother. If there was a way, Nassor would make peace with Kumi and do everything in his power to make sure that promise was kept.

As for Nyack, he had pretended to be asleep that whole night. For the first time, he didn't have anything to say. He thought of his own family and hoped that none of them would be there that morning to see the same fate that their father had endured. He had thought that he was prepared for this, but now he would do anything to avoid this cup of suffering. He fought a battle that he was meant to lose. A weakness came over his body, and he spent the rest of that night with his eyes closed and despair in his heart.

It was time and the guards came. They were brought to a place where a crowd of Noble citizens awaited them. Several had brought their esclaves and placed them just close enough so that they could see what happens to humans that break the law. They wanted the esclaves to witness deviants pulled into the dark void, the gateway into the Lougawou Mountains. Nyack looked into every face that they passed, and most of them looked back with contempt. No one even paid attention to Nassor; it was for Nyack they all came, and by now his name was recognized by all.

Nothing had changed, thought Nyack. Every human he looked at only made eye contact for a moment and quickly looked away, back to the ground. It seemed that mankind had abandoned him, not yet ready to stand against a bitter foe, injustice. To them, he was a broken man who had been defeated; and as long as they saw that image, they would never stand for themselves. Somewhere deep inside, Nyack knew that what happened today would matter years from now, but it all depended on him, the mark that he left behind. After this day, they would be property. So for them and himself, Nyack had to give the despised people what they needed most, a martyr.

With his head held high, Nyack looked them all in the eye, with the conviction that they had not yet broken him and there would be others to finish what he started.

It enraged the Nobles to see his outright defiance. "Kill him now! Hurl his carcass into the pit!" they chanted. But as he stood, the first rays of sunlight shone on his body, and the sanscoeur attached to him created an aura around him. It was an aura that was brought forth from their natural abilities. One of the guards tried to use the spear to control him, but Nyack refused; he would die in defiance against them. The pain was great, but Nyack didn't have to fight it forever—just long enough. His aura was so beautiful and undeniable that the Noble people quieted themselves. One by one, humans began to look in awe, linked to him as they witnessed glory on this day.

One man who would carry the burden of a people, One man who would deny Death to know Life

3rd World Order

Some were told to sit down and look away, but they couldn't. Even if they had been struck down, their eyes still remained focused on Nyack. It was as if he had enchanted them. Humans now asked themselves a dangerous question.

What crime is man so guilty of that he should be punished like this?

3rd World Order

In that moment, Nyack became what the Nobles feared the most.

Next, a group of Ona arrived with their routine disposal of guedado, accompanied by Obsidian and Desever. Both Nyack and Nassor were taken out of the caravan that brought them and were placed within a few steps of the dark void. The rays of the sun began to shine through the Diamond Tree that encased the Akin-Eno. The entrance to the Lougawou Mountains would now be fully opened.

The spectrum of light that came from that tree seemed everlasting, something that anyone could look upon and be humbled. Its rays would at some point reach everyone, including Menee and Amari who were up doing work, Khumani while tending to the baby, even Mala-Dek as she sat in meditation. But of course they would come, the three of them, Hasani, Chisulo, and Kumi, who were there for ulterior motives.

As that light was seen by all, its display eventually came to an end so that everything else could begin.

"You, Nyack C'Kre, have been sentenced to spend the rest of your life exiled to the Lougawou Mountains. Any last words?" asked Hasani.

With his chains removed, Nyack looked around and realized he was finally ready to leave this world; it was no longer for him, and his purpose had been fulfilled.

"Freedom will not be given; it must be taken!" said Nyack. No greater words had resonated among a people, especially for Nassor. What Nyack said sounded like a Declaration of War; and for all the humans who heard, a spark was lit inside them, a calling that they had forgotten. It was . . . *the old one, the Spirit of Rebellion.*

3rd World Order

"Defiant until the very end. Throw him into the void!" said Hasani.

The guard through his spear lifted Nyack off his feet and toward the entryway. The Noble peoples all stood cheering. "Justice has been served; justice has found a way." But as they cheered, the group of guedado began attacking the Ona, a surprise assault that grabbed the attention of everyone and allowed Nyack's feet to touch ground again.

The Hunters and the Ona were all caught off guard, and it was in that moment that the members of the Chideria Order unveiled themselves. Hidden as guedado, they were able to orchestrate this plan. The peaceful members of the Chideria Order struck hard and fast, throwing lit canisters filled with oil. This gave Nassor the opportunity he needed to grab the spear from the guard so it couldn't be used against Nyack. He took the guard out fast as the people began to flee in every direction. Fire was spreading everywhere, but the Hunters and Ona were not yet defeated; they took to the skies and, led by Chisulo, pulled out their weapons to descend upon their prey. Each was equipped with the Orum-Spear, which was the most trusted weapon of the serwans.

But Hasani was grateful for the attack, and his focus was solely on Nassor. "You will not escape," he shouted as he flew toward Nassor wielding the spear that would weaken him. Hasani descended right before him, but Nassor still had the spear that he took from the guard and pulled back to drive it right through Hasani's heart. Hasani was the one who made the first move, which pushed the fight in his favor. Using the spear, he threw Nassor down to the ground. "No matter what you do, I will make sure you are thrown into the dark void." Again using the spear, he hurled Nassor even further, over the edge. Nassor grabbed whatever he could, but the strain was too much. To give himself a chance, he had to drop the spear he had taken from the guard. The branches were sharp and cut through his skin. If his arms didn't tire out, the branch would eventually break, and he couldn't pull himself up without falling.

Smoke engulfed the sky; canisters had been thrown everywhere. Nassor saw Hasani fly away, thinking that Nassor had fallen in. Nassor then heard a voice say, "Grab my hand, quickly." Someone had peered over the edge to save Nassor; and as the smoke cleared, he could now see his savior, Faizah, who had bravely reached down to help her friend. Risking her own life in the process, she lowered herself to reach him and stopped him from falling into the dark void. No one had ever done such a thing for him. In the most life-changing moment of his life, Faizah was there for him and made the difference no one else could.

"You're not alone in this fight; I'm here for you always," said Faizah.

"Thank you," said Nassor.

When both of them had gotten their feet back on the ground, they were in the midst of a battlefield. Most of the people had fled and the fires were dying out. The big surprise was seeing the esclaves join the fight. The esclaves even knocked Kumi down to the ground and engaged any Hunter or Ona they saw. They had no weapons, only heart, as they fought hard and bravely. Win or lose, victory or death, it didn't matter to them. The only thing that mattered was taking their destiny into their own hands.

Nassor, thinking that he was given a second chance and out of a sense of compassion, ran toward his brother to make sure he was not hurt. He carried Kumi to a place where he would be safe. "Stay with him; I'll come back for both of you," said Nassor to Faizah.

Nassor ran back into the battle, hoping to make a difference, but the sanscoeur suddenly became active, crippling his body with pain. Psionic energy began pouring from his body because of it. Nassor could even sense where the spear that controlled the sanscoeur was, with Hasani.

Hasani was battling against Nyack as they fought over possession of the spear. Nyack wanted to help Nassor and return the favor. At last, Nyack was able to grab the spear from Hasani; but in the process he was injured, slashed right through the leg. Hasani had lured him into that move so he could use the orum blade, the latest weapon used for close-range combat. The two were still exchanging blows, but Hasani had dominated most of the fight and knew that he would win as Nyack collapsed to the ground in pain. He tried to get back up, but before he could, Hasani punched him in the jaw. Nyack then felt a pain coming from his sanscoeur, but it didn't make sense since the other spear had fallen into the void.

A masked Hunter behind Nyack had a ring that had the same control of the sanscoeur as the spear, something that Hasani had planned just in case. Nyack tried to get up again to show that he would be beaten but not broken by the likes of Hasani, and for that Hasani violently struck him down. He wasn't getting up again as Hasani stood over him.

"You were supposed to go in before Nassor, but you will join him soon after I am finished with you," said Hasani.

"We should leave; let the lesser of our kind deal with them," said the Masked Hunter.

"And run away dishonored? I would prefer death than to run from those who are beneath me. Now hand me the ring; I will do this personally," said Hasani.

But just as the ring was about to exchange hands, a canister that was thrown in the air exploded on the Masked Hunter and lit his body ablaze. Hasani had fallen back to shield himself as he lost possession of the ring. The effects of the sanscoeur started to wear off as Nyack looked up to see Nassor helping him up. "Let's go; we don't have much time," said Nassor.

Just as Nyack was about to follow, Nyack noticed a light in his eye. As he looked down, he saw the last bit of sunlight pass through the diamond tree as it shone on the ring. He took the ring in his hand and knew of a way to end it all. Stepping into the light that shone from the Akin-Eno and onto him, Nyack realized this moment would be the way to end mankind's suffering.

But he had to act quickly, as his allies were being taken down. Their numbers were dwindling, and even Nassor was swiftly defeated by the Masked Hunter who made his return with his body still covered with smoke.

The Masked Hunter pulled out his Orum-Spear to deal with Nyack, but as he approached, Nyack placed the ring on his finger.

"Kill them, kill them all, and throw any survivors into the pit!" shouted Chisulo as he commanded the Hunters and Ona.

Nyack now had no choice. He heard the screams of his allies become silence; they were being extinguished like the fires around them. He didn't know what would happen, but as he placed the ring on his finger, his body rose into the air; for the first time, he knew what it felt to be Noble. It was a glorious feeling, one that he would never forget, but it would be short-lived. Reinforcements of the Noble Regime stopped his ascent and pulled him back down to the ground.

"*No*, I will not lose, I will not!" cried Nyack. His aura from the sanscoeur still burned as it took the weight of a dozen Ona to bring him down. Even with the ring, his fall was inevitable.

From a distance, Nassor could see his friend fall to his hands and knees as Nyack lost control over the sanscoeur. Both Nyack and Nassor had been recaptured. Nassor saw Hasani walk up to Nyack and take the ring from his hand. Hasani looked Nyack in the eye and laughed as the Ona still struggled with Nassor. Hasani had both the spear and ring, but just as Hasani was about to gloat over his victory, Nyack jumped at him again and grabbed the spear. Kumi had just returned and witnessed the whole thing as they fought for possession of the spear. Others tried to attack Nyack, but the aura from him repelled them off randomly. His last breath would be in defiance.

The aura around Nassor grew more intense and brighter, surpassing that of Nyack, as more Ona came to subdue him as well. His body went into uncontrolled spasms of pain. The fighting reached its peak as the spear suddenly turned to glass and shattered into dust in the hands of Hasani. The aura of Nyack had disappeared, and when it did, the Masked Hunter took the orum blade and stabbed him in the back.

It seemed like the fight had ended, as the auras of both Nyack and Nassor died out together. But then a power exploded from Nassor, a raw power that pulsated through him. All the Ona who held him down were thrown into the air. The aura could be seen in his eyes as an unknown force possessed him. Faizah wondered what was happening as she became frozen. Every part of her said to run before she was captured, but she stood still as did everyone else. If Kumi hadn't seen this with his own eyes, he wouldn't have believed it. Hasani looked as his rival became something fearless. *That kind of power is too great to exist in man for long; it will kill him soon,* he thought.

While everyone's attention was on Nassor, he seemed to be focused on the monument. He then looked to the ground as a burst of energy dispersed from the sanscoeur, pulling him through the air with great speed.

"After him now; do not let him escape," commanded Chisulo.

"What about these prisoners?" asked the Masked Hunter as some saw fit to escape.

"They are not important; go after that human," said Chisulo.

A dozen Ona jumped into the air, flying at top speed to catch Nassor. Faizah was still near as she ran for safety, keeping Nassor in her sights.

"He's going to do it, going to do what no human has ever been able to do since the last age . . . become the one thing you fear the most," said Nyack in his weakened condition.

"But you'll never witness it, whatever he does," said Hasani. And then he kicked Nyack C'Kre into the dark void, into the Lougawou Mountains.

All who looked into the sky would witness. All esclaves, kenyetta, and serwan were watching a man take flight. Had their eyes deceived them? Was it an illusion? No, it wasn't, because the destiny of mankind could no longer be denied. Nassor kept moving as the distance between him and the top of the monument got shorter and shorter, realizing that this was what he was being tested for and it would change everything.

The Ona were gaining on him fast. They continued to close the gap, but Nassor's focus was on the light that guided him to the monument. Finally he landed within arm's length of his goal. But the Ona got there a moment after he did, pulling him away from the Diamond Tree. He could see the Akin-Eno and it was glorious; it was the very gift that legend spoke of and more. Nassor fought back desperately as more Ona appeared and grabbed hold of him. He refused to give in—that was not his destiny. He reached his hand out that was covered in his own blood, and the Diamond Tree seemed to become more illuminated, not from the sun but from something within. Sensing the power coming from the Akin-Eno, Nassor's sanscoeur began glowing even more, drawing Nassor even closer to the tree until finally he grabbed the Akin-Eno.

Its power surged through him, and it was immense, so great that tears of blood fell. When the blood touched the Akin-Eno, it triggered something, and Nassor's mind went beyond him, to a place only known as the Domain, where he met a being called the Keeper, a wondrous woman who was on the verge of giving birth.

"Nassor, you have been chosen to wield a legend, a legacy. The power of the Akin-Eno now lies with you, and the Age of Man has begun. From this day, your power, your greatness, and your destiny can no longer be denied. But remember, for your people to be saved, a sacrifice must be made and you must suffer!" said the Keeper.

With his body covered in the same eternal fire he had seen in dreams, Nassor's mind was sent back. When he looked around, the Ona had been turned to dust and the Diamond Tree was gone. The name of man was instantly engraved onto the obelisk, making all of humankind no longer esclave but now *ascended to nobility*. The Akin-Eno still with him flowed like water in his hand, and his mind forged it into the greatest weapon he could think of. It shimmered as parts of his body were covered in an armor fit for a warrior. This marked the Dawn of a new Age.

Witnessing as his brother made everything he had done in life meaningless, Kumi was beside himself as he shouted, "*No*, not him! *Not him!*"

CHAOS UNLEASHED

If you take from this tree, you will not die but you will be like them.

3rd World Order

So many changes were taking place because of what Nassor did; Nassor changed the course of human history. By awakening the Akin-Eno, the monument could no longer stand. The tallest structure in all of Kiskeya, which commemorated the Sentient War won by the Noble people, began to crumble. Nassor jumped down, flying faster than the falling debris, and used his power to save those he could. The Akin-Eno broke through the debris, turning it to dust.

Its power was raw, and Nassor was only beginning to learn what it was capable of. Upon his union with it, the Akin-Eno fused with the sanscoeur, erasing all of its weaknesses and amplifying its strengths. Nassor could now channel his aura for flight without fear of pain. Also, the Akin-Eno's solar origin provided a permanent source of *life* energy for the sanscoeur.

Its arrival did so much for the world of man in ways that may not yet be understood.

When the Akin-Eno was claimed once more, a mystical force surrounded Gina Ifosia and her two sons. Their bodies joined together, releasing four beams of light. One fell on Menee, granting her power over the earth. One fell on Amari, granting him speed. The last two fell on Faizah and Kumi, giving her a mystical energy and Kumi strength. Together, these four would be called the ordained, the chosen few predestined for something yet unknown.

Back at the Maroon camp, after the traitors had been revealed by Deathblow, an event occurred that broke Uhuru's concentration in the chasm. Every earth Eno possessed by a Maroon warrior began to shimmer. The Akin-Eno's power resonated among them all.

Uhuru emerged from the chasm with his Eno and said, "The Blessed Gift has returned." He realized that this was a sign not to be ignored.

After Nassor had done what he could to protect people from the falling tower, he went back to where Faizah had been. But everyone was gone, and he didn't know what had become of Nyack. He decided to conceal his armor, not wanting to draw any attention; for now, he had to go back to being normal.

He went back to the place where Faizah had hidden him and found her frantic, packing her things and getting ready to leave.

"Where are you going?" asked Nassor.

"I'm not going anywhere for now, but you are: you must take the Living Busara to the Maroon camp," said Faizah.

"But why? We are all citizens now. The war, this two-thousand-year struggle, is over without countless lives being lost," said Nassor.

"What you did changed everything, but you can't expect people to change in one day. Not in a system that they have lived by for so long. I can feel it, and in the next few days, things will get very dangerous," said Faizah.

"It has started . . ." said the Living Busara while entering the hidden room. Moments later, the sound of rioting and violence could be heard. The news that man had become citizen was growing, and people were going crazy over the shift in power. The land of Kiskeya was going into turmoil. It would start in Peponi and spread throughout the provinces.

"You have to go now, Nassor. I will meet up with you in a few days," said Faizah.

"But what about you? I can't leave you here. Come with us," said Nassor.

"I can't now. There are still some things that need to be taken care of. Followers of Chideria must be informed. They need to know what must be done next. You are still a fugitive; that's why you need to go before the Hunters find you," said Faizah.

Faizah seemed determined to see this through. Nassor could understand why, even if he couldn't accept that we must all be tested in life, that we must all fulfill a purpose. So he took the Living Busara and gathered the necessary things to go on their way. They all hugged each other good-bye, hoping that it wouldn't be their last. Nassor and the Living Busara then left Faizah and disappeared into the chaos outside.

Several days went by as rioting began to take over most of the major areas. All of the Ona were sent out to disperse and maintain order, it was gradually taking effect. In the more rural areas, the truth was being kept from the humans. Their serwan masters had no intention of telling them about their rise to power. To them, this meant losing their caste and becoming equals in a world where inequality was power.

The rest of the Ordained became curious about their power. Their world turned to chaos because the mark of man was written on the obelisk and the time was now for their gifts to be tested. They were forced to test their abilities mostly to protect themselves. One of the biggest riots happened in the area where Menee and Amari lived. Mala-Dek, who reveled in the disorder, hoped that inciting these riots would draw out the Assassin. At the very least, it was amusement to her. She didn't even know why the riots had started until after she got herself involved, but when she did find out, it only encouraged her. She set out with a lowlife group of serwans that rapidly grew in number. They started setting fires and destroying property. It didn't matter whose property it was, as long as they could take anything of value at the end.

At the time, Amari and Menee were out doing their daily work and were unaware of what was going on, even as smoke filled the air. They didn't realize anything was wrong until they heard an unfamiliar voice say, "Run, run, there is danger." The voice seemed like a whisper echoing in the wind. They went back home only to find it had been put to ashes, the result of a riot about to end, with several people running around looking for safety.

"Mama, where are you?" said Amari as he and his sister searched the area.

"I can't find her anywhere, but she has to be here," said Menee.

They continued searching, but their mother couldn't be found.

"Who could have done this . . . why?" asked Menee as she fought back tears to be brave for her brother.

Suddenly, they heard voices only a few steps away from them. Outside, they saw a red scarf blowing in the wind. They ran to see who it was.

"Mama, it's her, I know it," said Amari.

"Wait for me, Amari," shouted Menee.

As she caught up to him, they ran into the last person Menee ever wanted to see, Mala-Dek.

"Menee, isn't this your brother?" asked Mala-Dek.

"Yes, it is," she replied.

With a sinister smile, Mala-Dek asked, "Well, what's wrong, little one? Are you looking for your mother?"

"Yes, I am. We can't find her, but you have her scarf," said Amari.

"Your mother is a wonderful person; she gave it to me. I know where she is. I can take you there now if you follow me. My friends and I can keep you safe along the way," said Mala-Dek as several rioters emerged by her side, carrying bags of things they had looted.

"You know where she is? Take us to her, please," said Amari. "Of course I will, right now," said Mala-Dek.

But Menee knew better than to trust Mala-Dek, who thought of humans as fools. "How do you know our mother? What does she look like?" asked Menee.

"She looked human to me; you all look alike to me. But I remember her saying your names and how much she needed to find you," Mala-Dek answered.

That made Amari even more eager to go with Mala-Dek, and he stepped to her side.

"No, Amari, stay with me," said Menee.

Mala-Dek quickly grabbed the boy by his arm. "Don't you trust me, Menee? I've always been good to you," said Mala-Dek as her grip got tighter.

Amari started squirming, trying to break free, but that only irritated Mala-Dek. She kicked him in the leg.

"Stop that!" shouted Menee with a sense of panic.

"Or what? You'll fight me? Your brother would be dead before you threw your first punch," replied Mala-Dek. "But you know what I just realized? How did all those children manage to escape from my den chamber that night I was attacked? Do you have something you want to tell me, Menee?" asked Mala-Dek.

Amari realized he had played the helpless child long enough and winked at Menee as he bit Mala-Dek's hand. The bite drew blood, but Mala-Dek didn't scream or let go; she just got really angry and raised her hand to hit him. Before her hand could even get in reach of his face, he kicked Mala-Dek in the shin. It happened so fast that it was a blur. His power had begun to surge. "Aghh, what did you do to me?" screamed Mala-Dek.

"Get him now," she told the looters. But all Mala-Dek heard were screams as their hands and feet were tangled up in vines. "What's happening? Help us!" said the looters, but they were all dragged away into the forest, and their screams dwindled into whispers.

Amari and Menee started to run. They had smiles on their faces, as Amari had the scarf in his hand. "I wanted to get close enough to get it," he explained.

"Look out!" said Menee as she pushed Amari out of the way. An explosive canister, known as a scorcher, was thrown at them; it exploded when it touched the ground.

"Get them; they are sorcerers!" shouted other looters and rioters who had seen what they did.

"Keep running and don't look back," said the same unfamiliar voice that was a whisper echoing in the wind. Amari and his sister did exactly that.

Another scorcher was then thrown, but it dissolved into gas. Faizah had stepped out of nowhere to confront the looters. Two of them ran off immediately, but another two stayed. "One more witch that has to die," they said. They pulled out clubs to attack her, but on contact with her body, the clubs broke in half without fazing her in the slightest. The looters became terrified; they couldn't even run. "Please, don't kill us. Have this bag; it has valuable things," they pleaded.

Faizah remained quiet as she touched their foreheads. Both looters fell to the ground, immediately put to sleep.

The last thing Amari and Menee heard was, "Keep running. You know where to go," said the voice that sounded like a whisper echoing in the wind.

A NEW CALLING

At the Great Hall where the Secret Society of the Immortals come together, a ceremony was taking place that was of great meaning to Kumi. He was going to be baptized in the waters of the Firmament that was held in place by the prophesied GodKing and GodQueen, the ones who would one day come down from the 3rd Level of Heaven to reign over the land. By being baptized in these waters, Kumi would become a descendant of their greatness and a full member of the Immortals.

As Kumi stood in the ceremonial clothing of blue and white waiting for the final preparations to be made, he didn't feel nervous—he felt ready. He now felt that he had a calling and everything that had happened to him was meant to happen so that he could answer. He looked around feeling a great confidence in himself. In life a person's caste meant everything, even among the Immortals. In their world, there were five different levels, which allowed those in power to watch him from above as the ceremony went on. They would watch as he entered the Firmament to be baptized, but even though they were above him now, he felt that he was much greater than they would ever be and he would do greater things. His confidence was becoming arrogance, which he knew and liked.

"Kumi, it is time," said someone. Then the sound of a single trumpet began echoing in the hall, and the people were silent. He entered the main floor from a hidden passageway and stood between two lines of musicians. They were lined from one end of the Great Hall to the point where he would be baptized. The ceremony would start whenever he took the first step, accompanied by two females to escort him.

As Kumi made those initial steps feeling like a prince and the music began to play, with petals falling from above, he wanted to take in the moment so it could last forever. The Great Hall was a whole new place

to him, as the only source of light emanated from the ancient markings; it made the focus on the Gods and Firmament more apparent. One of the women walking with him was the tavern girl whose name he still didn't know, so he gave her a name, G'neva. They looked at each other for a moment and smiled. He was happy that she was here with him, especially since she helped save his life.

They now stood right before the waters of the Firmament, where the council leaders only known as the Eternals stood waiting to conclude the ceremony. Kumi went down on one knee and bowed his head in respect to the leaders, and then a man's voice began to speak.

"Kumi, you have been chosen to be a part of a great line, descendant of the GodKing and Queen. When you enter the waters of the Firmament, the first level of heaven, you will no longer be a mere mortal whose destiny is to go back to the dust from which you came, but you will be something more, something everlasting. You will be Immortalized."

Kumi got up and stepped within the golden ring of the Firmament, walking slowly into its waters. Two other men came in shortly after he did and submerged his body into the waters.

"The waters will wash away your mortal self, cleansing you of its impurities," said the same voice.

As Kumi's head went under the water, he thought of the night that came two days after Nassor pulled the Akin-Eno from its resting place, the night he was supposed to be killed.

That night he had received a message from the Immortals to meet with them. He journeyed there not knowing he was being followed. He didn't think to look over his shoulder at all, because at that time the riots were still taking place. As long as he kept to himself, no one would notice him—or so he thought. When he reached the location, no one was there, but that was how it always was every time he had to meet with them. Some time passed before he heard someone approaching. He could see four vague figures, and one of them was hunched over. "It's about time you got here; I've been waiting," said Kumi.

But the four figures weren't the people he was expecting. It was Hasani, accompanied by people he never saw before, two serwans and a guedado standing behind Hasani like a pet. "Were you expecting someone else? Of course you were; you were waiting for your informant," said Hasani.

Kumi was shocked to see them, but he kept his cool; he didn't want to give them any more reason of suspicion. "Yes, I was. I was going to get more information about the raids that I have been putting a stop to, to help keep Kiskeya safe," said Kumi.

"True, you have been of some help to me, but the safety and leadership of Kiskeya depend on nobility such as mine, not you. But we all have our place. Your people have a talent in keeping everything nice and clean. Maybe if we ever have children, I can let yours clean my house for practice," said Hasani.

"It's no accident that you are here. How did you know where I would be?" asked Kumi.

"I've been having you followed by my little companion, to keep me up-to-date of your activities," said Hasani as he gave the guedado some money. The guedado took the pay and ran off into the night.

"I admire you, Kumi. You have some of the same qualities and ambitions as your father who doesn't claim you—very sad. Yet you have been moving up the chain of command much faster than anyone had anticipated, and I've come here . . ." said Hasani.

"To dispose of me," said Kumi.

"Exactly. You are smart . . ." said Hasani.

"I'm not surprised; it would have eventually come to this. It scares you that I would have one day taken your authority. That's the reason all my enemies exist today, but none have ever posed a serious threat to me. This vendetta you have with me is no different," said Kumi.

"I fear *no man*. I don't care what that obelisk says. You are all dogs, and we are your masters. You are forever subservient to our will," said Hasani.

"Then nothing else needs to be said; do what you came here for," said Kumi.

It infuriated Hasani to see Kumi look him straight in the eye with so much defiance and lack of fear. He told the two serwans with him to grab Kumi, who didn't resist.

"There is no need to rush. You are on my time, living in my world. You die when I say you die. If anyone asks, I will tell them some story that you were working with your brother, the fugitive, to infiltrate the Hunters for the Maroons. It may make us seem incompetent, but either way, it's worth it to get rid of you, and I have those who will confirm it," said Hasani.

"You won't get away with this, and my father will never believe that," said Kumi as the two serwans still held him.

"Your father? Who do you think told us to watch you? He was even the one who planned this after the Akin-Eno was stolen by your brother. You were guilty in his eyes long before my 'vendetta' against you," said Hasani. Then he laughed as he told his henchmen to take Kumi to the woods, that it should be a quick death.

Hasani turned his back as the two serwans took Kumi away. Kumi wanted to wait until the right time to make his move, but then two more serwans were waiting for him. One put a dagger to his throat. "Hasani is paying us a lot of money to get rid of you," said one of them. Suddenly a noise was heard in the distance that got all of their attention, and then the one holding the dagger fell to the ground.

Kumi grabbed the other one and threw him into a tree, the force killing him on impact. The other two pulled out weapons to attack together, but when they got close enough, Kumi picked up a dead log over his head with ease and crushed them with it. It seemed that he had already gotten used to his power. Kumi immediately went after Hasani, only to find that G'neva was there with a knife at his throat; he was on his knees.

"You are full of surprises, aren't you?" said Kumi to G'neva.

"More than you know. Now, what should we do with him?" asked G'neva.

"I told you, Hasani, that no enemy has ever posed a threat to me and you are no exception, so I will let you go. In death, you would not see the downfall of your nobility and the rise of mine. I am granting you life and the chance to witness the birth of a new age that I will usher in. An age that you can tell your children to write about after you have cleaned my home," said Kumi.

With that, he turned his back on Hasani and walked away with G'neva.

"Are you sure we should let him go like this? He may know too much already," said G'neva.

"It makes no difference; he doesn't have the power to stop us now," said Kumi.

Hasani watched Kumi walking away, knowing that he had been disgraced, his dignity lost. He had watched as Kumi, a deviant human, stood before him in a position of control, where he had been conquered.

"*No*, it will not end like this!" shouted Hasani as he jumped into the air, pulled out the orum blade, and expanded his wings so that he could finish what he had started. At the time, Kumi heard a voice whispering to him that distracted him, and G'neva pushed him out the way. After she saved Kumi, G'neva managed to stab Hasani in the leg, but his rage didn't allow the pain to slow him down as he pulled the dagger out of his leg and hit her on the side of the head. He was about to kill her, but that night Kumi made sure no harm would come to her as he picked up a boulder without strain and threw it at Hasani. As the boulder came at Hasani, he used the power of the orum blade to protect himself. The boulder broke into several pieces before it could do any damage. The two of them fought, but there could only be one victor. Even with all his rage, Hasani knew that he was defeated. He slashed and stabbed Kumi multiple times with a weapon that could shatter stone. But against Kumi's skin it had no effect. Finally

Kumi grabbed Hasani by his neck. Hasani tried to say something but was already dead. Kumi had snapped his neck without even realizing it.

"Are you all right?" asked Kumi as he came over to G'neva.

"I'm fine, but we have to get out of here now," said G'neva, whose head was bleeding. She was starting to lose focus, so Kumi carried her. After that night, Kumi always called her G'neva, a name that had special meaning only to him. It was appropriate, because she was always watching over him since the beginning of it all.

That night G'neva took Kumi to the Eternals and told them of the plot that was conspired against him, but they promised to take care of the whole thing, saying that it was of no consequence. They would allow nothing to hinder their goals, and that much Kumi believed; their help was out of fear, not loyalty. If he had been arrested, it would eventually lead back to his involvement with them, and they weren't the type to have loose ends. He left G'neva in their hands that night, still feeling like an outsider.

"Come to me; you are needed . . ." was the voice Kumi heard underwater. The voice sounded like a whisper echoing in the wind. He emerged from the waters of the Firmament and was now an Immortal. He took a deep breath and looked around at all the smiling faces; music was being played in celebration. He wondered about that voice. It was there the night he was meant to be killed, but he thought it was G'neva. But on this night of his baptism, the voice reached out to him like a new calling. He felt drawn to it and knew it had to do with his gift, his power.

As he stood thinking about the voice, other Immortals came up to him to say congratulations. But even on this day commemorating his greatest achievement, it wouldn't be for him alone. At this point, all members of the secret society knew about what Nassor did, even if they didn't know who he was. By the end, Nassor had become the most important thing and Kumi was forgotten.

"Oooo, I wonder who he is?"

"Me too. Once we find out, we could make him join us."

"He has to be at least part human; otherwise, none of this would have happened."

"Nobody knows who he is so far. But what if he's someone we know?"

"Amazing, just amazing. I feel like crying."

Kumi could hear the constant nonsense all around him. Women who were supposed to be dignified above all others were giggling and talking like they were in love with his brother. Even the most distinguished among them, like the eternals, couldn't seem to hide their excitement over what had happened. One random person went up to Kumi and said, "How does it feel to be among free men, to be a citizen?"

Kumi replied, "I'm feeling something that no man in this room would understand."

The person laughed and said, "Don't be so sure, friend. Everyone here is feeling the excitement. He is now a hero among us all. No greater achievement could surpass what he . . ."

As he continued to talk, Kumi just walked away, only to come across a conversation among the eternals.

"We must find out who he is, get him to join us," one said.

"Why? He already has done more than enough in our favor," said another.

"True, but if what they say about the Akin-Eno is fact, then we will need access to that kind of power at our disposal," said another, and they all agreed.

"He may be the one who ushers in the arrival of the prophesied Gods; he may even be the GodKing," said one.

"Don't be absurd. Our scriptures speak nothing of the Akin-Eno, and as for its power, we will have to wait and see before we make our move," said another eternal.

They had become obsessed over the subject. Suddenly the mysterious voice reached out to Kumi again, this time even more compelling. Kumi knew that it all began with Nassor, and this voice might be calling him as well. Whatever this voice was, he wouldn't let Nassor get to it before him.

"Kumi, are you all right? You seem distracted," said G'neva.

"Yes, I'm fine. I just want this night to be over," he said.

"Why would you want that? This has all been done to honor you," she said.

"It seems as though people are here for reasons that have nothing to do with honoring me," said Kumi.

"Well, I can't speak for them, but I know I'm here for you," said G'neva.

Kumi couldn't help but smile. What she said made everything better for the moment.

"Come with me. I want to introduce you to someone," said G'neva. So she led Kumi across the room, still running into many important people along the way that had already forgotten about him. "Kumi, this is Kaliber, the man I will marry one day," said G'neva.

Kumi felt a little betrayed, even though he had no reason to be. G'neva never gave him a reason to think she was interested and unspoken for. He realized whatever small feelings of attraction that existed between them were just in his head, but still he was disappointed.

Kaliber was a very boastful man. Even in the way he shook Kumi's hand, there was an arrogance. He talked about the different bloodlines that coursed through his veins from Noble serwan families and how he was only one-eighth human. He was also a man not afraid to consume an extra meal or two. Kumi couldn't understand what G'neva saw in him. Kumi tried to keep the conversation short, but this man had a way of not letting someone go. Finally Kumi couldn't deal with him any longer and wandered toward other guests.

As the rest of the night dragged on, Kumi waited for the right moment to slip away. There was a feeling inside him that something important was going to happen and that he would be needed. As he left, a hand grabbed him from behind—it was G'neva.

"You're just going to leave without saying good-bye to me? Don't I deserve at least that from you?" she said.

"Of course, but you seemed to be enjoying yourself with Kaliber. I didn't want to bother you," replied Kumi.

"Oh please. He's an idiot. I'm only marrying him for money. I came here for you, and now you want to leave," said G'neva.

"Does that bother you? Can't see why when I don't even know your name," said Kumi.

"Let's just say that I've been watching you a long time on their behalf, so I do have a personal interest in you. But where is it that you have to be?" she asked.

"There's something I have to do, and it starts tonight, something important," said Kumi.

"Must be, if you're leaving all of this. You know, I haven't told anyone what happened that night when that Noble tried to kill you. You threw that rock like it was a shoe. How does a mortal man gain such power?" asked G'neva. "I hope nothing terrible happens to you," said G'neva with sincerity.

"There's only one way to be sure—come with me," said Kumi, not realizing what he asked of her.

"I wish I could and I would, but too much of my life is here, too much to lose," said G'neva.

"I can understand that—working so hard for something and being within reach of claiming it for yourself. Who would give up something like that? But what if there was something better than this, something more, for people like you and me?" said Kumi.

Kumi didn't know why he was suddenly fighting so hard for this girl whom he didn't know anything about, but there was a feeling that if he left tonight, he might never get the chance to know her. Their lives were headed in such different directions.

"What is it that you're asking me, because I won't change my life for the needs of one man?" said G'neva.

"Then I guess there's nothing left to say except good-bye," said Kumi.

There was a small noise; it sounded like the scratching of squirrels as they fought over food. G'neva turned her head, only to realize it was nothing. She was startled when Kumi put his arms around her. He moved closer in, whispered good-bye softly, and kissed her on the cheek. The kiss was one that lingered long enough that G'neva closed her eyes and smiled just a little. For a moment, she almost put her arms around him, but at the last second she gently pushed him away.

"You know, all those times you got messages from the Immortals to meet, that was really an excuse . . ." started G'neva.

"Those times don't matter . . . but this one does," said Kumi, who wanted what he wanted. To steal one kiss from her, a kiss to remember. "I'm not done with you yet," continued Kumi as he looked in her eyes, which spoke volumes.

As he leaned in for it, G'neva turned her head; she had heard Kaliber's voice nearby. The kiss fell on her cheek again, but neither was too disappointed. She left Kumi to go see if Kaliber was looking for her, but she found him acting like a drunken fool. When she went back outside, Kumi was already gone, without ever knowing her real name.

As he left, Kumi remembered something. That night at the bonfire celebration in the Lower Levels where he met that family, it was the same family that he encountered the night Nassor became a fugitive.

THE 2ND COMING

The night after Kumi departed, a secret town meeting was being held by concerned serwans who could no longer deny the changes taking place in a once-glorious society. Groups of serwans gathered under the cloak of darkness to talk about the coming days and impending war. One thing was for sure: this wouldn't be the last meeting held in secret. On this night, the voices of paranoia would be heard with a quiet thunder as they fed into their worst fears about human rebellion.

"Silence, silence . . . We must devise a proper strategy of dealing with this situation," said Desever to a crowd of serwans.

"Deal with the situation? Humans are citizens, and there is nothing we can do about it. There's no way that it can be dealt with," the people cried.

"We no longer have dominion over them; they are free to do as they like without fear of persecution. Just this morning, I looked onto my field and all of them were gone; those that had stayed looted my crops. I can't live like this; my lifestyle depends on their labor," said one.

As the people spoke among themselves, members of the three families also gathered to think of something that would appease them all. Moments later, Chisulo walked in with a group of Hunters and Ona, which he now led alone since the death of Hasani. Chisulo went up to his father and greeted him, while someone from the crowd stood up and asked how this could have happened.

Confidently, Chisulo told his father that he would take care of things from here.

"Let me start by saying that the body of Kiskeya has been dealt a major blow, and yet we are still here, still standing. We cannot hide away in the face of adversity but only stand firm. Some of you are still in denial, but that will be your end here and now if you cannot accept the changes taking place. We know that this was a Maroon plot, but my conviction to stop our enemies hasn't been deterred. What we do now is . . ." said Chisulo.

"The Hunters have failed; their leader Hasani is dead," shouted a voice from the crowd.

Hearing the name of his brother made Chisulo lose his train of thought. His father got up to see who dared to insult his son Hasani, who hadn't even been buried yet.

"Yes, my brother was killed, by the human who stole the Akin-Eno in a plot to destroy our most sacred and historic monument. But the threat is far from over; it has only just begun, and that is why we must stand strong," said Chisulo.

"The Hunters have been beaten three times by the same man. I heard that the human who destroyed our monument, who stole the Akin-Eno and killed Hasani, is the same human who was made fugitive for attacking your group before. So, you tell me what we should do to keep ourselves safe when you can't," said people from the crowd.

Chisulo didn't know how to respond. How did such information get to the public? No one outside of his own men knew.

But then another voice stepped in where Chisulo couldn't. "War, I say. Let us deal with them the way they have dealt with us; let us bring death and destruction to their door," said Mala-Dek as she emerged from the crowd with a limp.

"The humans have their freedom, so the Maroons have no reason to fight. They have won already," said another.

"At what price our dignity and honor? At the very least, justice must be demanded for the desecration of our monument. If we don't act now, what will be written in our archives will be how they made fools of us. They may be of our caste, but they are not our equals. We are of Noble descent and they are still deviant in nature; the Maroons are still outlaws who have taken lives. I refuse to live in a world where my enemy walks among me without fear of punishment and crimes unanswered," said Mala-Dek.

The people shouted in agreement; they were all in support of Mala-Dek. War seemed to be the only option that would appease their frustration.

"Who are the Maroons to us? Scavengers and vagabonds. They cannot stand against our might; they are a few against many. A city against a nation," continued Mala-Dek.

The excitement among the crowd grew as they cried out for war.

For the first time that night, the voice of the people was heard, and it resonated among them all. It was a call so great that even Adversary rose from his place before the people and they became silent. The most revered person of a Noble people was now going to speak. "Yes, the humans are citizens, but they are subject to the same laws as us, laws that we make. We are a Noble people, and that is what will always separate us from the humans and kenyetta. To maintain control, we must implement the proper conditions. As for the Maroons, they have left us vulnerable; but we are still here, still standing firm. Let this war be the Final Conclusion of the Sentient War. Let it be the second coming, where we reclaim the Akin-Eno and avenge a fallen son."

With that, the people cheered again. From that night, word was spread from house to house: this would be the war not soon forgotten, it would be the second coming.

When the riots started, Khumani was told by her father to stay with him until things started to die down. Khumani moved in with the baby, and it was during her time there that she heard the news about Hasani's murder. At first she could not believe it, but then Chisulo asked her to make the funeral arrangements.

"How did it happen? . . . Who?" Khumani asked.

"Who else but that fugitive? . . . He will now be my top priority. I swear his debt will be paid," answered Chisulo. "The Akin-Eno taken, our monument destroyed, and my brother . . . it will not go unpunished," he continued.

Khumani didn't know how to feel. She wasn't sure if Nassor was capable of killing, but she couldn't rule it out; everything was happening so suddenly. She didn't even have time to mourn over Hasani, but his funeral was scheduled to take place in three days. When she looked at the baby whom she named Nassor, she cried, thinking that the rivalry between Hasani and Nassor may have started with her. If she could see him right now, she would have to know the truth. But in the end, would it matter? At this point, nothing she did could save him.

During the three days of Hasani's funeral arrangements, Chisulo and his father were making their own preparations for the attack on the Maroon camp. Both of them went down to the military base, where they found Falun in full recovery.

"Falun, or should I say Lethalblow . . . it's good to see that you are ready; the timing is just right," said Chisulo's father. Falun's body had been so altered by the experiment that waves of his aura flowed through his body. Every day he was taken outside at dawn so that his body could feed on the sun's power.

"I've been waiting for this. When will I be put to proper use?" asked Falun.

"Now. You are going to bring back the Akin-Eno from the man who crippled your brother. We also have another objective for you. An amanche named Kumi, who was part of my team, has gone missing. We believe that he was working with Nassor, his half brother. You must eliminate both of them," said Chisulo.

Falun clenched his fist, and a bit of his power could be felt by the others. "Don't worry, I will deal them a lethal blow," said Falun. "But what about the others?" he asked, referring to others going through similar experiments.

"They will be deployed at a later date," answered Obsidian.

Falun was then taken to a location far outside the perimeter of serwan territory. Without the need for sleep or food for extended periods, he was able to run all night, using his abilities to track down Nassor.

As the serwans continued to make arrangements for war, the Maroons were also making themselves aware of what was going to come. It was inevitable, and they believed that the outbreak of war was near; signs were everywhere. Every morning since the Akin-Eno had been awakened, all Enos of the camp shimmered in unison, as though truth had found its way home to them, a revelation indeed. Women and children were taken into a deep valley to be kept safe with designated troops. Throughout the days, warriors trained hard, pushing their bodies and testing their limits. Uhuru went over battle strategies devised long ago; he wouldn't leave anything to chance as he discussed things with trusted men, especially if the worst should come to pass. The feeling was undeniable. Tomorrow bore promise for no one; fathers kissed their wives and children good-bye knowing it might be their last. If there was time, some spent it enjoying precious moments that would last forever; some even renewed their vows. But when the time came to finally say good-bye, most cried tears that couldn't be held back. No words could comfort the anguish that would be felt if a loved one didn't return, and families were broken apart having that knowledge with them.

Uhuru sat in his tent and did something he hadn't done in a long time: he closed out the rest of the world for a moment and pretended there was nothing else going on, no war or survival. He pulled out an old letter that was given to him by Bijou, a letter he always kept close to him but never looked at except when it was necessary. Reading it, he always felt vulnerable, which is something he felt a leader should never be; but just in case he was coming to the end of his days, he wanted his last thoughts to be of her. This, he felt, was his one and only love, gone but not forgotten. While reading the letter, he thought of her smile and laughter, even her devotion to helping others. He would never admit it to anyone, but he needed her; thoughts weren't enough anymore, they only seemed to hurt now because they reminded him of a happiness that was lost through duty and obligation. Lots of times he sat in the same place and wondered, if he'd had a second chance, had he fought harder to keep her, what his life would have been like. But when times like these came and he regretted being a Maroon, he would remind himself of the thing he would have had to give up to be with her—his freedom.

It was the morning of Hasani's funeral. His death was the final accumulation of everything that had happened, but today the serwan people would put all their doubts and fears to rest with the loss of their fallen son. His body was taken to the site where the monument had fallen, a place where debris still surrounded the area and the dust had not settled. His body would be entombed in the center among a bed of rocks, and from above rose petals the color of blood were thrown down like rain. One by one stones were placed around his body as the petals covered the ground near him. Countless people walked up to pay their respects dressed in clothing suited for the occasion. Khumani was one of the last to approach his resting place; she blew him one final kiss good-bye. She didn't notice it, but Chisulo's eyes followed her from the very moment she arrived. He watched as people came up to her, complimented her for putting together such a beautiful ceremony, and told her how sorry they were for her. Chisulo felt that she was in part responsible for the death of his brother, but for today, the only thing on his agenda was the funeral—everything else would have to wait. As the people continued paying their respects, Chisulo was signaled to give the eulogy. He walked through the falling petals and stood before his people.

"Today we come together in the face of tragedy and a relentless enemy. My brother was taken at the peak of his life. He was honorable and courageous but most importantly, humbled by the dedication of keeping our nation safe. It is a task that I have taken up in remembrance of him, so let this place that we stand in now be a reminder of what will not be taken from us anymore," said Chisulo.

Then the final stones were placed on his brother. Two of the last stones were earth stones like the ones used for Falun's experiment. When the stones were placed next to each other, they would fuse all the stones and rocks into a crystal-like structure. This happened as rays from the sun anointed his grave. Here Hasani would be Immortalized as the first fallen hero of the second coming, and construction of a new monument could begin. Chisulo then continued his eulogy, subtly directing his attention from his brother to Khumani.

"I want you to know, brother, that everything I do from this day forward will be for you, in your memory, in your name, and in your honor," said Chisulo. Tiny raindrops then fell from the sky; rain clouds were forming. It was time.

FORCE OF NATURE

Far, far away from where Hasani was being buried, Nassor accompanied by the Living Busara had stumbled upon a valley that remained untouched and unseen by people for centuries.

"Where are we?" asked Nassor.

"I don't know, but it feels like the beginning," said the Living Busara.

One by one, each of the ordained arrived from different corners of the valley. Kumi came in from the north, Amari and Menee came from the west, and Faizah came from the east. All of them had left their homes at different times but ended up in the same place without knowing how or why. It was as though they had been taken to another place, a realm separate from what they knew. They didn't even recall traveling that far to get here. There were streams of water flowing throughout the valley, fresh air, and lush, green grass. In the center were ruins that had over time become part of the valley.

All of them descended to the ruins, not knowing what to expect, except maybe truth. As they came closer to the ruins, their gifts were summoned forth, each one holding their Kyah crystal or Eno in their hands. The ruins started to glow like moonlight. Sparks of light fell from above as wind began to blow around them. Things started to illuminate as those same sparks of light began to take shape. The beads of light were completing the ruins as they became walls of light that surrounded them. Amari tried to touch them, but they were like air.

"Does anyone know what's happening?" laughed Nassor.

"No, I don't think any of us do," answered Faizah.

None of them felt frightened; there was no reason to be. They were all full of anticipation, especially Kumi; he was more eager than anyone to meet the force that had gone through so much to bring them here. He kept hearing Nassor's voice in his head, saying that he didn't belong here, that people like him were made to be esclaves.

The beads of light had become spheres and continued to take shape as a few of them came to the center and danced around in a circle. The spheres of light collided, and what emerged were three beings, Gina Ifosia and her two sons. The spheres continued to move around her until she became her true form, a visage like no other. She was part living and part spirit, but the two boys remained unchanged and almost unaware of what was going on around them. She was no longer the old woman that they knew, but something more; and when her transformation ended, the six of them stood in awe waiting for her to speak.

"Welcome, chosen ones, I am the Guardian of the Tomb of Creation, and what you see are memories of its greatness being restored. In the last age before the end of the Sentient War, the tomb of creation was hidden in the bodies of three mortal beings, a mother and her two sons, giving them eternal life. I, as the Guardian of the Tomb, was kept inside for over two thousand years as its keeper, until the day the Akin-Eno was pulled and creation unleashed once more into the world. All of you were chosen because of your compassion and kindness shown to this woman and her children; no one other than the five of you ever tried to help them," said the Guardian.

As the Guardian spoke of their willingness to help others, Nassor couldn't help but stare at Kumi. He laughed at the idea of Kumi having compassion to help anyone but himself.

"Why are you looking at me?" shouted Kumi, but Nassor paid him no mind so he shouted it again. "Don't you hear me, deviant? I said why did you look at me?" He grabbed Nassor and shoved him back. Nassor reacted quickly and pushed him too.

"Stop! Look at what you're doing!" said Menee. Their fighting had echoed among the two boys standing behind the Guardian; their movements mirrored Nassor's and Kumi's exactly. The rivalry between them also traveled into the walls and ancient structures being formed by the spheres of light like shock waves. It caught Nassor's and Kumi's attention enough so that they stopped arguing. When they did, everything was set back in place, and the two boys stopped fighting as well.

Looking over at Nassor, the Guardian continued to speak, "You have been given a gift; the Akin-Eno is a wondrous and ancient power. Even I have no understanding of its limits, but I am still bound to it. All of you have been given a different gift, but all with the same purpose: to free the human race, reclaim what is rightfully ours, and defeat the abominations that have taken refuge in our world," said the Guardian.

"But is war necessary? The human race has already been freed . . ." said Nassor, because war meant some people he cared about would have to be his enemy.

"The abominations are not of this world. They have become a plague, and as long as they are here, mankind will never know freedom. For now, you must leave with your gifts as I rebuild the Tomb of Creation. When it is complete, I will call all of you to return, for it is here that the abominations can be defeated. Follow this stream, and it will lead you to the Maroon camp; they will need you for the war," said the Guardian.

The six of them did as the Guardian said and followed the stream, but as they traveled back into the world, they heard the Guardian say one more thing. "Remember, for your people to be free, a sacrifice must be made." Again Nassor heard those words but this time from someone else, and each time he told it to himself, it felt like an ominous warning, a promise of hardships to come.

The six continued to walk until they reached a place where they had no recollection of how they had gotten there. When they looked back, the stream that had led them there was gone. But in the distance they could see campfires, which meant they were near the Maroon camp.

"I am not traveling down to that wasteland to help a group of fugitives and outlaws, but you would fit right in with those deviants, Nassor," said Kumi.

"Good; don't come. No one wants you here anyway. Just go back to the serwans and Hunters; maybe they'll give you what you deserve," answered Nassor.

"The smartest thing these rebels can do is surrender. I don't care what that spirit said, we can't get rid of an entire people," said Kumi.

"I don't plan . . ." started Nassor, who suddenly jumped, colliding head-on with his brother to save his life. All around trees were falling; and if Nassor hadn't reacted, Kumi might have been crushed. "Everyone, look out!" ordered Nassor as more trees started to fall where the rest of them were. Nassor went for them as fast as he could, but there wasn't enough time for him to get there as the trees fell on top of his friends. So fearful that they could be hurt or worse, Nassor dug for them, using the Akin-Eno to cut through massive amounts of wood as Kumi was left alone to face their attacker.

"Come out and show yourself. I want to show you what happens to those who attack me from behind," said Kumi. Then from the darkness he came, Lethalblow. He emerged from the trees at the peak of his powers, his body shimmering like gold.

"Where is the Akin-Eno?" he asked. Each arm was covered by a sanscoeur, and one was on his chest like Nassor; his eyes were focused and he was ready to do battle.

Kumi looked at him and laughed, "If you are looking for the Akin-Eno, it's right over there; but you'll have to get past me to get to it, and I must warn you, you've made me angry." After taunting his enemy, Kumi picked up a giant log as he had before with ease. Falun's eyes widened from Kumi's display of strength as the log was thrown right at him.

Channeling his energy, Falun destroyed the log on impact with his bare hands. Momentarily stunned, however, Falun looked around to see where Kumi escaped to, only to find that he was right behind him and grabbed Falun by his neck.

"I don't care who you are, but this is the last time you ever attack anyone whose back is turned," said Kumi. Kumi had learned to control some of his gift, and instead of taking the opportunity to finish Lethalblow, he instead chose to boast about his victory. As tight as his grip was, Falun just smiled.

Over where the trees had fallen, Nassor finally got to the others and could hear their voices. "Is everyone okay?" he asked.

"Yes, but Faizah is unconscious. She protected us as the trees fell," said Menee.

One by one, Nassor helped them to get out.

"Who has attacked us?" asked the Living Busara.

"I don't know, but the rest of you must go. Get to the camp; I'll deal with things here," said Nassor. He then carried Faizah in his arms, hoping she was not hurt, and laid her on the ground. Menee used her ability to summon sticks and other plant life that could be used to carry Faizah. They tied the vines around Amari, and he ran her to safety. The Living Busara followed right behind, but Menee waited. She said, "We can't just leave you; the Guardian said we must do this together."

"Don't worry about us; the Busara needs to get to that camp. Besides, how tough can it be?" said Nassor as he ran to help Kumi.

When Nassor arrived on the scene, Kumi and Falun were in the thralls of deadly combat, neither willing to submit. Falun released a burst of energy from his body, enough to send Kumi right to where Nassor was standing.

"I leave you for a few moments, and this is the trouble you get yourself into," said Nassor.

"He's much tougher than he looks. The only good thing is that he's here to kill you," said Kumi after dusting himself off.

"Many have tried; all have failed," said Nassor.

But as Kumi prepared himself for the next attack, Falun came in closer. "You must be Nassor, bearer of the Akin-Eno," he said.

"Yes, I am," answered Nassor, and in that instant, he summoned the power of the Eno. Parts of his body were engulfed in fire that turned to armor. Kumi watched as his brother became something he couldn't deny, a savior.

"Then you are the one who took my brother's life! And you will pay with yours!" shouted Falun, who in his rage unleashed an untamed level of energy from his body sent in the direction of Nassor and Kumi. Both of them tried to brace themselves, but only Kumi was affected as he was pushed even further away by the force of the impact. Nassor remained unaffected; the sanscoeur he had neutralized the attack from Falun.

"You took something from me, you and all other humans like you!" shouted Falun.

For Nassor, no more words needed to be said. He leaped into the air holding the Akin-Eno above his head to strike his enemy down. The power of the Akin-Eno was still new to him. Nassor fought out of instinct instead of control, his fighting style brutal and savage. As he leapt into the air, his body became so bright it put the sun to shame, blinding his enemy. He came down with enough force to kill a man ten times over, but for some reason, Nassor's best attacks were dulled when they came to direct impact with Falun's body. At best, they only seemed to faze each other, but neither could land the finishing blow that would end their struggle. Both of them pushed themselves to the very limits they could; blows that should have snapped bones in two or caused

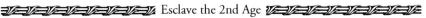

instant death were shrugged off by both of them. More of Nassor's body began to be covered by the armor; his will burned for victory, and the power of the Akin-Eno reflected that. Nassor struck Falun twice in the jaw, and he fell back; in that moment, blood was first drawn.

Falun realized that direct attacks were futile, so he resorted to using his surroundings again to punish his nemesis. Falun caused a tree to fall right above Nassor, but luckily he was aware of Falun's tricks and jumped out of the way, slicing the tree in half.

Each time Nassor used the Akin-Eno, the things it cut through became dust. Falun thought he could use that moment to get away and create some distance, but Nassor was too close to let him escape. Nassor was there right above him in the air. It seemed that as the battle drew to a close, Nassor only got stronger while Falun's power dwindled. Another tree started to fall, and this time headed toward Falun. Nassor had used Falun's own tricks against him. There wasn't time to move out the way, so Falun had no choice but to destroy the tree into countless pieces. That last move further dwindled his strength. When he looked at the aftermath, all the wreckage and destruction he and Nassor had caused, it seemed to mean nothing, as the bearer of the Akin-Eno stood shining above him. His body slowly burned with fire, almost Godlike in appearance. Falun was convinced that this wasn't the same person he began the fight with; it was a completely different person. Nassor came toward him, descending on his enemy, holding the Akin-Eno in his hand ready to kill. He grabbed Falun by the throat. Falun tried to fight back, but it was in vain. Nassor's power was overwhelming.

Falun struggled to push him away, but in the process he touched the sanscoeur on Nassor's chest. Suddenly, memories of Nassor's past flooded into Falun's mind. Knowing that he was going to take a life, Nassor thought while fighting Falun of the only person he had ever killed. That was the first memory Falun felt come into him. Then he saw recent memories of Nassor's time being imprisoned, moments with Khumani, hiding out with Faizah and the Busara, even the day he attacked the Hunters, and lastly the events that transpired when Nassor pulled the Akin-Eno.

Falun wondered if his fate would be the same as that serwan Nassor killed before he had a chance to avenge his brother's death. But somehow luck was on his side, because as Nassor's memories flooded Falun's mind, the reverse was also taking place. Nassor witnessed past events of Falun's life; he saw his origins. Seeing the experiments that created him and the reason he fought, Nassor saw a person who always felt second best in life, who felt that he had failed at everything until Falun found first love. But tragically that was taken away as well. It was the memories of a person who had been beaten, broken, and scarred in so many ways by life. And then Nassor saw the image of Falun's brother hanging from a rope, and he realized why Falun sought vengeance.

The effects of the memory transfer stunned both of them, but Nassor was affected much more because this was his first experience. He became so disoriented that Falun leaped forward and attacked using any strength he had left. He would have been able to finish the job if Kumi hadn't stepped in. Kumi grabbed Falun and punched him in the chest hard enough to shatter rocks. If Falun were a normal man, Kumi's hand might have gone straight through, but Falun survived the hit, his sanscoeur again saving him. Its aura protected Falun from serious injury, but that didn't help him from being knocked past a few trees in the process. Nassor was still trying to get himself together when Kumi went after Falun, but again more memories began to flood into Falun's head.

In that brief moment when Kumi touched his sanscoeur, Falun saw a memory of Kumi with his wife and realized he was the one who got her pregnant, ruining their lives. His rage rekindled, he again swore vengeance at his enemies. "You! The both of you! I will make you pay. I swear it!" shouted Falun, and with a cascade of force, he threw three giant stones at Kumi. As those forces of nature came toward him, Kumi didn't even flinch; he swatted them down like flies with one hand. He looked around to see what else Falun would throw at him next, but Falun was gone. At this point, Falun had been fighting on will alone; even his body had limits, as was shown today. But both Nassor and Kumi knew that he would return.

Kumi looked back at Nassor, who seemed to be all right given the circumstances. "He's gone. I was too much for him, and he ran like a coward," said Kumi. But as he boasted, Nassor touched the back of his neck in silence. His eyes widened, he collapsed to the ground, and the Akin-Eno vanished. *What just happened?* wondered Kumi, but then he saw a dart protruding from Nassor's neck. Kumi braced himself for what was to come next, but it was too late. A dart hit him, but its effects didn't come as fast as with Nassor.

"Show yourself," said Kumi with a loose tongue, but he was answered only with two more darts to the neck. He collapsed just as Nassor did.

FAITH IN A LEADER

When the two of them woke up, still feeling some effect from the drug, they were surrounded by both familiar and unfamiliar faces.

"Are you all right, friend?" asked a voice to Nassor. "You are in my tent, in the Maroon camp. Sorry for our mistreatment of you, but somehow people keep finding their way here so we have taken extra precautions," and then the voice became a laugh that directed itself to another figure across the room.

When Nassor's vision got a little clearer, he thought it was Falun standing there for a second chance at killing him. Nassor jumped to his feet to defend himself, as did Kumi. Both men summoned forth their gifts, and when they did, everyone stepped back in amazement.

"Hold on; no one is here to fight you. You have my word as leader of the Maroons," said Uhuru.

"Who is that freak?" asked Kumi.

"That is Deathblow, which is a story for another day, but he is an ally," explained Uhuru.

"Yes, it's okay, Nassor. We are right where we're supposed to be," said Faizah.

"Then where are the others—Amari, Menee, and the Busara?" asked Nassor.

"They are out exploring the camp, but safe nonetheless," she answered.

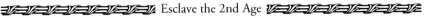

Hearing Faizah's voice reassured Nassor that the people he was with could be trusted, but Kumi still held his doubts. "What about him? Whatever that thing was that attacked us before your soldiers ambushed us from the shadows looked just like him," said Kumi.

Uhuru again explained how Deathblow was now on their side after a failed assassination attempt and that he now wanted to help mankind. But Kumi still made it clear that Deathblow better keep his distance, as well as the rest of them.

"If you are leader of the Maroons, then you should know that we are here to help you win this war," said Nassor, whose determination was sensed by the Akin-Eno. It shimmered, and again its power resonated with all other Enos near it. Uhuru watched as his own Eno shimmered.

"The Akin-Eno . . . somewhere it was written and decided that you would be its bearer," said Uhuru. Uhuru looked at the Akin-Eno as though it were the Holy Grail, and he felt shamed just to be standing in the presence of the Creator's pure gift. Kumi stood to the side and scoffed. Again people were fawning over his brother. Would his torment ever end?

Two days had passed since their arrival. Messages were coming from distant Maroon outposts that the serwans were lining up their forces, but the ordained spent those two days immersing themselves in the Maroon culture and battle plans. To them, it was like being in a whole new world where it was okay to be yourself. Throughout their time, they learned to hone their abilities even further. For some it came easier. Amari was able to show off by using his speed to entertain people. Faizah learned that her mystic powers had more than one use, but were very exhausting as compared to the others. Menee had the most difficulty, because she feared that a power over the earth would be dangerous if she couldn't control it; she simply had too much doubt in her heart. Kumi spent his time sparring with the best of the Maroon warriors. He bested most but learned that his strength alone wasn't enough to face warriors like these. Things like speed, stamina, and experience factored in as well. It was a lesson he would never forget as he sparred with the four elite. Their coordinated moves made Kumi's strength almost useless; while one distracted, two others attacked, and he could never get his hands on one of them completely. Their movements were like blurs coming from all sides, but no matter what, he kept fighting, never letting exhaustion win.

Nassor watched him from a distance. This was the first time in awhile that they had been so near each other, but Nassor spent his time with Uhuru, who started to become more of a mentor to him. As Uhuru taught a history about the human race that Nassor knew nothing of except what was told by the serwans, he learned things about the Maroon culture and its origins being tied to the Akin-Eno. Some things he had been aware of, but hearing them from Uhuru gave it new meaning. Uhuru again told Nassor that the Akin-Eno was a gift, which could be received by anyone but only used by a few. At first Nassor didn't understand, until Uhuru made it clear that the Akin-Eno can be wielded by anyone but its power works differently in each hand that possesses it.

In righteous hands the Akin-Eno can change the world for the better, but in unrighteous hands it can be destructive to the person who bears it.

3rd World Order

Later on that night, a few people began to sing and dance, playing music that lifted them to a higher place. A bonfire was started to relax the mood. Some ran around, while others watched the fire burn. Menee stared at the fire, almost lost within the flames. When Nassor spooked her from behind, she screamed and then laughed at his joke.

"Why don't you come join us, Menee? You always seem to be by yourself, but you can be open with us," said Nassor.

She smiled and then followed Nassor to where Faizah and Amari were playing a game.

"Is there room for two more?" asked Nassor.

"For her, but not for you," laughed Faizah.

"Ha-ha, very funny. I didn't know a priestess could make jokes without praying first," replied Nassor, who was the only one who laughed. Everyone else looked confused.

"Leave it to Nassor to ruin a perfectly good moment," said Faizah, and that's when everyone laughed.

"You were funnier before they put you in prison. What did they do to you?" continued Faizah as everyone kept laughing at his expense.

"Okay, enough about me. I'm not the one who cheated in a game with a little boy," said Nassor.

"Hey, I'm not a little boy," said Amari.

"Hold on, Amari, I'm talking . . . I am the man who freed all of mankind from a terrible foe," said Nassor. But they all continued to laugh and talk to the sound of music despite Nassor's foolishness.

Faizah asked if she could braid Menee's hair and she agreed. While they were together, Faizah asked her a question. "Aren't you hot with those long sleeves?"

"I don't mind; I like to keep myself covered," said Menee.

"But why?" asked Faizah.

"When I was younger, I was in a fire. Some of my family died, and my body was scarred by the flames. Ever since, I've covered my body so that others wouldn't see how hideous I am," answered Menee.

"That's so sad, but you should know that those scars will be there whether you're happy or sad. Wouldn't it be better if you were happy instead?" stated Faizah.

Menee didn't respond because she just didn't know how to answer. Faizah continued doing her hair.

To the side, Nassor was teaching Amari how to fight like a man. "You will make a pretty tough warrior one day," said Nassor.

"Maybe I'll do that with the Akin-Eno too," said Amari as they both laughed.

Kumi watched them from a distance and walked away. He felt it wasn't important for him to make friends with anyone here, but he did take note of how Faizah seemed real comfortable with Nassor. Maybe they were together, he thought. Menee and Faizah continued getting to know each other even after Faizah finished braiding her hair.

"I never would have known that you were really against the serwans. I mean, you were always so into teaching people to be loyal to the regime," said Menee.

"I'm not . . . . I just lead a secret life where truth reigns supreme. The serwans hate religion because it is something else to believe in, and the Chideria Order is another way of thinking and looking at life. That is something that I will never regret. My whole life I felt unwanted, like an outcast, but in the order, there was no one who would always accept me more than the creator, the Origin. He loved me enough so that I could love myself, and from that day I knew that was all I needed. He had a purpose for me, like he has for all of us now. A purpose that in the end will not make us feel shamed or worthless. When I gave my life to him, I could let go all my insecurities," said Faizah.

"Wow, that sounds beautiful. I hardly ever heard of your faith, but was always curious. We could be punished for talking about it. My mother would beat us if we did; she said that kind of talk could put me in jail. But hearing you talk about it now . . . How can I learn more?" asked Menee.

"Easy. I can teach you all that I know, but words can only do so much; you have to believe and have faith," answered Faizah.

Just then Nassor walked over, and Menee asked him, "Where's Amari?"

"He got tired from today's adventures; he's asleep in that tent over there," replied Nassor.

"It's good that he has you to look up to. Thank you," said Menee.

"Him? I'm the one who made him who he is. When we first met, he didn't even believe there was a God," said Faizah.

"Is that so? I think I was reluctant to believe, but I wouldn't say I didn't believe at all. Don't be jealous that I'm influencing Amari's life," said Nassor.

"Well, don't worry, because you can come to me when you want to learn how to do that. The good news is that Menee wants to learn more about the order, and I think it would be great if you told her some of your experiences," said Faizah.

Nassor sat down right next to Menee and took her by the hand. "If you are serious about this, it will be the best decision you ever make," he said to her.

The three of them stayed up long after the music and festivities ended so that they could continue exchanging stories of how faith changed their lives and their fears of the days to come.

After Faizah and Nassor fell asleep themselves, Menee stayed up thinking about what they had said. She walked around the camp revisiting places she had already seen, and she came across a young Maroon about her age. She noticed him from a distance as he polished his Eno. His shirt was partially opened, and she noticed a few scars on his chest. He then noticed her too and tried to call her over, but she turned away to try and avoid him. The young warrior chased after her. He wasn't trying to scare her, and by now everyone in the camp knew about the latest visitors; he was just curious about how they would help win this war for the Maroons. He caught up to her and convinced her he was harmless. The two of them started to exchange a few words that became a conversation lasting until morning.

The following day, more families were being moved to the valley, and there were hardly any kids left for Amari to play with. It was the middle of the day before Nassor got up.

He went in search of food, only to find that Menee and Faizah had already prepared something. "So, why are you so happy today?" Faizah asked Menee.

Nassor quickly thanked them, and after a small talk went about his business as he let them finish their conversation. As he walked about, he came across Kumi, who was again in combat training with the Maroons. They had shown him some valuable techniques, but this time he used them without the benefit of his gift. All the other Maroons were agreeing that Kumi must have had previous training and that he was quick to learn, but the Maroon fighting style was still new to him. He might have been training with them all morning. When Kumi noticed Nassor, he called out to him.

"Nassor, are you just going to walk away from all the fun, or do you want to see if you have what it takes to face me?" said Kumi.

"I think we got ourselves a challenge, men. Will the bearer of the mightiest of Enos accept?" said one of the Maroons.

All the warriors there shouted in unison for Nassor to accept; they wanted to see both men in action with their gifts, but Kumi had something else in mind. "No, we will fight without the use of our powers," said Kumi. An unexpected move, thought the others, but it brought more intrigue.

Nassor looked Kumi right in the eye; he wasn't the type to turn down a challenge. "Maybe this time I won't have to hold back against you. Maybe you can show me a move that doesn't involve hitting the ground," he said.

"Then what are you waiting for? Come put me down if you can," answered Kumi.

Nassor came over with all the men rooting and chanting for him. Just as their fight was about to begin, an alarm was sounded. All the troops quickly jumped into their respective ranks and designated regiments. Uhuru came and grabbed Nassor from behind.

"Uhuru, what's going on?" asked Nassor.

"It's the serwan army. They are close, much faster than we expected. We have less than a day before they arrive," answered Uhuru.

"What do you want to do?" asked Nassor.

"My men are as prepared as they will ever be. Win or lose, this war will happen. There's no turning back, but this isn't about what I will do. This is about what you will do," said Uhuru.

"What I'll do? I will fight by your side, you and your men. Do what I have been sent to do," said Nassor.

"You misunderstand me, Nassor. I grow weary of this life. I am a man torn between duty and want, and I don't want to be part of that struggle anymore. My time here ends. I can no longer be leader of the Maroons. I realize that now," said Uhuru.

"How can you say that as we go to war? Lives depend on your leadership. If you don't lead them, then . . ." and for a moment, everything paused for Nassor.

"Exactly," said Uhuru. "Nassor, this is a great deal to ask of any man. Especially for you who has only been with us for a short time. You must go into the chasm, and when you return, you will be leader of the Maroons," explained Uhuru.

"But why?" asked Nassor in disbelief.

"You hold the Akin-Eno, which means you hold our future. It is the origin of all great warriors. Whatever you are meant to do, it starts in that chasm, where the hearts and minds of all those warriors make their return. When you go into the chasm, they will reach out to you just as they did with Deathblow, but he only saw flashes of truth. You will receive much more; you will receive and comprehend all that is," said Uhuru.

Nassor didn't know how to feel about this, but he trusted Uhuru. Something inside said that he must do this, so he went inside the chasm, not knowing what to expect.

THE ONE REBELLION THAT WOULD NOT FAIL

After his defeat by Nassor and Kumi, Falun was placed in the chemical tank that birthed him so that he could recuperate from his injuries. During this time, the scientists worked to further enhance his abilities. Chisulo had ordered this as a result of his failure, even if it killed him. While in the tank, it seemed as though Falun was calmly asleep, but the trauma he received from fighting Nassor and Kumi was imprinted in his sanscoeurs. He kept going over those memories again and again without realizing it was a dream.

"He failed just like the first one, Deathblow," said Chisulo.

"Failure is something to be learned from, my son. We can still extract necessary information from his memories. I'm sure we can find the location of the Maroon camp and get there much faster than predicted. We already know that he was also fighting Kumi; Kumi has betrayed us," said Chisulo's father.

"I knew he would and I don't care. He was just a token used to appease those who think humans can keep our land safe. I didn't even know he was missing until you mentioned it," said Chisulo.

With what they learned from Falun, the serwans began mobilizing their armies even faster, deploying all necessary troops. By the time Falun got well enough, most of the room had been dismantled. The only equipment that was left was those needed to tend to him and others like him. When he emerged from the tank, he felt his increase in power and was ready to put it to use, but Chisulo ordered him not to go. Chisulo stated that he still was not ready.

"I was unaware that they would have such great power at their disposal, but I won't make the same mistake again. This time I will crush them," said Falun.

"Oh, I believe you, because next time you face them, you will have the proper reinforcements," said Chisulo, who pointed out three other kenyetta now like him, two males and a female. They would be his team. They had been given the same enhanced abilities, which was how they extracted Falun's memories while he was sedated in the tank.

"Falun, you will be leader of this team and responsible to no one other than me. Your enhancements allow your mind to be linked to theirs; this will coordinate your movements, and it has only one weakness, distance. The farther apart you are, the weaker the link," said Chisulo.

"So then, what are we waiting for? We should be deployed now," said Falun.

"No, not yet. We all underestimated the power of the Akin-Eno. It alone could turn the tide of this war. We need to lure Nassor away at just the right time, and I know exactly how to do that," said Chisulo.

Then one of his Hunters came in. "Commander, our forces will soon be in position, and there is someone here for you, Mala-Dek. She said you would be expecting her."

"Perfect, just perfect. Send her in. I'm ready for her proposal," said Chisulo as he signaled others who would be needed for this meeting.

Uhuru's army was also on the march, moving to a place where battlefield conditions would favor them. "In ancient times, this place was called the Land of Mountains," he told them. Uhuru's eyes remained steady as he led them into their final conflict. These were men who were hungry for a good fight. But for now, they made their final prayers as dark clouds loomed right before the start of the battle.

The light from the sun was completely blocked. The rains would wash away evidence of this war as though it had never happened, but still it must. Not even the sound of their marching could be heard as the ordained walked with Uhuru.

"I have never seen the sky like this," said Menee.

"Yes," said Uhuru. "This storm will be a dark omen for both sides, but if we position ourselves correctly, it may do more damage to the serwans. The places that will be hurt most are the serwan territories. The water will rise, causing flooding that has never been seen before," said Uhuru.

"How do you know this?" asked Menee with an intense look of worry in her eyes.

"The Busara. I was told about it the other night," replied Uhuru.

If what Uhuru said was true, than this would be disastrous, thought Menee. She was much too far away to do anything, but there was one person who could do it, one person who could save them. Menee took her brother by the hand. "I need you to do something, something important. Lives depend on it."

While Menee dealt with her brother, troops from the serwan army were making their arrival. The ground troops came first, armored from head to toe, with weapons at the ready. In the distance they could see giant artillery cannons being pulled by the deadliest creatures in the land, their senses focused for killing. The beasts that the serwans had at their disposal roared with thunder, ready to be released at any moment. Chisulo stood on top of the horizon overlooking the entire battlefield, where the future of a nation would be decided. He stood with three other serwan generals covered in the same silver armor as he. Their armor was strong, yet light, and increased their speed to fly. Engravings written all over the armor signified destiny, power, and greatness. It was an old writing that hadn't been seen since the first war. Two soldiers approached Chisulo with a box, and in it were several earth stones—one for each general, and two for

Chisulo. They were positioned as part of their gauntlets and chest plates. After his generals received their earth stones, Chisulo signaled two of them to go down to the battlefield. As he watched overhead, they jumped from the top of the horizon and expanded their wings, making a slow descent to the front of the serwan army. The other general, the Masked Hunter, was sent back to Kiskeya.

Uhuru saw the entire thing. His enemies had come prepared for war. The Maroons wore no armor at all, only the color of dark red, which marked a fearlessness. Uhuru himself wore white to signify his leadership and to make sure that his enemies would know who he was. He turned and looked at his men, looking each one of them in the eye. They all bowed in respect, waiting for him to speak, holding their Enos before them. A silence came to them all; even Kumi and Faizah did as they had. Kumi in a moment's breath glanced at Faizah without her notice and looked away as Uhuru spoke his final words before the war.

"Some of you believe in fate, some of you believe in destiny, but all my life I have believed in the Free-will of Man. It is tied to us as light is to the sun. Freedom will never be given to us; it must be taken! *So let this day ring forever in your hearts as the one Rebellion that would not Fail!*"

3rd World Order

Drops of rain fell from the sky, and a force flowed through each member of the Maroon army. A single thought filled them, compelled them—that they must not lose. On this day, mortal men would decide their own fate.

"Let this war be so great we break the earth," cried Uhuru. They all shouted behind him in unison; this was the point of no return. Their life's purpose would finally be fulfilled.

Those who had been outcasts of the shadows would now be forged in greatness.

3rd World Order

Uhuru's warriors charged in with Enos at the ready. From a distance, it seemed like a pool of blood engulfed the land.

At Chisulo's orders, the serwans launched scorchers into the air from giant catapults.

Kumi used his incredible strength and threw a stone at one of the catapults as it was just about to throw another scorcher. The stone whistled through the air, and on impact it tore through the catapult, resulting in multiple explosions. Fire spread to some of the surrounding serwan troops, burning them to death as they screamed in agony.

In the midst of the turmoil, the fire seemed to consume everything, but the flames had released the beasts used by the serwan army. Their bodies had absorbed the fires. These beasts had been brutalized by their masters only for the use of war and altered by experimentation. Giant, fierce, and ferocious by nature, they would show no mercy; their eyes burned red and their bodies were scarred white. One was like a python with four arms; its tail was strong enough to squeeze the life out of a man, and its bite was venomous. The next creature was the perfect balance between speed and strength. It was strong enough to crush bone, and its teeth and claws could tear through flesh. It had the appearance of a two-headed jaguar, with bones protruding through its skin, and instinctively knew to first strike at the neck. These creatures were known as the mai'juard. One of the serwan commanders saw them break loose from their chains and merely extended his hand, causing them to submit under his will. Once the other troops backed away, the commander released the beasts to pursue their prey, the Maroons.

Gradually, more of the beasts were released to wear down the Maroons as the scorchers continued to fall from the sky. Faizah did as much as she could by snuffing them out and turning them into red dust, but she could not get to them all. Menee wasn't sure how she could help as Maroons raced by her to engage the enemy.

Kumi placed himself at the front lines as the mai'juard closed in on him. Kumi was quick, but the beasts proved to exceed even his speed and one wrapped its tail around his body. It slammed Kumi left and right onto the ground. Other Maroons came to his aid to vanquish this serpentlike creature. They fought even as scorchers still fell from the air consuming their bodies in flames. All the while, the mai'juard remained unharmed; fire fell off their bodies like water. While Kumi was still in the grip of the mai'juard python, the creature whipped its tail around, using Kumi as a weapon against those warriors who had stabbed and bled it. The creature thought it had gotten most of them, but there was still one Maroon who managed to cut off one of the beast's arms. The creature was in shock with pain, and its grip around Kumi loosened. Kumi grabbed an Eno lost by a Maroon and stabbed the creature in the tail to free himself. The creature fell back, retracted its tail, and used it as a spring to jump into the air. As it came down, the only person who stood in its way was Uhuru. The beast opened its mouth to infect Uhuru with its venom, but Uhuru rolled out of the way and sliced its head off.

Other mai'juard still came and in greater numbers. Another was already upon Kumi before he had a chance to catch his breath. It smacked him down with its tail, much like the other one had, but before it was able to get a good hold, Kumi managed to grab its arm and break it. He finished the job by snapping its neck. Kumi picked up the creature's dead body to return the favor that the first one did for him; he swung it around to keep back any other creature who would meet death by his hand. Finally, he released the creature, throwing its body through the air toward the horizon aimed at Chisulo. A good approach, but Chisulo calmly extended his hand, and a sphere of energy was released that deflected the creature. Chisulo smiled as though disappointed that this was all Kumi could think of.

"Do you think that got his attention?" asked Kumi.

"I think it definitely got his attention," answered Uhuru.

Chisulo then gave a signal. Moments later, countless troops of the serwan army were released into the air, making up the first wave. The battle had just started, and already the Maroons were being overwhelmed. Faizah jumped in between a group of Maroons and three of the two-headed jaguars.

"Don't worry. Stand back and wait for my signal," she said as the group of beasts came for her. They jumped at her, slashing from all sides, but none of their attacks had any effect. They tried biting her, but as they wrapped their mouths around her neck, their jaws would break. Another tried to tear her arm off, but she touched one of the creature's heads and it went limp. Even though they had been wounded, the mai'juard jaguars kept attacking. More scorchers were falling right on top of them. To protect herself and stop the scorchers would put a great strain on Faizah's body, but she had no choice. She couldn't snuff them out as before, but she directed them, as many as possible, to fall right on top of her. An explosion engulfed the area. Fire splashed down on top of them as Maroon warriors dove for cover. Her selflessness protected all those near her. Most were grazed by the flames but still able to fight.

After the explosion, Maroons found Faizah on the ground beneath a mai'juard. The beast snarled at her, deciding how it would kill her. One of the Maroons signaled his brethren to surround the mai'juard. They wouldn't let her life end this way, not after what she had done. Fire still burned around them, slowly dying out as Faizah began to open her eyes with the beast breathing down on her. Moments later, two other mai'juard also appeared; they had survived the blast. Using a chainlike eno, one of the Maroons punctured the lung of the mai'juard that hoped to make Faizah its victim; the other Maroons carried her to safety. When they knew she was out of danger, they all attacked and slaughtered the remaining mai'juard.

"Are you all right?" asked the Maroon who had carried Faizah away, her body still strained from the force of the attack. But Faizah wouldn't get the chance to answer, as serwan troops landed all around them from the sky.

"Take them and make their beating hearts your trophies," said one of the commanders as he released a powerful force from his body.

"Nassor, where are you?" whispered Faizah as she struggled to keep herself focused.

Nassor might as well have been in another world, as everything he knew was being tested in the chasm. In there, Nassor had no recollection of

time. A lifetime could have gone by, and he wouldn't have known; his mind was taken to deeper depths of awareness and understanding. As with Deathblow, the consciousness of all Maroon warriors from the past sought him out, but not as broken visions or flashes. No, Nassor would understand what was being revealed to him as though he had lived through it all.

"You have become Bearer of the Akin-Eno, a power that has not been wielded since the Last Age, when the Maroons were still young," said a voice.

So many voices, thoughts, and memories were racing through his head. It would take him time to process it all. "What is it that you want from me? What must I do?" asked Nassor.

But the voices talked in riddles that he couldn't make sense of. "It's not what you must do; first, it's what you must know," said one voice.

"And what you must know will help you do what must be done," said another.

"Then, what must I know so mankind can be saved?" asked Nassor.

Suddenly, the Earth Eno that held the minds of warriors past started to boil and creatures took form. First in the form of ants: an army of them crawled all over Nassor's body. Then a giant mamba snake wrapped itself around his body. The snake opened its mouth and bit Nassor with its venomous fangs. Another creature emerged. The Noble lion stood right before a humbled Nassor, who knelt down before the animal. It slashed Nassor across the face, marking him. Nassor didn't scream in pain or even flinch as each manifestation disappeared after anointing him. The marks they gave him started to fade away as though they never happened, and the creatures then reappeared and merged into the form of a man. "What we will reveal to you is what we know: truth."

TEST OF GREATNESS

Back in the safe lands of Kiskeya, where the Noble Regime still ruled and the citizens were waiting impatiently on a war that they could not witness, the people remained unaware of what this ominous storm meant as it came upon them. Rain fell from above as thunder and lightning dominated the skies. The people stayed indoors as inhabitants of the Lower Levels looked for places of refuge from all the flooding. As Uhuru said, the worst of the storm would be focused here, and it was being felt. Thunder and lightning shot down, wreaking havoc and destruction. No one was safe as the world became an unfamiliar place filled with a darkness that reflected the curse that Noble people had been on mankind. As most of the people remained fearful of the storm, even greater dangers were beginning to take place.

The Assassin, who had failed to kill Mala-Dek, was lurking in the shadows at a place where she knew her enemy would be. Several guards roamed the area, which surprised the Assassin but didn't deter her—she was set on finding a way in. She made it past the gates and overheard one of the guards mention Mala-Dek's exact location. With haste she went. As she got closer, she could hear voices and knew that Mala-Dek was near. They were whispering in secret like rodents. The Assassin watched Mala-Dek from a window not too far away as she ordered around a few servants, and then Mala-Dek was left alone. The Assassin came in and followed her inside once she knew that there would be no one to interrupt them. She moved like the wind and didn't make any sound. The room was dimly lit as she entered, and her weapon was kept tightly at her forearm. She could feel her heart beat harder on her chest as she made note of every moment, feeling, and sensation all at once. Thunder and lightning struck again, and the falling drops of rain drowned out all other sounds. She then saw something move fast, or at least she thought she did.

"Let's not play games; I know you're here," said Mala-Dek.

The Assassin was taken by surprise by what Mala-Dek said as she lit a torch, making things more visible. "You are quite amazing, very good at what you do. Punishing those who profit off the suffering of others . . ." said Mala-Dek.

The Assassin didn't want to waste time with words; she wanted to bring Mala-Dek's life to an end tonight. Their fight began with a fury that was even more intense and brutal than the last time. Both were fueled by a vendetta, and the Assassin didn't hold back. She coated her hands with the same dust that ended their last fight. Now each blow would slowly dwindle down Mala-Dek's strength, but for now they seemed so evenly matched.

"I will make you and everyone like you reap what you have sown. I will never tire in what I do, not until those who have suffered by your hand are avenged," said the Assassin.

Mala-Dek screeched at her like a wild animal in pain and slammed the Assassin against the wall, pinning her forearm at her neck; but the Assassin clawed at Mala-Dek's face and bit her fingers. She pushed her off, and it seemed as though Mala-Dek's reflexes were starting to get slower; it appeared the toxin from the dust was taking effect.

The Assassin came at Mala-Dek hard with a barrage of attacks, blows to the face, kicks to the ribs and other soft areas. Victory seemed assured. "You are a scourge. The fact that you live offends me, persecutes me," said the Assassin. As she was prepared to finally kill Mala-Dek, she raised her hand to come back down with final judgment.

Mala-Dek's eyes began to widen and shimmer with the color of blood. Suddenly everything seemed to slow down, and when the Assassin blinked, Mala-Dek's right hand was gripping her throat. A force possessed her, powerful enough that she effortlessly threw the Assassin across the room. Before the Assassin's feet had a chance to touch the ground, Mala-Dek was already upon her, delivering back the same punishment that had been done to her, and more. She threw

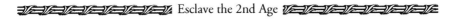

the Assassin to the ground, laughing. "Did you think I would be so vulnerable unless I allowed it?" said Mala-Dek as her enemy spit blood from her mouth.

"Did you think that you would have found me unless I laid the clues and whispers that led you here?" asked Mala-Dek. But the Assassin was too battered to even respond; her vision started to blur, and she was about to pass out. Her eyes grew heavier, blood poured from the side of her head, and then Mala-Dek pulled off her mask.

"Wait, don't leave me yet," said Mala-Dek as she slapped the Assassin, but words had become incoherent to her. Even the pain she felt started to dull.

Someone then came through the door and started talking to Mala-Dek. The Assassin was too dazed to really pay attention to who it was as Mala-Dek took the gauntlet from her. She thought Mala-Dek was going to kill her with it, but instead, she hid it behind her back. Mala-Dek killed the person that had entered the room just as the Assassin passed out. The only thing the Assassin knew for sure was that it was one of the Noble Elite.

Far away from the battle that was taking place, Amari had just arrived back in Kiskeya; even with his speed, it took him longer to get there because of the flooding. His legs were covered in mud. He was exhausted, but he wouldn't let that slow him down. He had to save those children left behind in the other den chambers; if the flooding waters got to them before he did, they would drown in a hell they didn't deserve. He frantically raced through to the den chambers Menee had told him about. He could still hear her voice telling him that there could be those abandoned and trapped in what was left of those hellholes. He kept the scarf from his mother tied to him, and as he ran, he could only be seen as fire burning through the wind. So far, each den he came across was empty or already flooded. Why didn't he and his sister try to liberate those children when they first got their gifts was the sole thought in Amari's head. Why hadn't they worked harder to do something about their torment before the situation got to this? If just one of the children died, it would be his fault, thought Amari. It was a burden he didn't want to carry.

He had gone to all the places that his sister told him about with no sign of any children. Amari kept running at top speed, hoping to come across something; he wouldn't take the chance that there were none out there who needed his help. Something kept him going, a feeling at the pit of his gut that told him he was needed. He felt drawn to go west of Kiskeya, where the storm was most felt. When he looked up at the sky, it was like the storm was taking on a life of its own, daring him to come and challenge its awesome power. Lightning punished the earth all around him, but he wouldn't stop—this was what he was compelled to do.

Back at the battle, it seemed that the Maroons and their allies were holding their own, fighting in a war where their enemies' natural skills and abilities were far different from their own. Casualties were heavy on both sides, and the serwans penetrated deeper and deeper into the Maroon forces. The battle was becoming one-on-one combat.

Kumi was immersed in the battle; he wanted to be the sole reason that the Maroons claimed victory. The enemy surrounded him on all sides. The mai'juard came at him in great numbers, but with brute strength, he fought back against them, crushing them and breaking bones with his bare hands. Relentless were these abominations as Kumi tore the venomous fangs from their mouths and used them as a blade against the beasts. All those who would dare stand against him, whether it was serwan or mai'juard, they all fell before his brutality like leaves in the fall. The venom that he injected into them was excruciating; its victims went into convulsions, and their skin seemed to deteriorate as they foamed at the mouth. Kumi struck whatever place he could.

It would seem that the gift Kumi had received was a great challenge to those he faced. It made him feel destined to defy the Noble people, and the body count began to pile up for him. Then from the sky landed one

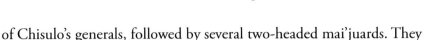

of Chisulo's generals, followed by several two-headed mai'juards. They had torn their way past everyone to obey the call of their master. The mai'juard circled him with eyes blood-red for the amount of their kind killed by Kumi. They cried for revenge.

"For treachery and deceit, you must be punished by me," said the general as he instructed the mai'juard to attack. They did so with full force.

Kumi drew back his hand to hit the first one with all his might, but as it drew near, it split its body in two. The second mai'juard came just as Kumi had been caught off guard by the deceptive move the first one had made. It dug its sharp claws right into Kumi's chest, and then separated itself into two, so that there were four mai'juard. Kumi staggered to his feet. He grabbed his chest and saw that there was no blood, but from the corner of his eye was a flash as the general attacked him with the power of the earth stone. It was a hard hit that knocked Kumi through the base of a tree; any other person would have been killed from an impact like that. The extent of his invulnerability was being tested.

Destruction of the land was all around Kumi, and even though he wasn't hurt, he still felt the pain of each attack as the four mai'juard sought to destroy him. They were all over him, wearing him down with their claws and teeth. One tried to bite Kumi's head off, but he was able to grab the beast by its throat and slammed it to the ground. He was fighting for survival, swinging wildly, but the mai'juard fought just as savagely; they fought on a primitive, yet effective level. The general was still there too, intervening whenever he found Kumi's back turned.

"By the end of this, you will beg for your life. Chastised severely by me and disciplined like a dog. Even my mai'juard will pity you, for you are now lower than them," said the general. To him, Kumi would never be something that he would have to fear.

With all his effort, Kumi managed to kill one of the mai'juard by crushing its windpipe. When the general tried to attack again, Kumi threw the dead body of the beast into the path of the earth stone's

attack. The three remaining beasts became cautious of Kumi and out of fear merged into one body. This new creature was much more formidable, with its strength, speed, and size taken to greater limits. In his weakened condition, there would be no easy way for Kumi to kill it. The three-headed mai'juard charged at Kumi, who picked up one of the fangs he had dropped at the beginning of the fight to face the beast head-on. They leaped at each other and collided in midair. Kumi stabbed the center head with the fang deep into its neck; the blows they exchanged were devastating.

More serwan reinforcements came, and the general commanded them to kill Kumi. The general then used the power of the earth stone to bury Kumi under a hail of boulders.

As he fought desperately against the mai'juard, Kumi jumped to evade the general's attack. He turned the boulders into dust as they came toward him, shattering them into pieces as he punched right through them. Small drops of blood fell from Kumi's face. The overwhelming forces were starting to take their toll, but there was still plenty of fight left in him. He still could push his body even further.

"Is that the best you can do? Is this all the strength the Noblest of people can summon?" arrogantly asked Kumi.

"You have yet to see what we have in store for you . . . we will chastise this land with the blood of our enemy," replied the general. "There is no force that can stand against the Noble Regime!" continued the general as all those at his command closed in on Kumi.

As they threatened to overtake Kumi, Uhuru heroically jumped to his defense, unleashing his full fury to protect those who were brave enough to stand with him. Uhuru threw himself at the general, not even being remotely concerned with his own safety as other Maroons joined in the fight. Kumi in that instant grabbed two of the serwan soldiers and threw them into the mouths of the ferocious mai'juard. The Maroons who came to his aid were like a swarm of bees fighting against the serwan troops. Bones were broken, blood was spilled, limbs and wings were hacked off.

It was a clash of titans, a force of the heavens battling a force of the earth. As they continued to fight hard, Uhuru's Elite Guardsmen began circling the three-headed mai'juard as the venom began to stagger the beast. These four brothers worked as though they shared one mind. Kumi had watched them at the peak of their abilities and knew that their skills were far beyond his own. They subdued the beast by gouging out its eyes; to them it was like practice, and afterward they joined the rest of their comrades in fighting the serwans. Kumi was swatting them down like flies, and the Maroons were holding their own as the rainstorm became a drizzle.

Uhuru was still in deadly combat with the general.

"My family name will go down in history for killing you. Your Eno will be put on top of the next monument we build," said the general.

"I hope so, so that the generations to come will know the symbol of our victory and know that a Noble can be defeated," replied Uhuru.

The power of the earth stone made the general formidable, his armor almost impenetrable. But both refused to give in; they wished for a fair and honorable fight. It was taking everything Uhuru had and more, but something in him knew that he wouldn't lose. Streaks of sunlight began to break through the clouds. Uhuru's Eno began to shimmer from being in the light's path as drops of his own blood fell onto it. It was like a moment of rebirth for him, and as he looked at his enemy surging with a power that seemed infinite, Uhuru had no doubt in his heart and his mind became clear. The general was putting everything he had into this final attack, but Uhuru remained ever-ready. Next a flash engulfed the area, so bright that those around had to shield their eyes. When the dust cleared, Uhuru was the only one left standing, and the general was dead as blood poured from his slit throat.

This small victory would only be short-lived, as Chisulo and the second general descended onto the battlefield. This would be Chisulo's first step into all the carnage, and his entrance was almost God-like as an aura surrounded him. His troops made way for his arrival as the sky began to darken again. Shadows blanketed the ground, and for a moment they all thought that the storm had returned—but it had not. Chisulo had ordered a second aerial assault, but even so, Uhuru stood firm and fearless, daring the Noble army to face him.

Chisulo had endured human defiance long enough. "They will lose . . . brutally," he said.

Then a trumpet was sounded that made the world become silent. Moments later, the ground began to rumble and trees fell. Whatever force was causing it drew closer to the heart of the battlefield. Chisulo had just unleashed his secret weapon, his new breed of warriors loyal to the Noble Regime, a group of sanscoeur warriors the same as Falun. Forty-eight deadly sanscoeur fighters with the power to decimate an entire army of trained men, this would be a true test of Maroon skill.

LOSS

In the chasm, the one who would bring an end to all this was also being tested. His mind had been shattered into several pieces to represent the different aspects of his true self, reflections of his inner demons and greatest hopes. There were feelings of arrogance and envy, yet his sense of compassion dominated them all. When Nassor pulled all those different parts back into himself, his eyes shot open. Each persona went through their own trial, yet stayed connected to their source like a thread and were completely aware of all that was happening simultaneously. The being who had been testing him the whole time called himself Legacy.

"You are still weak-minded; use your will and summon the armor. Unlock the first gates of the Akin-Eno's power," said the Being Legacy.

Nassor did as he was commanded, and while fire engulfed his body, he was only able to summon a portion of its power, even less than during the fight with Falun.

"I am still not ready," said Nassor as the fate of an entire people depended on him. In their greatest hour of need, he had failed them.

"Do not doubt yourself. You have done more for the good of mankind than all of us combined, and know that you will do more. Within you and you alone is the power to tip the balance of Kiskeyan rule back to its native people," said Legacy.

"But if what has been revealed to me is truth, then the real threat, our real enemy is not those fighting in this war. We have been misled since the last age by an even greater danger," said Nassor. "And even with the full armor, I may not win . . . there's a chance I will fail," continued Nassor.

But Legacy wasn't willing to give into doubt as Nassor was. Legacy had waited in life and now in death to see mankind redeemed. Legacy took Nassor's mind to a place where he perceived gates that went back as far as the eye could see, each gate with a distinct mark that denoted its power.

"What is this place?" asked Nassor.

"As bearer of the Akin-Eno, you must be tested at all times. For each power you unlock, it will test your worthiness," said Legacy.

Looking around to see each magnificent gate that waited to be opened, Nassor came across a gate with its mark carved off, imprisoned with a lock and chains. It was old and dark, yet enticing to him. There were a few others just like it, but this one made him want to reach out for it. Before he could, his mind was brought back to the chasm.

"Doubt holds you back and it cannot be removed, so we will fight with you. We will finish the armor to unlock the first gates of power. The seed will return to the earth, and the child shall lead the mother," said Legacy.

Now an even greater fire engulfed Nassor, a different one from before, that summoned all the Earth Eno in the chasm to become a part of him, to finish the armor.

To the west of Kiskeya, where the youngest of the ordained had been sent, the flooding waters and falling rain had made the area a dangerous place to be. All paths leading there had been washed away, and Amari was forced to forge his own path. There were those who needed him, Amari could feel it at the pit of his stomach, as thunder and lightning showed no mercy, still daring him to stand against their power. He moved at a speed that would put the wind to shame, but a part of him had a fear that he would fail. But who else would have the courage right now to stand firm and do what must be done, push it to the next level?

"I have to do this. I must . . ." thought Amari. Once he made that promise, he let go of everything, putting his faith and trust into something beyond himself, the Creator. He ran with eyes closed, allowing a benevolent and merciful God to guide him. Trees and lightning exploded all around him, and yet he moved past them with such grace as though he could predict the danger. The winds might have been strong enough to move mountains, but not strong enough to stop him.

The Guardian had remained ever watchful of all of them as she rebuilt the tomb. She knew that after the events of this day, some of them would be forever changed; in the realm of mortality, one never receives a blessing without its burden. She saw as Amari stopped running and his eyes slowly opened. He looked around and was completely disoriented, but in the wind, he could hear scattered voices.

"*Help*, please help!" cried the voices of children.

Beneath him the ground was different, hard, with water draining into it. The voices got stronger as he dug through the debris of broken branches and leaves. "Don't worry! I'm coming!" said Amari.

"Someone's here; somebody came to save us," shouted one child, as though their prayers had been answered.

But Amari was shocked to see that a gate blocked his path. He could see the faces of dozens of children who could only reach their hands through the bars looking for Amari to hold onto, someone to pull them from their prison.

But the winds kept carrying the scattered voices of children. Amari left, only to find more gates that blocked his path. More children imprisoned in den chambers, one after the other. Amari raced everywhere to find something that was strong enough to cut the bars, but found nothing. His speed meant nothing as time dwindled away. He struck the bars relentlessly with his bare hands, ignoring the pain as blood poured from his fingers.

"He's going to save us; he will free us," said the children.

But as much as Amari wanted to, he couldn't. The waters were rising so high the children were floating inside the chambers.

"Please hurry. Some of us can't swim," said one girl who had been praying to be saved. But when she looked hard into Amari's eyes, she knew that nothing could be done. Puddles became streams, streams became rivers, and all around Amari was water as the rain washed the blood from his hands.

"You have to save us!" shouted one child as panic and fear took him over.

"Don't give up; we need you," said another child as he grabbed the bars to try and break himself free. They all tried. Tears started to fall from Amari's eyes, as from all of the children's eyes. He reached his hand out to touch the girl praying for mercy, a girl no older than him. She slowly gave up and stopped struggling against the bars—it was futile. All the children could do was hold onto each other and prepare for the worst. The water was so cold. Their bodies shivered with fear of the inevitable. They gripped each other tightly as they said their final good-byes. It wouldn't be long now, as water flowed in from the barred gates.

Amari held onto the girl's hand, looking into her eyes and those of all the children there. In trying to save them all, he saved none, he thought. The water rose so high that even Amari was well underwater, but he didn't let go of the girl's hand. In fact, they all were still hanging onto each other. A bright light started to shine from Amari's chest, so bright that he could see all the children's faces as they floated in the water, still chained to the floor. It was his Kyah crystal. From it came a warmth that eased their suffering and anguish. In the crystal was a reflection of all the children, a moment that Amari would never forget.

Life started to fade from their eyes as the children let go of one another, slipping away and floating in the darkness of their watery grave. The little girl held onto Amari with both hands until she began letting go herself. When she did, Amari's eyes closed. He had seen all the children slip away into death before he did. His crystal still shone brightly, remembering them all.

The invading forces of the Noble army were overwhelming. Their numbers were great, and the destruction they caused would leave the land in ruins. It had almost completely stopped raining in the area of the battlefield. As the sun began to shine even brighter, the ground troops commanded by Chisulo attacked like forces of supernatural birth. Faizah's strength had returned to her. She couldn't believe her eyes as she witnessed the skies swarmed by the Ona who landed before them, but without fear, Maroons still protected her. The sound of weapons clashing seemed never ending and there were still more Ona coming, but that was not the biggest worry as the ground troops arrived. These sanscoeur fighters, called hordes, were divided into six groups of eight each, and they remained within range of each other. Faizah thought back to her brief encounter with Falun and knew the destruction that these abominations were capable of. She knew that she had to do something, but in that moment she didn't know what to do as one by one, Maroons were struck down.

"Who can save us now?" said Faizah, believing that not even Nassor could stand against such power.

Individually there was a chance to defeat them as they did Falun, but as a group the hordes were nearly invincible. It was with ease that they attacked, showing mercy only to those that they might torture or imprison later. It seemed as though there was no consciousness in their eyes. The only thing that mattered to them was Chisulo's command, and that gave them a deadly focus.

Some of the Maroons were able to strike back hard and fast. As futile as most of their attacks were, some had been able to slow down the hordes. Throughout the entire battle, Menee had remained out, fearing the death and bloodshed. Once the scorchers started to fall, burning men alive, it only brought back memories of the fire that had scarred her so badly. She

told herself not to abandon her friends and the Maroons in need, but her feet were doing something else as she ran for safety.

As for Uhuru, he still fought bravely with his guardsmen and Kumi; they were fighting the best the Noble army had at their disposal. But it wouldn't be long until they were overwhelmed. Enemies from the skies surrounded them and were closing in, while Chisulo had kept an entire set of the horde with him to deal specifically with Uhuru and Kumi.

"I will give you one chance to surrender, but only if you submit yourself and your Eno in service to me. Kneel before your first and only master. Spare the lives of your people by showing humility, or they will suffer dearly," said Chisulo to Uhuru with an air of dominance.

But in that quick moment Chisulo's arrogance left him vulnerable to an attack by Kumi, who wanted the glory that would come from killing the commanding leader of the Noble Army. He brought Chisulo down with his full force, thinking that Chisulo must be dead from a hit like that; but the battle armor Chisulo wore kept him protected. The only thing injured was his pride, because he had allowed himself to be so vulnerable even while being surrounded by his horde. Chisulo wouldn't let an assault like that happen again and the one who was bold enough to have done it would be dealt with, but for Kumi it was a moment of realization. As a man thought to be a deviant and defined as an esclave, he was able to stand in a position of authority over those that called themselves master. Kumi knew that by attacking Chisulo, he would be a target for the entire set of sanscoeur fighters that protected Chisulo—but he didn't care. This had been a needed moment, and now he was viciously attacked by them for his onslaught.

As most of the horde went after Kumi, a shadow appeared over Chisulo. It was Uhuru, who looked him in the eyes and spat in his face. Even though there was a chance for Uhuru to kill Chisulo now, he had to let his enemy know that he wasn't fighting a bunch of savages who ran wild throughout the jungle. No, he had to let Chisulo know in that moment that he was fighting a people, a nation whose power rivaled that of nobility. That he was fighting an equal and at the end of this day, only one would overcome, only one could be victorious.

"My *destiny! It can no longer be denied!*" said Uhuru.

3rd World Order

To see that encouraged Uhuru's men to fight even more valiantly. For a few moments, they felt no pain or fatigue, but only the will to win. They could now feel something deep in the earth through their Enos—something was coming.

Uhuru took his Eno and banged it together loudly, which allowed Chisulo a chance to get up and defend himself. The skies were clearing up, and the sun shone brightly. The two leaders now stood face-to-face, knowing that whoever would be left standing could possibly decide the outcome of this war. Uhuru was ready for this fight to be taken to whatever ends necessary, but Chisulo would not let himself fight a mere man, even the Maroon leader hated by the serwans. Uhuru kept himself ready for whatever threat would befall him, but Chisulo merely took a step back from his enemy as two members of his horde stepped forward.

"There will be a time when I will deal harshly with you, but for now you must be punished and broken by the will of the Noble people," said Chisulo.

With that, the two sanscoeur fighters attacked Uhuru, while he did his best to defend himself. He banged his Eno a second time as he engaged against opponents who fought like demons. They moved like spiders on the ground, and it didn't take long for Uhuru to be subdued. They struck him to the ground, and all the while Chisulo stood there laughing at what seemed to be Uhuru's humiliation and defeat. Uhuru crawled to his Eno, watching as his men fell all around him.

"You have no strength left to fight with. Have you now realized what a fool you are? No different than any other human I've broken under my heel. Your forces are being pushed back, as mine advance. You've even chosen a place where the storm would not even touch my army," boasted Chisulo as he enjoyed and took in the moment.

"I know . . ." said Uhuru, and with that he grabbed his Eno and banged it together for the third time. The echo was received by a group of Maroons placed on the far side of the battle. It could be sensed by only a few of his men, but that was all that was needed. The Maroons who received the message unveiled several catapultlike constructs that was hidden in the shadows of trees. Near them was a reserve of organic Eno, and at Deathblow's command, they unleashed a counterassault.

"Fire!" said Deathblow, and into the air were sent projections of the Earth Eno that solidified in sunlight. The Living Busara, who remained near Deathblow, saw as in the air the organic Eno formed what looked like nets big enough to capture dozens of the Ona fleet flying through the air. Shards of the propelled Eno would break away before being solidified and were deadly enough to impale. Limbs and wings were severed off in an instant; there was no escape for them. The organic Eno moved too fast and was much too big to avoid being captured.

The entire aerial fleet was being decimated. Hordes of the sanscoeur fighters were sent in to deal with the situation and destroy the catapults before the Maroon army could cause any more damage. The fighters leaped and moved through trees with ease. Chisulo watched and felt a chill run down his spine as his general asked what could be done now since the entire aerial fleet had been nearly eradicated. For a moment Chisulo was silent, and then he said, "Seize him! Their leader . . . Take him back to Kiskeya."

"They are taking Uhuru!" said one of the guardsmen. They had remained close to their leader out of loyalty, defying his orders. Most of the Maroons had fallen back as part of his plan when Uhuru banged his Eno the second time, but the guardsmen stayed, fearing that this action would leave Uhuru vulnerable. But being overwhelmed, Uhuru's guardsmen couldn't get to him in time.

Kumi saw the whole thing and tried to come to Uhuru's rescue. He managed to get past the sanscoeur fighters, only to be taken down by Chisulo's general, who was getting ready to take care of Kumi permanently when Chisulo stepped in.

"No, I will take this mongrel. He has disgraced us," said Chisulo.

Serwan forces began closing in on the area where the catapults were located, only to be met with dangerous traps and ingenious devices, but they still kept coming. To protect the men stationed at the catapult, Deathblow had to leave them and fight his own kind. He told the Living Busara to stay near the catapults, where it would be safe.

The others like him could sense his presence as he drew nearer. They tried to link their thoughts with his. Deathblow had shielded his mind from their influence; he would not be vulnerable to their tricks. There were three who stood against him, and it was easy to recognize how similar, yet different, Deathblow was to them.

"You are the first creation, the first to be gifted, and yet you have betrayed us. You can redeem yourself if you join us now," said one.

Deathblow answered back with aggression, his pulse wave letting them know that there was nothing left to discuss. The three scurried away into the trees to evade the attack.

Even though the other sanscoeur fighters were physically superior, Deathblow had skills and experience that his opponents were not aware of. He would have to use that to win.

PAIN OF ENDURANCE

Menee was watching the fight from a close, yet hidden, distance. Her heart hadn't stopped pounding since the battle started, and it seemed that the number of casualties and turmoil had yet to reach its peak. She was beginning to panic from worrying about Amari, who still hadn't returned. What danger did she place him in, she wondered to herself. The men fighting for the liberty of the human race were taking heavy losses, while she sat by doing nothing. What good was it to have such an incredible gift, but be fearful not of its power but of yourself?

She decided that it was now time to stop being afraid and do what must be done. Focusing on the power of her Kyah crystal, she willed the ground she stood on. It burned from the scorchers, which marked her fear yet made her feel one with it. The earth now understood her pain, and that gave her courage as the earth began to move beneath her.

Even though they were nowhere near each other on the battlefield, both Kumi and Deathblow were in the fight of their lives. Trees were falling down all around Deathblow by his own hand as the trio he fought moved from one branch to the next. Realizing that his attempts were useless, he decided to bring the fight to them. So Deathblow hurled himself into the trees after them, but with not as much ease. The movement of the trio was so natural that they might as well have been walking on the ground; in fact, they seemed even faster in the trees. Deathblow was no fool, and he realized that from the start their plan was to lure him up there. Suddenly, one of them came from behind and grabbed him by his neck; the other two quickly came so they could finish him together.

While Deathblow was dealing with those three, Kumi was having trouble dealing with one foe. Kumi had truly underestimated the fighting power of Chisulo; each hit sent a shock throughout his body. As much as Kumi

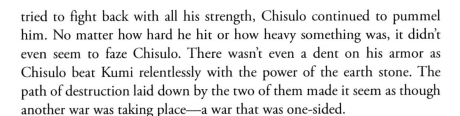

tried to fight back with all his strength, Chisulo continued to pummel him. No matter how hard he hit or how heavy something was, it didn't even seem to faze Chisulo. There wasn't even a dent on his armor as Chisulo beat Kumi relentlessly with the power of the earth stone. The path of destruction laid down by the two of them made it seem as though another war was taking place—a war that was one-sided.

The punishment had not ended for Deathblow either. While one held him down, the others attacked; but he fought back, waiting for the right moment to exploit a weakness in their design. Their swiftness and agility were matched by Deathblow's cunning and the Maroon fighting skills that were bestowed to him. Blows were exchanged at will as they fought on pure instinct, but each time Deathblow managed to hit one of them, they all became disoriented though only for a moment. A shock was sent to their minds from a memory surge, the same memories that Deathblow had received in the chasm. It staggered them, giving him time to run. Curious of what he was trying to do, they split up so that they might circle him. It didn't take long for one of them to cut Deathblow off.

"Where do you think you're going?" asked the horde fighter.

They moved faster than he expected. The enemy advanced toward Deathblow thinking that he had won, but it was Deathblow who was the victor. He lured the horde fighter into a hidden trap. As the other two arrived, Deathblow already had his hands on his victim. A payload of memories was forced into him. The shock was so great that all three went into violent convulsions. His victim struggled to fight back and resist the flow of memories, but it didn't matter. Deathblow savagely broke his neck. The severity of that pain traveled to the rest, crippling them into submission. He then broke the necks of the other two in the same fashion. Those within range could feel it too, but at varying degrees.

It was the perfect time for the Maroons to get the upper hand and act quickly, but some weren't able to act quickly enough. The hordes that had survived and recovered from the shock became something even deadlier. They had now taken the memories of the Maroons they were fighting and adapted those skills to their own. Other horde fighters came for Deathblow after they had killed a handful of Maroons, even taking their

Enos as prizes. The tables had turned quickly, and it was a certainty that they would get past him to destroy the catapults.

"Ready yourselves!" shouted Deathblow to the Maroons behind him.

One of the sanscoeur fighters then threw an Eno that whistled through the air. Deathblow barely got out of the way; there would be a scar that reached from his neck to the side of his head that he wouldn't forget. By the time he moved out of the way, most of them had disappeared into the trees to get past him, but others stayed for the kill. Out of nowhere, two of them jumped out of the shadows to attack him, but then a colossal monster crushed them both before their feet touched the ground.

Deathblow looked up to see that a goblin, made from the earth, had come to his aid. With her gift, Menee had summoned forth three giant goblins. After Deathblow had been saved by Menee, he saw that the sanscoeur fighters that had gotten past him had been entangled with vines; the fight had been squeezed out of them.

"Dip your hands into the Earth Eno," said Menee, who commanded the goblins as parts of their bodies burned with fire; her crystal kept it that way. She decided to call them fiends, and to the Noble army the fire-goblins were otherworldly. With their size, power, and strength, the fire-goblins would take this battle to new depths. For now, Menee had become the anointed Guardian everyone needed, but it seemed that Kumi was fighting the agent of death.

Kumi had already thrown his best combinations and techniques at Chisulo. He could shatter stone, but against Chisulo his strength meant nothing. Chisulo's armor had been made to absorb brute force, which made most attacks useless. Kumi then picked up the broken piece of a catapult to beat Chisulo down with, but at the end, only Chisulo was left standing. As he pulled Kumi out of a pile of debris, he said, "I'm not done with you yet."

The ground troops were still trying to make it past the fire-goblins, who proved to be fearsome; they could actually harness the fire that burned on their bodies. One could breathe fire, and another had flames covering an entire arm so it could engulf any one of the horde within the palm

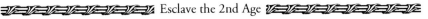

of its hand. The ground troops suffered casualties that were swallowed into the inferno of the fiends; others burned alive as they were squeezed in the hands of soulless giants. The flames took them up quickly as they struggled, fighting wildly for the chance to live and escape the torment, but it all remained futile.

Menee now seemed to be in full control of her gift: the fiends followed her movements and thoughts. A piece of her was in them and they in her. The Kyah crystal she wielded reflected that bond, as even her own hands started to burn like those of the fiends. As her grip tightened, so did theirs; and when she closed her eyes, her victims were made to go through a fiery demise. With each kill, she took her time to embrace the moment. But for her to take out just one of the horde was demanding. "The strain . . ." she whispered. It would take time, but eventually the fire-goblins would be put down by the horde. With each subsequent attack, the fire-goblins were being broken down, and it would put a great strain on Menee when she would have to restore them.

"They can't last much longer," said Menee as Deathblow stood by her side.

"Maroons, prepare yourselves. They will soon come, and we will be ready to meet them," ordered Deathblow. Luckily the catapults were still firing, which kept the Noble forces from advancing any further. It gave the Maroons time to plan their next move without a leader.

Just as Deathblow turned his back, one of the horde got past the fire-goblins. Its aim was to kill Menee, but then a young Maroon selflessly jumped in to protect her. He saved her just before it was too late.

"Protect the girl," shouted Deathblow as several Maroons surrounded her and he dealt with the sanscoeur fighter.

The young man who had saved Menee was badly injured already; the sanscoeur fighter who attacked had stabbed him with a fang of the mai'juard. When she came by his side to thank him, she realized that it was the same young warrior she spent the whole night talking to. She held his hand tightly as the venom began taking effect; his body started

to cringe and tighten. He tried to fight the pain, to not be vulnerable in her presence. Tears fell down her cheek as Menee started to cry, because it wasn't fair that it should end this way. The young warrior opened his mouth to say his last words as he placed his Eno in her hands, but then his eyes rolled back and he was dead. The sound of agony was gone.

As her tears fell for him, a bright light appeared in the distance and intensified.

"What is that?" said the Living Busara.

"It comes from the chasm," answered one of the Maroons.

This same light was eventually seen by all those on the battlefield. Even Chisulo had been mesmerized by its glory as he laid Kumi defenseless atop a giant rock. Chisulo was beating him into the rock, shattering it into smaller pieces as dust scattered from every blow. Blood trickled from Kumi's face; the limits of his invulnerability had been reached.

But then in an instant, something shot out of the earth so fast that it seemed like a shooting star to all those who could see. It was Nassor, and those who believed in him knew it. If Chisulo had seemed God-like in battle, then he had just become a flame in the presence of a torch as Nassor emerged from the chasm. His body was covered in what could only be called magnificence; his power was celestial and had no rival. His gift was pure and couldn't be corrupted; his aura was felt but never touched.

Nassor fell from the sky to the earth where the ground troops fought to destroy the catapults. On impact an energy was unleashed that obliterated all the hordes around him and the fire-goblins. Their bodies were turned to ash. Amazingly everyone else was left unharmed, including Deathblow. When they were able to get a good look at Nassor, they saw that his body was covered in an armor created from the union of an earthly force and a celestial force. Markings just like those on the Eno of any Maroon warrior covered him, but before anyone had a chance to say a word to him, Nassor took to the sky to other parts of the battle. The words to his people as he left were, "Keep fighting."

In his head a familiar voice reached out to Nassor. "The stage has been set. Your arrival has been written since the last age. You, Nassor, are the first coming in over two thousand years . . . born of greatness, forged in destiny, and made in the image of God . . . . Let time remember you as Legacy Maroon."

Nassor arrived on the scene where Chisulo had made his mark and conquered Kumi. His arrival couldn't be ignored. All eyes were now on Nassor as he made his approach to Chisulo, slowly hovering before him fearlessly. For a few moments, the fighting near them stopped. Nassor pulled out the Akin-Eno, a gift in each hand, and collided them together. Just as it was said the echo that originated from the Akin-Eno resonated among all Enos, uniting all Maroon warriors for the first time, and even though Uhuru had been taken, a new leader had been placed in his stead for the time being. This is what the Living Busara had seen in her vision—this was SkyBreak.

Chisulo turned to his enemy, casting Kumi aside. "I'm done with him . . . . Have you come to surrender? Because you are too late. I've already taken Uhuru, and he will be punished dearly for his crimes."

As Chisulo spoke to Nassor, the other general positioned himself.

Chisulo's hand began to tremble as he rose to Nassor so that they would be eye-to-eye. When his back was turned, Faizah and others came to help Kumi get away, to distance themselves from the fight. There was so much emotion in both their eyes as they looked at Nassor. Faizah felt relief and assurance for the future, and in her heart she thanked the Origin, Creator of Life, for his benevolence in all this. As for Kumi, he felt a silent rage and envy that could only come from knowing that the fate of all peoples lay in the hands of his brother, as it was foretold.

"No matter what you do, Nassor. Even if you defeat me, you will suffer. You will suffer a loss so great, and you will know that it was by my hand it happened," said Chisulo. "I broke Kumi, and now I will crush you."

Suddenly, the general with the Ona attacked from an unseen direction. At full strength from his armor, he tackled Nassor to the ground as dozens of Ona and horde followed. Uhuru's guardsmen and other Maroons jumped into action to aid the Legacy Maroon, but the power that Nassor possessed was completely underestimated. Moments later, from under the melee of Ona and ground troops, Nassor emerged and shot into the sky untouched. Some tried to hold onto him before he could escape into the air, but they were put down hard before they could grasp him.

"After him!" shouted an enraged Chisulo.

Those Ona who were still able-bodied jumped into the sky at top speed after Nassor, but the Legacy Maroon evaded them all with ease. During the battle, Nassor took notice of the clear skies he fought in and of the dark clouds that raged over Kiskeya where Khumani would be. It was obvious that a change was coming, and not everyone would be around to see it.

"Face me, human!" shouted the general, who had become aggravated that Nassor hadn't taken him seriously. He came at Nassor, hoping that the power of the earth stone would convince him otherwise. He and his soldiers surrounded Nassor, but even with all the confusion, Nassor blocked the attack with one hand.

"He is making fools of you all," said Chisulo.

Angered by his leader's disappointment, the general ordered the Ona and all others to kill Nassor now. Like vultures surrounding dead prey, the Ona encircled Nassor, attacking him with the orum spear and blade. They had completely engulfed Nassor by sheer numbers. Chisulo watched with a look of anticipation as sweat fell from his forehead. Nassor was a threat he didn't want to come across personally.

Thuds and the cracking sound of bones were heard as bodies hit the ground. From the heavens war cries could be heard that became shrieks of anguish. The sound of weapons clashing was replaced by the sound of limbs being broken. With the Akin-Eno, Nassor was tearing through them all.

Chisulo, blinded with rage, soared into the airborne battle and fought through all the falling body parts in his way. Grabbing his orum spear, he put himself into the center of the fight. "This ends now!"

The general followed his lead. They attacked Nassor wildly, unleashing powerful energies from their bodies. But Nassor merely grabbed the two of them and spun them around in the air.

Nassor took the two of them through all dimensions of the sky. They were moving so swiftly that they couldn't tell whether they were going up or falling down. The Nobles had always been natives to the sky, but as the Ona tried to keep up, Nassor made it his domain without question. From the ground they all watched—Kumi, Faizah, and Menee had witnessed the impossible. One man brought a nation to its knees, one man made the difference, and one man gave them another reason to keep fighting, to never give up.

Nassor, while in the air, threw the general to the side so that he could deal personally with Chisulo. He held onto the leader of the Noble army as they began exchanging powerful blows. Yet it was only Nassor's that were doing any damage. Chisulo's armor couldn't take this kind of punishment. The shock of the hits could be felt through his armor, which should have been impossible, but ever since Nassor pulled the Akin-Eno, the rules for what was impossible were now decided by him. Sparks were flying from the collision of armor against armor. No one could keep up with Nassor, and he still was holding back.

"I will not fail!" Chisulo shouted with conviction for his people and dead brother. Waves of concussive force refracted from the two of them as Chisulo threw attack after attack. His body surged with power from the earth stones that he channeled into his hands.

Nassor finally fought back with opposing defiance. He grabbed Chisulo's arm and kicked him in the ribs. He then plunged his knee into Chisulo's chest and finished with an elbow across the face. For a moment, Chisulo was so stunned that he almost blacked out. As he began to stagger, he tried to recover and come back for another assault, but Nassor punished him with a hit that sent Chisulo back to the earth.

"I can't believe what I am seeing!" said Menee, as shock began to set in.

As Chisulo fell, members of the Ona flew down to save him. The fight would now fall to his general, who stepped in the place of his commander to take Nassor. Surprisingly, the general seemed to have the upper hand as he landed two hits on Nassor. But that would be the end of it as Nassor forcefully grabbed his arm and cut it off with the Akin-Eno. The general cried in bloody anguish, "*Aghhh!*" There was no way he could put up a fight, but Nassor hadn't finished with him yet. He tore off the general's wing and jumped on his back as they both plummeted toward the earth. The general lay there lifeless, with Chisulo being the only one left to lead the Noble army—but he used that moment to escape. There were still plenty of his soldiers left, but after what they'd seen, most would lose their will to fight.

As the war continued, there were those who feared Nassor's power even among the Maroons. The best of the serwans couldn't stand against him, and now he walked among mortal men as though he were divine. When he touched the ground, the earth began to tremble.

"Surely he has become a God!" said those on the battlefield.

But the trembling of the earth didn't come from Nassor. A message was being sent from the Guardian of the tomb of creation. Each of the ordained, as well as Nassor, saw a woman only visible to them point in the direction of the valley where they had been brought together. This woman was covered in a mist of frost whose touch was like ice. Giving no other message, the woman disappeared.

"It's time; we have to go," said Faizah.

"We can't leave yet; Amari hasn't returned," said Menee.

"Then I'll go find him after I bring the rest of you into the valley. Where did he go?" asked Nassor.

"I'll explain on the way," replied Menee. "But we need to get my brother now; I know he needs me." With her ability, Menee created a tunnel that led right beneath the ground and through to the direction of the valley; it seemed that she was beginning to understand the power she had.

Faizah's right hand began to glow like a torch. "Time is of the essence," she said as she was the first into the tunnel, with the Living Busara and Kumi following behind her. Even though Kumi seemed all right, he was too embarrassed to look at anybody after his defeat; his ego had been severely crushed, and it wasn't by Chisulo. The battle had hit its climax, and it was now up to the rest of the Maroon army to end it.

Deathblow and the guardsmen stood near Nassor waiting to see if he had anything to say. They saw him as a living, breathing testament to an age of tradition, but they had to let him know something terrible: Uhuru had been captured, taken prisoner.

"The Nobles will want him alive. We have nearly won this war, and he will be their only leverage if they wish to negotiate. Until then, you all know what to do—follow the code, and win the war," said Nassor. He then entered the tunnel, and Menee followed, sealing up the entrance.

As they hurried to catch up with the rest, Menee turned to Nassor and said, "The serwans have wanted Uhuru for years, to see him punished before their entire nation. If the war is lost, the only thing they will have is him. They won't negotiate his life; they'll take it . . . . you've given those men false hope."

"War has its casualties. Uhuru and those who fought with him knew that," said Nassor.

It couldn't be denied. Someone would have to pay the debt of this war claimed by the Maroons. That would be a sacrifice meant to be kept.

CONSEQUENCES

Entering into the valley again was like entering a new world, a world filled with majestic mystery that existed outside the horrors of life they had always known. They would stay here forever if they could. The land was ancient and everlasting, and forms of energy danced around them. Under sunlight, an aura emanated from them. There was no word for how beautiful Faizah was in that moment, thought Kumi and Nassor. Menee had already wandered off on her own, as Nassor looked at the tunnel that filled up with earth. In his head, he prayed for the safety of the Maroons. *You are the true sons of nobility, and I know your righteous hearts will guide you to victory.*

Not long after they arrived, Menee actually found Amari. "Everyone, he's here. I've found him," she said.

They all gathered around to see Amari resting peacefully against a tree. His hands were cold, and his clothes were wet.

"What happened to him? How did he get here?" asked Faizah.

"He's still alive and he doesn't seem hurt—that's what's important. He hasn't left us yet, Menee," said Nassor, putting his hand on her shoulder for comfort.

"But why won't he open his eyes so that I can speak to him? Say something to me, Amari. Open your eyes," said Menee. She held onto his hand, but he remained as peaceful as ever. Even the Living Busara couldn't explain his condition.

"If he is here, then it is by the hand of the Guardian. She must have a way to help him. Guardian, where are you?" shouted Kumi.

Menee whispered in Amari's ear, "I didn't come this far to lose you."

Then there was a bright flash that took them all by surprise. Moments later, Nassor looked around to see that all except he stood still like statues. A mist blanketed the area as the Guardian finally revealed herself in all her glory.

"What have you done?" asked Nassor.

"My power only exists within the boundaries of this valley and is limited to those who carry the Kyah crystals. The magic that was used to bind them will last temporarily," replied the Guardian, as the two simpleminded boys snickered around her. The next moment, they were all surrounded by a building constructed of light that became rock and stone, the tomb of creation.

"If we are here, then the tomb must be nearing completion. What must be done now to end this war?" asked Nassor.

"The war has already been won, but that will not stop the suffering of mankind," replied the Guardian.

"In the chasm, I was told of a Noble who was the cause of all this. The one the Maroons of the past warned me of, the one I have to kill," stated Nassor.

"Yes, the Noble you speak of is the source of our people's suffering, yet killing him will not bring it to an end. The damage done has gone beyond him," said the Guardian. "Remember, Nassor, for your people to be free, a sacrifice must be made. For victory to be claimed, you must suffer. And for us to defeat the abominations, you must accept that burden," said the Guardian.

An ominous feeling filled Nassor's heart. *What could be meant by those words?*

"Then, Guardian, if that is what must be done, then do it. I accept the consequences, but I tell you now that I have suffered enough. This debt that you expect from me has already been paid by a lifetime of pain, agony, and humiliation. Nothing more will be taken from me," said Nassor.

The look on Nassor's face of pure determination could even be felt by the two boys as they fell behind the Guardian.

"Let me go; I must go back to Kiskeya," said Nassor as an ember glow emanated from his sanscoeur.

Then, with her power, the Guardian placed Nassor as close as she could to Kiskeya, and he traveled alone the rest of the way. An uncertainty filled his thoughts as he recalled a brief moment with Uhuru a day or so before the battle began.

"Nassor, I grow weary of this life. As each day passes, I feel something calling me to return," said Uhuru.

"Return where?" asked Nassor.

"I don't know. It's a place not seen by my eyes, a place not corrupted by serwan influence," said Uhuru.

"If a place like that exists, it would be in our dreams; but it may one day exist here, after we have won the war," said Nassor.

But in Uhuru's eyes was disagreement. He didn't believe that any war would erase the stain of nobility that had marked the souls of men.

"I tell you now, Nassor, for there to be victory, a sacrifice must be made, and I am ready to make it," said Uhuru.

Uhuru was the only mentor Nassor ever had, like a father almost. In the short time he spent with him, Nassor had learned so much. He would not let Uhuru die by the hand of his enemies.

Some of the areas in Kiskeya had been hit hard, especially those in the Lower Levels. Faint cries could still be heard, but there was nothing that could really be done to help those that had already been cast out by society. Panic took over as violent looting began among the guedado and kenyetta because the Ona were either too busy policing other areas or thought it would be better if they did destroy each other. As their world became a darker place, the stage was being set by Chisulo and the remainder of his men for the demise of Nassor. Chisulo was now putting everything on this one final moment; there wasn't much more for him to lose except his honor.

Nassor himself had arrived at the home of Khumani. It wasn't easy, but he had to see her to make sure she was all right. No one was around; it seemed that everyone had left for some place safer. He was going to leave until he heard something break inside. Nassor opened the door and found a woman with her hands and feet tied together. Her mouth had also been muffled, and as Nassor came closer, she cringed in fear, not knowing what he might do to her. Cautiously he approached her.

"I'm just going to untie you, that's all," said Nassor in a calm voice. Nassor then removed the wrap from her mouth and freed her.

"I hope you are Nassor," she said.

Surprised, he replied yes. "If you know me, then you must know Khumani. Where is she?" he asked.

"She was taken by the Ona, her and my son. They forced their way in and grabbed them. They pushed me to the ground. They only left me so that I could deliver this message to you, that they will be waiting for you at the Lougawou Mountains," said the woman.

"Do you have someplace safe to stay?" asked Nassor as his heart began to race. He knew their plan would be to lure him into the void.

The woman didn't answer his question, but instead accused him of all the terrible things that had happened throughout Kiskeya.

"Khumani told me that she named my son after you, Nassor, the freer of mankind and the destroyer of all that we know. You took the life of my husband's brother, a patriot of this land. Enabled a war that would further divide our peoples. Even though the human race is no longer enslaved, it will never be celebrated, only punished," continued the woman as tears filled her eyes.

"My son carries your name, and in the years to come, he will be punished by both kenyetta and serwan for what you did, just like all humans will be. If he dies now, it would only be a blessing," she added.

There was nothing more that Nassor could do. He turned his back to the woman and went after Khumani. He couldn't help but think about what had been said to him. There was truth in her words. It took two thousand years for them to be freed. Would it take just as long for them to be accepted? Times would be harsh for them all, and as the Guardian said, nothing he did now would be enough to bring peace unless he dealt with the root of this. Now all his worry and fear was channeled into rage. He would show no mercy as he had before.

Chisulo had just arrived at the Lougawou Mountains, where his prisoners were waiting for him. They were surrounded by guards all wearing armor similar to what protected their leader. When he arrived, Falun and Mala-Dek were there. Falun stood over the edge of the cliff into the entrance of the dark void, while Mala-Dek put on the mask and gauntlet she took from the Assassin. Uhuru had been taken next to the other prisoners, who would all be thrown into the mountains, with his hands tied. Uhuru could do nothing as Chisulo held his Eno examining its magnificence, but to Uhuru it felt as though the purity of his gift had been desecrated.

"This weapon is quite impressive, Uhuru. After you are gone and I have held Nassor's heart in my hand, they will call me a hero, a patriot of this land. Then we will build a new monument, a tower of greatness dedicated to me, and atop it will sit your Eno. My name will ring throughout history; they will sing praises of my victory and of your defeat," said Chisulo, but his words betrayed him. Uhuru was a leader himself, and the things

Chisulo said lacked a quality it once had on the battlefield. Even in the eyes of the soldiers who had returned with Chisulo, you could see they were disheartened.

"You fear him," Uhuru said defiantly. "You wouldn't have left the battle unless you were about to lose. You've deluded yourself into thinking that you might still win here and now. But you lost even before the war began."

"Keep quiet, dog, or you will be beaten within an inch of your life," said the Masked Hunter as he kicked Uhuru in the back.

Chisulo said, "Do you hear them, fearless leader? Do you hear the screams of panic and fear coming from the mongrels freed by Nassor? Take a good look at the price for setting a wild animal free—it will only follow its nature."

When Uhuru gazed upon what Chisulo spoke of, he saw his people committing acts of violence against each other, degrading themselves in ways that brought shame to them all. In his heart, there was sadness caused by what he had witnessed.

"This is what you fought for, and this is the legacy that you will die for. The humans are vicious and deviant in nature. You said that I had already been defeated, but look at the victory that you have claimed. It has been here for you since the last age," said Chisulo.

Falun came over and said something to Chisulo that Uhuru couldn't hear, and then the two walked away as though Uhuru didn't even matter. Uhuru felt a hand touch his arm, but without thinking, he jumped back defensively. If he had actually taken the chance to strike, it would have been the biggest regret of his life because the person who touched his arm was the only person who ever touched his heart, Bijou. He felt his heart skip beats as he pulled her in to embrace her. It felt like a lifetime had passed since he had seen her, but their love was timeless. When she overheard him talking to Chisulo, she knew it was him by the sound of his voice.

For all those years, Uhuru had no idea what had become of her, no idea of her alias as the Assassin, who vowed justice and dealt vengeance on those who would victimize the helpless. But Bijou was always kept informed about Uhuru; whispers about the great rebel leader were always circulating in secret. They shared a bond that pushed all other distractions away. Uhuru looked in her eyes, feeling excitement from being near her. He was on the threshold of kissing her—but in that moment, Uhuru dropped his guard. If this was the end, then he would give his last moments to her.

Mala-Dek saw that moment of vulnerability and stepped in, grabbing Bijou by the back of her head and dragging her away. "Did you think I would ever let you have a moment of joy?"

Uhuru acted immediately, but the Ona and Masked Hunter were waiting in anticipation. They violently forced him into submission, as he was blindsided by a blow to his head that disoriented him. Uhuru fell to the ground as the Ona taunted and mocked him, even spit on him.

"Should we teach this filth a lesson?" they asked as they enjoyed their moment. They then circled around him as Bijou struggled from the ground against Mala-Dek, who laughed at her and Uhuru maliciously. Bijou reached out her hand as though to save him, but Mala-Dek stomped it down with her foot. "I want you to remember this moment as I will, that nothing you did could have saved him from this fate," said Mala-Dek.

"*Leave him alone!*" shouted a voice. The Ona guards paused for a moment to see who had made such a command. They turned to see Chisulo and Falun walking over to their final prisoner, Khumani. She again ordered them to stop, but they continued their assault after seeing the look of approval on Chisulo's face. Khumani tried reasoning, even pleading with Chisulo to stop them, but he didn't even look back at her as a small grin came across his face. "Falun, I wish to enjoy this pleasure. If this traitor gives out any more orders, even in the slightest, I want you to snap that baby's neck," said Chisulo.

Khumani slowly stepped back, holding the child even more tightly. Being aware of Falun's history with the child made her even more concerned; a part of his misery was because of this child's birth. There was nothing she could do to protect herself or the baby as Falun stood before her. He grabbed her by the throat, and still she hadn't dropped little Nassor. She struggled to fight back, even trying to reason with him. "I helped you . . ." she said to Falun, but her words meant nothing to him. She could feel the flow of blood to her neck slow down. She started to get weak. As her body went limp, Falun took the child as she fell to the ground. Chisulo was either too focused on Uhuru or didn't care what happened to Khumani at this point. The small child immediately started crying in Falun's hands as he wondered whether to show mercy, but then out of nowhere, something fell right out of the sky next to him.

"It's a scout," said one of the Ona guards, and everyone's attention was averted. The body was lifeless, and it looked as though it had been beaten beyond recognition. Two more bodies fell with the same amount of damage.

"*Prepare yourselves!*" ordered Chisulo as Nassor dropped down to the earth.

Without a moment's pause, they attacked him, a militia of all his enemies. They surrounded him from all sides, believing that they might have a chance to bring him down; but they underestimated Nassor in all levels, especially his will to win. He fought against a small cavalry of Ona, Hunters, and horde; but even though they fought harder and stronger, that still didn't give them the advantage needed to kill him. Weapons clashed with fury. Nassor's enemies struck fast and deadly, better than he had anticipated; but as devastating as those blows were, his mind-set would not let him be distracted by anything other than what must be done. Watching in disbelief what Nassor had become, Uhuru took advantage of the moment by freeing his hands with a blade he took from the guards that had beaten him. He then strangled the Ona stationed to watch him and took his orum spear.

Mala-Dek was still in the rear, with a view of everything that was happening. She was witnessing firsthand the destruction that Nassor was capable of and reveled in the thought of causing that kind of destruction herself one day. She even saw Uhuru going to face Chisulo, wanting to kill him with the orum spear already dipped in blood. He drew closer to his enemy to fulfill his final act as Maroon leader, but again, Uhuru would not be successful. A soldier loyal to Chisulo stepped forward and sacrificed himself to save his Noble Leader. The blow couldn't be stopped as Uhuru thrust the orum spear into the soldier. Uhuru looked into the eyes of his victim and then back at Chisulo, who just realized the sacrifice that was made for him.

This Noble soldier was young, barely of an age that would require him to see battle. He was the one who had brought in Khumani, and nothing much could have been expected from him. The soldier clutched onto Uhuru's arm as he collapsed to the ground. Before he died, he saw Chisulo standing before him. He clutched at his chest and blood filled his mouth. He then extended his hand as though reaching out for help and said, "Great Leader, I do this for you and my people . . ." Even as the boy spoke his final words, Chisulo had not even looked at him. As he stepped over his body, the young soldier died. At the end, what he believed in didn't find any value in his life.

Uhuru attempted to attack again, but this time Chisulo was ready. He broke Uhuru's wrist as he came in to strike. "No one can save you now," said Chisulo.

Bijou also tried to fight back against Mala-Dek. Even while lying on the ground, she proved to be just as dangerous. She gave Mala-Dek an elbow to the knee, and then grabbed Mala-Dek's head when she stumbled over, pulling the queen den-master to the ground. But with her hands still bound, Bijou had the upper hand for only a moment.

They struggled as Bijou began choking Mala-Dek. She would not let go even as Mala-Dek dug her nails deep into Bijou's hands. Harder and harder Mala-Dek scratched and clawed until blood flowed, and then Bijou's grip started to weaken. She started to feel dizzy. Mala-Dek took advantage and smacked Bijou on the side of the head with a piece of debris next to her.

Still dazed from the attack, Mala-Dek continued to beat Bijou down. She grabbed Bijou by the head just as Falun threw a small child into the depths of the Lougawou Mountains. Suddenly, Bijou's vision started to blur and her own thoughts became incoherent, but she was able to hear

Mala-Dek's last words before she blacked out, "This is the fate that awaits all of mankind."

When Falun threw the child into the dark void, Khumani jumped in right after him flying right above Falun. It was the first time she had ever taken flight, diving right in to save the boy.

It wasn't until the last second that Nassor had seen her go in. "Khumani . . . *Don't*!" But as he called out to her, the Masked Hunter blindsided him through the power of the earth stone.

It fazed him for only a moment, but a moment was all his enemies needed. Some used it as a chance to retreat, while others like the horde unleashed their full power. Those who ran from the battle were fortunate. They still had reason and knew that Nassor's force was unmatched and unnatural. Those who stayed could only delay the inevitable. Even while being attacked by others, Nassor became so angered by the Masked Hunter that he took the Akin-Eno and slashed through a portion of his face. In one move, he cut through several of his enemies that got in the way of him and the Masked Hunter. They all screamed in agony as Nassor threw the Masked Hunter to the side. Blood poured into the Masked Hunter's hands as he tried to cover his face. He had now been permanently marked by the greatest of Maroons. He had received the mark of Legacy.

Uhuru had been knocked to the ground several times by Chisulo, and each time he fell, he was determined to get right back up. Chisulo at this point had been amusing himself. Each time Uhuru got up to use the orum spear against him, it was deflected. Like a small child, Chisulo smacked Uhuru across his jaw with the back of his hand.

As he fell to the ground again, he saw Bijou thrown into the Lougawou Mountains. Her loss was another casualty of war, and for the first time, his enemies had taken some of the fight out of him; his world became dark. More than ever, he realized that it was up to Nassor and the ordained; Uhuru's time had come. Moments later, Mala-Dek took the mask of the Assassin that she had taken for herself and threw it into the void as well, a final good-bye to her enemy. But she kept the gauntlet as a keepsake.

A moment of peace surrounded Uhuru. All senses except sight were dulled as time seemed to slow down so that he would take in and remember every moment. Before Uhuru had a chance to get up, Falun stood on his hand, crushing it under his heel; you could hear the sound of something breaking. But Uhuru never cried out; it seemed that he was in a state of shock. Falun and Chisulo seemed to be saying something to each other, but Uhuru didn't pay any attention to it. The next thing that happened was Falun dragging Uhuru so that he could be thrown into the dark void as well—realizing that Uhuru didn't struggle back.

"Have no worries. You will join them, as will many others so that you may share in the same punishment," said Chisulo.

Falun now had Uhuru facedown with his heel right on his back, grinding it in. Uhuru's head was over the edge of the cliff as he saw what awaited him. He reached his hand out toward the dark pit, thinking of Bijou. Uhuru's mind had drifted from the most important fight of his life. But then something caught his attention, bringing back his focus.

"Falun, your lord and master needs help." It was the voice of Nassor, challenging Falun as he held Chisulo to the ground with an armlock.

"He is not my master; a power as great as mine cannot be made to submit," said Falun.

"Let Uhuru go, and Chisulo will live," said Nassor as Chisulo cringed from the strain on his arm. But Falun would not let himself be fooled again; he tied Uhuru's hand to a branch and then made a slow approach toward Nassor.

Nassor, still pinning Chisulo down, noticed Uhuru's Eno and reached for it from Chisulo's side. "Do you really expect to win? All of your forces have retreated or been broken by me," said Nassor.

"This isn't about a victory for Kiskeya's Noble people. This is about our vengeance, and it must start with you!" cried Falun as he released a powerful shockwave, which gave Mala-Dek the chance to attack from behind.

There wasn't much time to think. Nassor could only react, so he grabbed Mala-Dek before she could finish her assault and threw her into the path of the shockwave. She and Chisulo received most of the impact. Nassor jumped to the side and threw Uhuru's Eno in Falun's direction. To save himself, Falun released another shockwave; the Eno was deflected, yet it was still able to cut through the whole side of his face. The after-effects of the shockwave were still strong as it knocked Nassor to the ground. Nassor hadn't anticipated another attack so fast based on their last fight.

"I am much stronger than any of the others like me. I could have stepped in the fight at anytime, but getting rid of Khumani and the child just as you appeared made my vengeance perfect, so that you would know with all your power, you still could not save her," boasted Falun.

Chisulo and Mala-Dek were still down but recovering fast as Falun was engaged in deadly combat with Nassor. The two of them were exchanging devastating blows. Falun was not holding back; he had changed so much that Nassor was no longer immune to his attacks. He was giving everything he had to crush his enemy, but Nassor's hits delivered greater impact. Much like the fight with Chisulo, Falun felt a pain that even he could not ignore. As the two of them continued to fight, Uhuru kept trying to reach for his Eno, which had landed near him. It was his one chance to free himself.

Chisulo and Mala-Dek were back on their feet and watched as Nassor pummeled Falun. Mala-Dek's eyes showed she realized that any further confrontation against Nassor would be futile, but Chisulo refused to accept it. He was one of a Noble race and lineage that bowed before no esclave.

"We can still win this if you do exactly as I say," said Chisulo, and Mala-Dek agreed.

Multiple gashes and open wounds covered Falun's body from the Akin-Eno. The fact that he had lasted this long was already an amazement, but his fate was sealed either way. With brute force, Nassor drove his knee into Falun's face, and he fell back, almost stumbling to the ground. He recovered fast, storing the remainder of his strength into one final shockwave in his hand, which he clenched into a fist. He came at Nassor again, but Nassor caught the blow in the palm of his hand, holding Falun's fist. The entire shockwave had been deflected right back at him, and its devastation destroyed his body, deteriorating him to what looked like death. The fight was over, and Nassor drove the Akin-Eno right through Falun's chest, killing him. His last words before he died were spoken in the native language of his people, something Nassor couldn't understand.

Then there was Chisulo standing right there as though he had been waiting patiently for him to finish.

"You can run now if you want," said Nassor. "There's no army to protect you."

"Yes, I have no army or reinforcements. I can't claim the victory that I wanted, but I won't walk-away empty-handed," said Chisulo. His armor burned brightly, but to his surprise, Mala-Dek had her own plans and she pushed him into Nassor. Not realizing what was happening, Nassor struck Chisulo with the Akin-Eno; it couldn't be stopped. In the end, both their fates were tied to the Akin-Eno.

The Akin-Eno had sunk in deep, right through his armor. Blood poured from his body like a river; he could no longer stand. As he fell to the ground, Nassor noticed a wound in his back—Mala-Dek had stabbed Chisulo. This was a moment of clarity for Chisulo. As life drifted from his eyes, Nassor looked over at Mala-Dek to see her wiping off her gauntlet with a look of accomplishment.

Why did she do it? It was such a shattering betrayal, thought Nassor. As Nassor's guard was down, Chisulo with his last breath focused as much energy as he could into a final attack at Mala-Dek. What was a perfect opportunity to deal one last blow to Nassor, Chisulo instead used to exact revenge. Even Mala-Dek was surprised as the shockwave made full contact—this was an ending foreseen by no one.

Nassor looked down at Chisulo and knew for certain he was dead. All of the forces that had been set against him were gone except for the one that threatened his entire world, but it would soon be dealt with accordingly. With this battle finally ended, the mystic armor that protected him dissipated into the sky back to the chasm. He had fulfilled his purpose as Legacy Maroon. Still possessing the Akin-Eno, Nassor was back to his old self and confident that he had done all he could. He made his approach to the edge of the cliff hoping to greet Uhuru for this monumental victory, but he didn't see him. Where could he be? *He wouldn't have run away*, thought Nassor. The only explanation was that he fell over the cliff edge. Someone must have done it while he was fighting; anything could have happened while his back was turned. There was no place else Uhuru could have been, no other explanation to his disappearance.

"Ugghh, ugghh," was the sound that Nassor heard from behind him. He turned hoping to see Uhuru, but it was Mala-Dek. Her breathing was faint. There wasn't much time; she would be dead soon. Nassor came to her side quickly and asked, "Where is Uhuru? You must know."

Weakly yet sinisterly, she responded, "I saw him tied to the branch. He cut himself free, and then he stepped over the cliff edge."

"You're lying!" said Nassor angrily as Mala-Dek coughed up more blood.

"I know that humans aren't smart, but I didn't think one would ever go into the void on purpose," said Mala-Dek.

Nassor went back toward the cliff edge. "How could . . . There has to be a way . . . I will find it." As the wind blew eerily through the area, Nassor closed his eyes to remind himself that his purpose hadn't yet been fully completed. He would overcome this obstacle. The wind blew stronger and fiercer, but he resisted its onslaught. Damnation wouldn't be the end for those who had risked everything; he had to return to the tomb of creation and find answers.

A sharp chill went up his back and through his body, forcing his eyes open again. Mala-Dek stood right before him. Blood covered her mouth. As she grabbed Nassor by his head and kissed him, he felt a strange dizziness come over him that slowed down his movements like he was drugged; an unknown influence had overtaken him. He became angry. All the rage bottled up inside him came to the surface; he no longer felt any inhibition, only pure desire, as he clenched her throat.

"Falun told me . . ." started Mala-Dek.

"This is your doing. You pushed Uhuru over. I know it!" he said as he threw her to the ground, pulled out the Akin-Eno, and slit her throat in vengeance. After he had killed Mala-Dek, his rage disappeared and he realized what he had done. In that instant he had no control over himself. Nassor looked at the Akin-Eno and saw his reflection change within it as a scarf blew away in the wind. It was wrapped around Mala-Dek's neck; she also had a sanscoeur. When he no longer felt the dizziness, he left as fast as he could back to the valley. Nothing more could be done here.

AFFLICTION

"You were warned, Nassor, that for your people to be free, a sacrifice must be made. In all of this, there would be only one possible outcome," said the Guardian. Her voice echoed through the tomb as it reached completion. "Nothing can be done for Uhuru or anyone else lost to us. All is as it is," continued the Guardian.

"He is a failure. What else could you expect from an esclave? . . . It was a mistake to have him be the bearer. I should have the Akin-Eno! Give it to me," said Kumi.

"*Shut up*! The only mistake here is you. Worthless until the very end! I have stepped on things with more worth," shouted Nassor as he gripped the Akin-Eno.

"Nassor, calm down. This isn't the time to get upset," said Faizah as she felt the tension and tried to reason with them both.

"Why are you always stepping in?" shouted Nassor to Faizah. "No matter how many people you help, it won't make up for the father that left you. You know nothing about us, so stay out of this." Nassor turned his back to Kumi and Faizah to talk to the Guardian.

"Listen to me, old woman, I'm tired of doing things by your orders and blind faith. So far it's cost me a great deal of misery. You give me the strength to crush nations and peoples, but I'm not allowed to save those that matter to me most. From now on I'm making my own decisions, and I say . . ." continued Nassor.

But the Guardian soon realized that some sort of influence was beginning to take control of Nassor and the Ordained, an affliction that created discord among them. Nassor's eyes glistened and its power resonated among them all. Through the Akin-Eno, each person that had a Kyah crystal would be infected.

Menee was the last to feel its effects. As they all showed symptoms, she felt a dizziness as she watched over Amari, who was still asleep. Soon they all began going through their own personal delusions that brought out unthinkable rage or worse.

Kumi was hit worst by its symptoms. His mind kept replaying the words Nassor had said to him: "Worthless . . . mistake . . . worthless . . . mistake." In his mind, Nassor was always there to persecute him, convincing him that he had always been a reminder of their mother's shame and burden, that Kumi had no place here. In his torment, Nassor took the form of an otherworldly specter that whispered hurtful secrets. "Our mother had been defiled by your father; you were her punishment," the specter said. Its hands were disfigured and eyes sewn shut as it spoke with an eerie voice.

"Why do you hate esclaves, dear brother . . . is it because you are more of an esclave than you would like to believe?" The specter said many things and moved like the wind, haunting Kumi. "Yes, you are an esclave. After all, you are a half-breed; you only exist as a result of bondage. So why hate being an esclave when you were made for it?" said the specter as it laughed fiendishly at Kumi.

The fighting had already begun between Nassor and Kumi. With his overwhelming strength, Kumi gripped both his hands around Nassor's neck. "Was I destined to be an esclave?" he muttered to himself. As their battle raged on, the two boys who accompanied the Guardian stood watch over them, intrigued by their fighting. Then one of the boys did the most unexpected thing: he smacked the other without any cause or even looking at him. The other boy didn't cry out as he got back to his feet; he just looked at his hands and saw blood that dripped from his nose. With a look of confusion, he turned to Faizah and Menee, who were dealing with their own torments, as he was attacked again by his brother from behind.

Faizah struggled with the thoughts of never having stability in her life, never having a place of belonging. In her delusion, she was confronted by the different aspects of herself, the versions of her that were used to conceal her true self from the world. They were not specters, but personalities created for the world and not for herself. In the center of it, she stood as a helpless little girl overwhelmed by the duties the world expected her to fulfill. Each personality would go about its own business without ever bothering to help her, as though she wasn't even there. Then she saw a figure, a man whom she called after. "Poppy, wait, I'm coming . . ." she would say as she chased after him, but the more she chased, the more distant the figure became. More versions of herself would come in and block her path. Confusion took over as she cried, "Wait, Poppy! Don't leave me!"

"But, my child, I am right here at your side, where I have always been," said a man who put his hand on her shoulder. Faizah turned to see a man covered in a glory that only she could understand and called him, "Father." This man of renown embraced her in his countenance in such a way that it defined her worth. She awakened from her delusion and realized that even though her earthly father had left, her Heavenly Father had been and always would be by her side. As a tear fell down her face, she was reassured by trusting the Origin, and that trust freed her from the affliction. The Living Busara stood next to her with a hand on her shoulder. "We must help the rest of them," she said to her.

"I will . . ." replied Faizah as the mystic power of the Kyah crystal emanated through her body.

Menee was already deep into her delusion. She gripped herself and whispered, "I hate myself, I hate myself . . ." over and over again. For years, the insecurities of her burn scars made her feel like an outcast, always looked down upon and rejected by others. She looked at her hands; scars seemed to cover them and the rest of her body, as vines and other plants surrounded her, hoisting themselves around her neck. They were acting in response to her emotions, and the plants knew that she wanted to end her life so they wrapped tighter around her body. "I don't want to live anymore," she whispered.

The plants secured her arms and covered her eyes as the end came near, but Faizah healed her from the affliction. The mystic power of Faizah's crystal now had a healing touch, and it helped as Menee came close to death. Faizah freed Menee just as she did herself, pulling her mind from what persecuted her most.

The Guardian remained ever vigilant over them all. She tried her best to communicate, but nothing was heard; her mortal form was slipping away as she became more spirit. As the affliction spread, it phased her out of their existence. She could see and hear them, but they were unaware of her. As she left, the memory of her did as well. She walked among them watching as the fight between Nassor and Kumi grew more intense. The affliction even had adverse effects on their powers. Nassor's touch was like fire, and Kumi would cry out as though he had hot coals held to his body. But Nassor's deadly touch was matched by Kumi's brute strength, which could turn stone to dust, and Kumi began taking on a monstrous form. The thunderous blows could be felt echoing throughout the tomb as parts of it began to crumble, turning back into sparks of light that their bodies now absorbed to fuel their rage. Even the Guardian's two sons were fighting as though they were mortal enemies, something they had never done before—yet they still remained unaware of their actions. They were only responding to the animosity that existed between Nassor and Kumi.

Faizah was the only chance they had to stop all this madness, as even the valley that the tomb was kept secret in began to dissipate into the air.

"They're so strong. How can we stop them?" asked Menee as they drew closer.

"I have an idea, but look at them. They've inflicted so much pain on each other, but there's no damage; they're invulnerable," said Faizah. But it was much more serious than that. The fury between them confused their minds; their words became incoherent to the rest, but not to each other. Whatever they were saying as they fought, only they knew. Kumi picked up an altar and threw it, shouting with rage at Nassor; but as it crashed into him, Nassor's body absorbed it, powering him up even further. Kumi picked up something else to throw, but before he could,

Nassor sliced it through with his Akin-Eno and grabbed Kumi by the face. Kumi screamed from the touch of Nassor's burning hands.

Faizah acted fast because this might be her best chance. She hit them with a strong pulse wave of her own. Before either one could recover, she placed her hands on both of them the same way she had Menee. But to her surprise, Faizah's power hadn't done what she meant it to do. Instead of freeing Nassor and Kumi from the affliction, her power unleashed it further, and they got up to fight even more ferociously.

"Let me try to stop them," said Menee. As she summoned nature to her aid, nothing seemed to happen; all of the plant life in the valley had dissipated. "My powers don't work, Faizah. What is happening?" said Menee.

"I don't know. Their fighting is destroying everything. Go to Amari; keep him safe," said Faizah. Faizah stayed behind watching as the brothers warred against each other, hand against hand.

"We must leave this place now," said the Living Busara.

Even the fight between the two boys began to rival Kumi's and Nassor's battle as far as intensity, and there was no way to stop them. But there was something even more peculiar, because their fighting started to make them more aware, reflecting more of the thoughts and emotions coming from Nassor and Kumi. Like mirror images, they repeated their movements. Then Faizah and Menee heard the faint voice of the Guardian, "It cannot be stopped . . . Nemissary's Omen!"

". . . . BECAUSE OF OUR MOTHER!" All four of them shouted those words at the same time during a dramatic clash between the brothers that drained all the energy out of Kumi and Nassor. The energy then transferred to the two boys. Their bodies absorbed all of that raw power. Nassor and Kumi were so weakened that they fell paralyzed. Faizah ran over to them knowing that something worse was going to happen. The energy the two boys had absorbed started a chain reaction. They started to reabsorb everything that was inside the tomb and valley.

"What have I done?" said Nassor.

The boys' bodies absorbed everything, causing a massive implosion that trapped everyone inside. A giant light filled the sky and broke into three directions; this light could be seen across the entire territory. It burned brightly into the homes of the serwans, through the Lower Levels of the guedado, and across the battlefields where the Maroons claimed victory.

That part of the sky burned brightly for several days until it was gone. Sometime after that, a group of travelers came across a part of the Akin-Eno, which was eventually placed in the hands of an Elite Noble Serwan who took the Akin-Eno to the burial site of Hasani.

"In time, my Lord, In time . . ."